For Your Own Good

Samantha Downing was born in the Bay Area, and currently lives in New Orleans. Her debut novel, *My Lovely Wife*, was a Richard and Judy Book Club pick and a *Sunday Times* bestseller, and has been published in thirty languages. It won a Dead Good Reader Award, and was shortlisted for four other major awards: The CWA John Creasey Dagger, The Edgar Award for Best First Novel, The ITW Thriller Award for Best First Novel and The Macavity Award for Best First Mystery. Amazon Studios and Nicole Kidman's Blossom Films have partnered to produce a feature film based on the novel. Her second novel, *He Started It*, was also a *Sunday Times* bestseller.

For Your Own Good

SAMANTHA DOWNING

Waterford City and County
Libraries

MICHAEL  JOSEPH

MICHAEL JOSEPH

UK | USA | Canada | Ireland | Australia
India | New Zealand | South Africa

Michael Joseph is part of the Penguin Random House group of companies
whose addresses can be found at global.penguinrandomhouse.com

First published in the United States of America by Berkley 2021
First published in Great Britain by Michael Joseph 2021

001

Copyright © Samantha Downing, 2021

The moral right of the author has been asserted

Set in 13.5/16 pt Garamond MT Std
Typeset by Jouve (UK), Milton Keynes
Printed and bound in Great Britain by Clays Ltd, Elcograf S.p.A.

The authorized representative in the EEA is Penguin Random House Ireland,
Morrison Chambers, 32 Nassau Street, Dublin D02 YH68

A CIP catalogue record for this book is available from the British Library

HARDBACK ISBN: 978–0–241–44688–1
TRADE PAPERBACK ISBN: 978–0–241–44689–8

www.greenpenguin.co.uk

PART ONE

I

Entitlement has a particular stench. Pungent, bitter. Almost brutal.

Teddy smells it coming.

The stench blows in the door with James Ward. It oozes out of his pores, infecting his suit, his polished shoes, his ridiculously white teeth.

'I apologize for being late,' James says, offering his hand.

'It's fine,' Teddy says. 'Not all of us can be punctual.'

The smile on James's face disappears. 'Sometimes, it can't be helped.'

'Of course.'

James sits at one of the student desks. Normally, Teddy would sit right next to a parent, but this time he sits at his own desk in the front of the class. His chair is angled slightly, giving James a clear view of the award hanging on the wall. Teddy's Teacher of the Year plaque came in last week.

'You said you wanted to talk about Zach,' Teddy says.

'I want to discuss his midterm paper.'

Zach's paper sits on Teddy's desk – 'Daisy Buchanan from *The Great Gatsby*: Was She Worth It?' – along with Teddy's rubric assessment. He glances up at James, whose expression doesn't change. 'An interesting topic.'

'You gave him a B-plus.'

'Yes, I did.'

James smiles just enough. 'Teddy.' Not Mr Crutcher, as

everyone else calls him, and not Theodore. Just Teddy, like they are friends. 'You know how important junior year grades are for college.'

'I do.'

'Zach is a straight-A student.'

'I understand that.'

'I've read his paper,' James says, leaning back a little in his chair. Settling in for the long argument. 'I thought it was well written, and it showed a great deal of creativity. Zach worked very hard to come up with a topic that hadn't been done before. He really wanted a different perspective on a book that's been written about ad infinitum.'

Ad infinitum. The words hang in the air, swinging like a pendulum.

'All true,' Teddy says.

'But you still gave him a B-plus.'

'Zach wrote a good paper, and good papers get a B. Exceptional papers get an A.' Teddy picks up the rubric and holds it out toward James. 'You can see the breakdown for yourself. Grammar, structure, mechanics . . . it's all here.'

James has to get up to retrieve the paper, which makes Teddy smile inside. He folds his hands and watches.

As James starts to read, his phone buzzes. He takes it out and holds up a finger, telling Teddy to wait, then gets up and walks out of the classroom to take the call.

Teddy is left alone to think about his time, which is being wasted.

James asked for this meeting. James specified that it had to be after hours, in the evening. This is what Teddy has to deal with from parents, and he deals with it ad infinitum.

He stares at his own phone, counting the minutes as they

pass. Wondering what James would do if he just got up, walked right past him, and left.

It's unfortunate that he can't.

If Teddy walks out, James will call the headmaster and complain. The headmaster will then call Teddy and remind him that parents pay the bills, including his own paycheck. Belmont isn't a public school.

Not that he would get fired. Just six months ago, he was named Teacher of the Year, for God's sake. But it would be a headache, and he doesn't need that. Not now.

So he stays, counting the minutes. Staring at the walls.

The room is orderly. Sparse. Teddy's desk is clear of everything except Zach's paper, a pen, and a laptop. No inspirational posters on the wall, no calendars. Nothing but Teddy's recent award.

Belmont Academy is an old school, with dark paneling, solid doors, and the original wood floors. The only modern addition is the stack of cubbyholes near the door. That's where students have to leave their phones during class, an idea Teddy fought for until the board approved it. Now, the other teachers thank him for it.

Before the cubbies were installed, kids used their phone throughout class. Once, several years ago, Teddy broke a student's phone. That was an expensive lesson.

Five minutes have passed since James walked out. Teddy starts to pick at his cuticles. It's a habit he developed back in high school, though over the years he got rid of it. Last summer, he started doing it again. He hates himself for it but can't seem to stop.

Time continues to pass.

If Teddy had a dollar for every minute he was kept waiting

5

by James and every other parent, he wouldn't be teaching. He wouldn't have to do anything at all.

Eleven minutes go by before James walks back into the room.

'I apologize. I was waiting for that call.'

'It's fine,' Teddy says. 'Some people just can't disconnect.'

'Sometimes, it's not possible.'

'Of course.'

James takes his seat at the desk and says, 'Let me just ask you straight out. Is there anything we can do about Zach's paper?'

'When you say *do*, Mr Ward, are you asking me if I'll change his grade?'

'Well, I thought it was an A paper. A-minus, maybe, but still an A.'

'I understand that. And I understand your concern for Zach and his future,' Teddy says. 'However, can you imagine what would happen if I changed his grade? Can you appreciate how unfair that would be, not only to the other students, but also to the school? If we start basing our grades on what *parents* think they should be, instead of teachers, how can we possibly know if we are doing our job? We couldn't possibly know if our students were learning the material and progressing with their education. And *that*, Mr Ward, is the very foundation of Belmont.' Teddy pauses, taking great joy at the dismayed look on James's face. Not so arrogant now. 'So, no, I will not change your son's grade and threaten the integrity of this school.'

The silence in the room is broken only by the clock. The minute hand jumps forward with a loud click.

James clears his throat. 'I apologize. I didn't mean to suggest anything like that.'

'Apology accepted.'

But James isn't done yet. They never are.

'Perhaps there is some extra work Zach can do. Even if he has to read a second book and write another paper?'

Teddy thinks about this while staring down at his hands. The cuticle on his index finger already looks ragged, and it's only the middle of the term.

'Perhaps,' he finally says. 'Let me give it some thought.'

'That's all I ask. I appreciate it. So does Zach.'

Zach is a smug little bastard who has no appreciation for anything or anyone except himself. *That's* why he didn't get an A.

His paper was good. Damn good, in fact. If Zach were a better person, he would've received a better grade.

2

Teddy's old Saab is the only car left in the parking lot. Everyone else has cleared out, including the sports teams and the other teachers. Tonight, he's the last one. He unlocks the door with his key – no electronic gizmos on this car – and sets his briefcase in the back seat.

'Mr Crutcher?'

The voice makes Teddy jump. A second ago, the lot was empty, and now there's a woman standing behind him.

'I'm sorry. I didn't mean to startle you,' she says.

She is tall and curvy, with dark hair, cut at the chin, and plum-colored lips. She wears a simple blue dress, high heels, and what looks like an expensive handbag. He's seen enough of them to know.

'Yes?' Teddy says.

'I'm Pamela Ward. Zach's mother.'

'Oh, hello.' Teddy stands up a little straighter. 'I don't think we've met before.'

'No, we haven't.' She steps forward to offer her hand, and Teddy gets a whiff of her. Gardenias.

'I'm afraid you missed your husband,' he says, shaking her hand. 'He left about twenty minutes ago.'

'I know. He told me.'

'Yes, we – '

'I'm sorry I missed the meeting. I just wanted to stop by and make sure everything has been taken care of.' She looks him straight in the eye. No fear. Not of him or of being alone in a parking lot at night.

'Taken care of?' he says.

'That you'll do what's best for Zach.' It's not a question.

'Absolutely. I always want the best for my students.'

'Thank you. I appreciate that,' she says. 'Have a good evening.'

'And you as well. It was a pleasure to meet you.'

With a nod, she turns and walks away.

Now, he sees her car. It's across the lot. A black crossover, which almost disappears in the night. So does she.

Teddy gets into his car and watches in the rearview mirror as she drives away.

Before this evening, he had never met James or Pamela Ward. Unusual, considering Zach is a junior. Teddy makes a point of attending every orientation, parents' night, and fundraiser, as well as every sporting event. The big games, anyway. People know Teddy Crutcher, and most have also met his wife, Allison.

He was surprised when James emailed and said he wanted to meet. Teddy looked him up online and learned he worked in finance. Not surprising – half the Belmont parents work in finance. It made James a little less interesting, a little more pedestrian. A little more manageable.

Now, Teddy knows even more about James, and about his wife. Not that it matters. Not unless he can use it to his advantage.

From the front, Teddy's house looks like it could be abandoned. Broken slats on the fence, overgrown garden, sagging porch. He and his wife had bought it as a fixer-upper and started with the electricity, the plumbing, and the roof. Everything had cost more than expected and took longer than it was supposed to. He still isn't sure which one ran out first, the money or the desire, but they'd stopped renovating years ago.

The inside is a little better. The rooms were painted and the floors refinished before they moved in.

He almost calls out for his wife, Allison, but stops himself. No reason to do that.

The good thing about having such a large house is having more than enough space for Teddy and his wife to have their own offices. Hers faces the back and was supposed to have a view of the garden and a pond. That never happened.

His office is in the front corner of the house. He had envisioned staring out at his lawn and a freshly painted fence around it. Instead, he keeps the drapes shut.

His inbox is filled with messages from students asking about assignments. They want extensions, clarifications, more explicit instructions. Always something. Students today can't just do as they're told. They always need more. Half of Teddy's job has become explaining things a second, third, or even fourth time.

Tonight, he ignores the emails and pours himself a tall glass of milk. He doesn't drink it often – dairy has always been an issue – but he likes it. This evening, it's a treat. Something to help him think about what to do with Zach.

3

Upstairs in his room, Zach Ward works on a history paper while chatting online. A text from his father interrupts him.

Come downstairs please.

He didn't even hear his dad drive up, much less enter the house. Zach types a message to his friend Lucas.

Gotta go. I'm being summoned downstairs.

Lucas replies with an exploding-bomb emoji.

Zach heads down, reminding himself that, no matter what happens, it's better to keep his mouth shut. Except when necessary. Whatever his parents have done is already over. No need to argue about it now.

'In here,' Dad says, waving him into the living room. He's still in his work clothes, minus the suit jacket. Mom looks exactly the same as when she left this morning, minus the shoes.

Physically, Zach is a combination of both his parents. His thick hair, jawline, and dimples come from his dad. The eyes are his mom's, including the long lashes. The best of Mom and Dad. A genetic jackpot, and Zach knows it.

'Have a seat,' Dad says.

Zach sits on the couch, while Mom and Dad sit in the chairs on either side of him. This makes him feel a little trapped.

'I met with your English teacher this evening,' Dad says. 'Your mother was stuck at work.'

'Although I caught up with him afterward,' she says, giving Dad a pointed look. 'So we both talked to him.'

'Mr Crutcher is an interesting man,' Dad says.

Zach says nothing. He's not taking that bait.

'We had a very good talk about your paper. He showed me his rubric assessment, and I brought up some points he may have missed. He agreed with most of what I said.' Dad pauses, letting Mom pick up the story.

'My conversation with Mr Crutcher wasn't very long, but he did seem amenable to rethinking his position on your paper,' she says. 'I think he understands that even teachers can be fallible.'

Crutcher admitted he was wrong? Not likely. But Zach has no doubt his parents believe it.

'All in all, I think we were able to come to an agreement on your paper,' Dad says. 'While he's unwilling to change your grade at this point, given that you already have the paper back, he is willing to give you an additional assignment. Extra credit, basically. That way, your grade can be raised from a B-plus to an A-minus without causing a rift with the other students.'

In other words, Crutcher said no. Not surprising to Zach, given how much his English teacher hates him. It's so weird, because teachers always like him. He's never had a problem until Crutcher.

He's also never had a B – plus or otherwise.

'We think this is the best possible outcome,' Mom says. 'Your GPA will remain intact, all with nothing out of place happening.'

Zach nods, trying not to smile at how she phrases it. They would've loved nothing more than to convince Crutcher to change the grade. They couldn't – and won't admit it.

Like Dad says: *Failure can be an illusion.*

That's just one of his many sayings, which he calls Ward-isms. Zach's been hearing them all his life. Most are stupid.

Both his parents are looking at him, and Zach realizes they're waiting for him to speak.

'Thank you,' he says.

'You're welcome,' Mom says. 'You know we're always willing to help.'

Of course they are. Anything to keep him on track to the Ivy League. This time, however, he didn't want their help. He didn't want them talking to Crutcher, didn't want them asking to change his grade. The B-plus wasn't *that* big of a deal – not on a single paper. It wasn't his semester grade or anything.

No, they'd said. *We can fix this.*

But their idea of fixing had resulted in more work for him, not them. And Crutcher probably hates him more than he did before.

Perfect.

'Did Mr Crutcher say what the extra assignment is?' Zach asks.

'He did not,' Dad says. 'He's going to mull it over, and I assume he'll let you know directly.'

'If he doesn't, let us know,' Mom says.

Zach nods. Sure he will.

'And let's review that assignment together before you turn it in,' Dad says.

Another nod. That'll never happen.

Dad's phone buzzes. He takes it out of his pocket and nods to Mom, then walks out of the living room.

'Have you eaten?' Mom says.

It's eight o'clock at night – of course Zach has eaten. Alone, as he does most nights. 'Yes,' he says.

'Good.' She smiles, patting Zach on the knee. 'I guess that's it for now. Keep us updated about Mr Crutcher.'

'I will.'

Zach walks out of the living room, passing by his father in the hall. Dad is yelling at somebody about something Zach doesn't care about. He doesn't bother eavesdropping any-more. Dad's conversations got boring a while ago.

Back upstairs, he checks online for Lucas. Gone. He looks for a couple of other people but can't find anyone, so he returns to the history paper he was writing. It's hard to con-centrate, though. His mind keeps wandering to that extra assignment and how much time Crutcher will give him to get it done.

Even though it's early, fatigue sets in quickly. Between Crutcher and his parents, Zach feels like he's been batted around like a pinball in their game.

He picks up his phone and texts his friend Courtney.

My parents suck.

The reply comes a minute later: Not exactly breaking news.
I wish they'd stayed out of it, Zach says.

Your teenage angst does not make you a unique snowflake.

Courtney is watching old episodes of *Dawson's Creek* again. She likes to do that when she's high.

Zach doesn't bother answering her. If he continued the conversation, Courtney might refer to his parents as 'paren-tal units' and Zach might throw his phone out the window.

He lies down on his bed and stares up at the modern,

asymmetrical light fixture Mom chose for his room. He hates it. He also hates the furniture, the carpet, and the walls, which are all in varying shades of grey. Every time he walks into his room, it's like stepping into a gloomy cloud.

Less than two years. Twenty-two months to be exact, and then he'll be out of Belmont, out of this house, and away at college. Doesn't even matter where at this point.

Shut up and smile.

Not one of his dad's sayings. It's a Belmont saying, one all the kids know. It's how they survive.

4

Up until yesterday, Teddy had thought of Zach as just a little prick who'd grumbled – loudly – about giving up his phone during class. He always sat in the center of the room with a smirk on his face, waiting for an opportunity to crack a joke, make a snide comment, or do anything else that would get attention.

Now that Teddy has met his parents, Zach seems even worse. Daddy will protect him, or so he thinks.

'We're going to do something different,' Teddy says to the class. That gets their attention. 'I've decided to let you choose our next book.'

With a great flourish, he raises the pull-down screen that covers the chalkboard. Unlike most teachers, Teddy won't give up either one. He doesn't use smartboards.

Two book titles are written on the board. Teddy gives them a moment to read. Some write the titles down; others just stare. Confused, perhaps, at being given a choice.

'Any immediate thoughts?' Teddy says.

Three students raise their hands. The same three students who always raise their hands. Teddy points to the least offensive one.

'Connor,' he says. 'Which one do you prefer?'

'*Moby Dick*.'

That makes a few of them smile. Even without their

phones, they know *Moby Dick* has to be shorter and easier to read than the second book.

They're right.

Two students still have their hands up, but Teddy doesn't look at them. He surveys the room, landing on the back row of the class. The Invisibles. That's what he calls the students who try to disappear.

'Katherine,' he says.

Her head snaps up. She had been staring at her desk.

'Care to offer an opinion?'

She looks at the board, perhaps for the first time. Katherine is a petite girl with blond hair and skin so pale she almost disappears.

'Um,' she says.

'Um?'

'Sorry. I mean, no. I don't have an opinion.'

She never does. Teddy stares at her until she looks away.

Finally, he zeroes in on Zach, who is looking at a girl sitting diagonally from him. He's staring at her legs.

'Zach,' Teddy says. 'Any thoughts on the books?'

Zach glances up, not looking a bit surprised. He smiles as he speaks. 'I'm sure they're both great books.'

Somewhere, a girl giggles.

'But if I have to pick one,' Zach says, 'I think *Moby Dick* is the best choice. I think it's the most relevant, given how the environment is so important. Especially the oceans.'

A few people in the class applaud. Others roll their eyes.

Most students don't want to read *Bleak House* by Charles Dickens, and for good reason. It's one hundred and fifty thousand words longer than *Moby Dick*.

'Thank you, Zach. Anyone else?'

No one raises a hand.

Perfect. Just as Teddy had planned.

The teachers' lounge is up on the second floor, away from most of the classrooms, and it's more comfortable than most. Plush seating, real dishes and cups, occasional free snacks, and lots of coffee. Teddy goes up there during the breaks, though it's not for company. The lounge is the only place to get his favorite coffee blend: Prime Bold.

During the afternoon break, the room is busy. A small line forms in front of the single-cup coffee makers. The fact that they need more than two is an ongoing conversation topic.

Teddy nods and smiles at Frank, an ex-college football player who now teaches math. He's very young and very enthusiastic about his work, his coffee, and his religion. He's already been warned once not to discuss his faith at school.

'I've tried them all,' Frank says, pointing to the shelf of coffee pods. 'And I keep coming back to the Ethiopian Roast. It's not too strong but not weak, you know?'

'I do,' Teddy says.

'And it's good to support the Ethiopians. We always have to help those less fortunate.'

A loud voice cuts through all the chatter.

'Are we seriously out of Gold Roast?'

The voice belongs to a science teacher, a middle-aged woman named Mindy. She's high-strung – with or without coffee.

'We can't be out,' she says, opening all the cabinets. Another teacher joins in to help her look.

Teddy moves to one of the machines and starts making his Prime Bold.

'I was up here earlier, and I swear there was half a box,' Mindy says as she slams through all the cabinets.

'Perhaps they've all been used,' someone else says.

'No way. Not possible.'

Teddy's coffee is finished just as Mindy claims that the Gold Roast must have been stolen. 'Everyone has access to this room,' she says. 'It's not unheard-of.'

She's right. There have been a number of thefts over the years, some solved and some not. But no one has ever bothered to steal coffee pods.

Except Teddy. Although the word *steal* might be a little strong. He has, on occasion, slipped a few pods into his pocket to use at a later time. In the teacher's lounge, of course. Mostly.

But that's not what Mindy is saying. She thinks people are stealing coffee in bulk. She goes through each cabinet at least twice before huffing her way out of the room.

Teddy smiles as he sips his coffee. Nothing like a little excitement to perk up the day.

'Wonder what happened in her class today,' Frank says, making his Ethiopian Roast. 'Some kid must've been acting up.'

Before Teddy can answer, Sonia Benjamin walks in. She grabs a pod of Slim Roast and smiles at everyone.

'How are you two doing today?' she says to Teddy and Frank.

'I'm well,' Frank says.

'Very well,' Teddy says.

'Good, good. It's such a lovely day, isn't it?' she says. Her smile looks as fake as the artificial sweetener she puts in her coffee. As she stirs it, her spoon makes a clinking sound against the cup. Repeatedly.

'Sure,' Frank says. 'It's nice out today.'

Sonia flashes them another smile. 'It certainly is.'

She walks out of the room. Today, her dress is a sickening shade of yellow, but Teddy doesn't think about that for long. He thinks about how self-satisfied she looks. Sonia always has the same expression on her face.

'Well,' Frank says, shaking his head. 'Someone put something in her coffee today.'

'Perhaps,' Teddy says.

Frank is wrong. No one put anything in her coffee. Not today, anyway.

But Teddy has done it before.

5

Teddy spends a long time thinking about how the voting will work. His first idea is to have the students raise their hands. It's an appealing option. He likes the thought of the students being able to see who chooses which book.

The downside is that it could skew the results. Most kids are followers, so depending on who they admire or who they don't, they might change their vote at the last second. The chance of it happening is small, given the choices, but it's possible.

A secret vote, then. It has to be.

He spends the evening designing the ballot while drinking tea. Tonight isn't a milk night. Dairy is only for special times. Too much, and he'll be doubled over in the bathroom for hours.

Not tonight, though. He sits in the office of his huge, empty house, and he tries his best not to think about his wife.

No, no. No.

He isn't going to think about her. Even reading his email is better than thinking about Allison. Forcing himself to stop picking his cuticles, he pulls up his inbox. Email messages are boring, predictable, and easy to answer. The opposite of his wife.

Every once in a while, he receives one that's interesting. Tonight, he hits the email lottery.

It comes from a former student, a horrible girl who didn't

deserve to be at Belmont. She didn't listen, didn't participate in class, and when she did talk, she was an arrogant snob. Fallon Knight was Zach Ward multiplied by a hundred. But damned if she didn't turn in the best papers Teddy had ever read. She aced everything, all the way through high school. Teddy had no choice but to give her an A on every assignment – though it was always an A-minus.

Still, the universe always finds a way to right the wrongs. For Fallon, it was when she asked Teddy for a reference letter.

Writing it was a pleasure.

Teddy spared no detail, describing at length Fallon's attitude, her behavior during class, and her inherent elitist beliefs about herself.

And he mentioned – perhaps even expanded on – his belief that Fallon cheated. This was a girl who got everything she applied for. Student representative to the board? Fallon Knight. Student representative to the Parents' Collaborative? Fallon Knight. Nominee for the summer seminar? Again, Fallon Knight.

She had to be doing something. Maybe using her parents to influence who was picked, which to Teddy was the same thing as cheating. So that's what he put in his letter.

Many teachers give reference letters directly to students. Not Teddy. He sends them to the recipient, and Fallon's letter went to every college and university she applied for.

Not a single school admitted her.

As he'd expected. The unwritten rule about cheating is to err on the side of guilt. No matter how wealthy a student is, they aren't worth having the school's reputation sullied.

A year passed before Fallon figured out why, and by then

it was too late. Not even her parents' money could help. She goes to a state school now, and not a good one.

Fallon still blames Teddy for all her problems.

It's me again, reminding you what a piece of shit you are. You remember that paper I wrote on *The Grapes of Wrath*? You gave me an A-minus on that. I turned in the same paper for my college lit class and got an A. Good to know there are still a few honest teachers out here.

Teddy reads the email twice. Fallon always makes him smile.

Students are antsy on Fridays. They want their phones – so anxious to make plans with their friends – and they'd rather be anywhere but in class.

Too bad. For one hour, they still belong to Teddy.

Today, he looks particularly smart. He's wearing his nicest jacket and a new button-down shirt, and his slacks are creased hard enough to cut glass. He didn't shave, though. Stubble is part of his look.

'I hope everyone has given some thought to which book you'd like to read,' he says, pointing to the board. 'Does anyone have any final comments before we vote?'

He looks around the class. Not a single student raises their hand.

'Then let's get to it,' he says. 'There's a ballot on your desk. Please circle the book you want to read. When you're done, fold it up, and I'll come around to collect them.'

Teddy had brought a bowl just for the ballots. The hand-crafted pottery is a deep shade of blue with a gold rim, a wedding gift from thirteen years ago. One of Allison's favorites. Teddy picks it up like it's a piece of Tupperware.

He walks around the room, holding the bowl out for each student. Some have folded their ballots in half. Others have folded them three, four, even five times. Everyone votes, even the Invisibles.

When he's done collecting, Teddy returns to his desk. He mixes up all the votes and sets the bowl down.

'Let's count them together,' he says, smiling at the students.

They look surprised, like they were sure he would count them in private. Sometimes being unpredictable is a good thing.

'The first vote,' he says, unfolding a ballot, 'is for *Moby Dick*.'

One by one, he goes through each vote, tallying the results on the board for everyone to see. The closer the vote, the closer the students pay attention. He can see it in their eyes, which are neither glazed nor half-asleep. They are alert and interested, and as the votes continue, the tension in the room rises.

Counting the votes together may be one of the best ideas Teddy has ever had.

'Three more left,' he says. There's a sparkle in his eye as he pulls out the next vote. '*Bleak House*.'

A few students groan.

Teddy makes a tally mark next to the title and takes out the next ballot.

'And the penultimate vote is for . . . *Bleak House*.'

If anyone wasn't paying attention a minute ago, they are now.

'Down to the last vote,' he says, unfolding it as slowly as

he can. The students are surprised the vote is this close, and they should be.

Because it's a lie.

The truth is, the class had overwhelmingly voted for *Moby Dick*. The expected result, but not fun at all. Nothing like a little drama to keep the class engaged. Teddy has no problem fudging the results to make things interesting.

Unlike the students sitting in front of him, he didn't get the best education. In fact, it was hardly an education at all. No one told him that right and wrong aren't always what they appear to be. He had to learn that for himself. He also had to learn that lying isn't an option; it's a necessity.

He walks to the board and, with no small amount of drama, makes the final tally mark – next to *Moby Dick*.

The students breathe a collective sigh of relief.

'Your choice has been made,' he says. 'Have a good weekend.'

As the students grab their phones and leave, Teddy says one more thing. 'Zach, can you stay behind for a minute?'

Zach nods, checking his phone while he waits for the class to clear out. Teddy doesn't speak until the room is empty.

'I've given your last paper some thought.'

Zach says nothing. To his credit, he does not smile or smirk.

'And I've decided to give you some extra credit work to help raise your grade,' Teddy says.

'Thank you. I really appreciate that.'

'What I'd like you to do is read the book the class *didn't* choose and write a paper on it.' Teddy leans back in his chair and clasps his hands behind his head.

'You want me to read *Bleak House*?' Zach says.

'That's exactly what I'd like. And I want that paper one week from today.'

Zach's jaw drops. For a second, it looks like he's going to argue. Then he makes the better choice. 'Um, okay. Sure, I can do that.'

'I know you can.'

Zach walks out looking a little dazed. He'll do as he's asked, because he doesn't have a choice.

Maybe this will teach him not to ask his parents to fix his mistakes.

6

Sonia Benjamin walks down the hall, smiling at each student she passes. The ones who aren't staring at their phones smile back or wave.

'Good morning, Mrs B!'

'Good morning,' she says. Her smile is warm and real. All the kids call her Mrs B. 'How are you, Connor?'

'Great, just great,' he says with a smile.

Connor is followed by Celeste, Noah, Patrick, Leigh, Simone . . . She can name just about every student in the school.

Ten years. She's been teaching at Belmont for ten years. Actually, it's nine years, eleven months, and eighteen days. Less than two weeks from now will be her tenth anniversary.

She knows the faculty is planning something, as they always do. A soiree. She likes that word. It rolls off the tongue so well. Sonia has been watching her diet for the past month, hoping she can fit into her red dress, the one she hasn't been able to wear for a few years. That's the price of working at a school like Belmont, where the food isn't just good – it's delicious. Even the headmaster eats lunch in the dining hall, and he doesn't have to. He chooses to.

Eleven more days. She can eat carrots and lettuce for that long.

Today is Monday, and the school is humming. Weekends can have an odd effect on the kids. Half would rather still be at home, and the other half would rather be anywhere *but* home. Sonia is on high alert, keeping an eye out for anyone who looks triggered or is about to be.

The warning bell rings, letting the students know they have four minutes to get to class. A special committee was set up to calculate the precise time needed for that bell, and four minutes was what they'd come up with. Sonia wasn't on the committee and, thus, had kept her mouth shut, but she thought it was all very silly. The original five-minute warning bell had been just fine.

'Mrs B!'

She whips around to find Zach Ward jogging toward her. 'Well, good morning.'

'Hey, I'm glad I ran into you. I was going to come see you today.'

'Oh? About what?'

'The article.'

'The deadline is Friday,' she says.

'I know. That's the problem.'

Sonia's smile fades.

The *Belmont Bugle* is published online the second Wednesday of every month. As the faculty advisor to the school's newspaper, Sonia has to make sure the paper is on time, every time. No exceptions. On her watch, there haven't been any.

'Zach,' she says, 'if you don't get the article in by Friday, we won't have enough time for editing.'

'I know.'

She waits.

'The thing is,' he says, 'I won't be able to get it done by then.'

Sonia shakes her head, pretending she didn't hear.

'I'm really sorry,' he says. 'But I've got an assignment due on Friday for Mr Crutcher, and there's no way I can do both.'

'This isn't like you,' she says, pursing her lips. 'It sounds like poor time management.'

'It isn't, I swear. He just gave me the assignment a couple days ago. It's . . . it's an extra-credit thing. I have to do it for my grade.'

As much as she wants to say something about Teddy Crutcher – and his teaching methods – she bites her tongue.

Instead, she glances at her watch. Zach is dangerously close to being late for his next class, and so is she. 'Come see me later. We'll talk about it then.'

Zach nods and runs off. He waves to half the kids left in the hallway as he goes, and they all wave back. It's impossible not to like Zach. He's the kind of student you want to help.

She walks into her class, where everyone is already seated and waiting. The final bell rings as she shuts the door. With no phones to play with, they all stare at her like a litter of lost puppies, wondering what they're supposed to do next.

It's a good thing Sonia is here to guide them.

As soon as she has a chance, Sonia texts the student editor of the *Bugle*, letting her know that Zach's article may not be done in time, and that it's possible they'll need another article to fill the space.

Courtney freaks out, as she is prone to do.

But we don't have time to get another article!

Don't worry. We'll pull it together, Sonia replies. **We always do!**

!!!
!!!!!!!!!!!!!!!!!!!!!!!!!!!!!!!!!!!!!!!

Courtney's string of exclamation points fills the entire message. She's a junior, which everyone calls their 'last chance' year. Last chance to get your GPA up. Last chance to cram in all the extracurricular activities colleges love so much. Junior year is a pressure cooker when it comes to college, and it isn't just the students. It's also the parents.

They spend a lot of money sending their kids to Belmont, and for that, they expect something. Not a good college, a great one. Ivy League is always the goal, or at least one of the top-tier West Coast schools – Berkeley, Stanford, UCLA. An institution with a big name and an even bigger network of contacts. A school that will ensure a child's future.

It's exhausting. And ever since the college admissions scandal, it's been even worse. Which is why Sonia is rather peeved with Teddy for assigning extra work at a time like this.

Normally, she has a hands-off rule when it comes to other teachers and their methods. To each their own, she always says. But in this case, she decides she *has* to step in and say something, even if it's Teddy. It's her duty, given the stress these kids are under.

Every year, Sonia keeps one eye out for any students who are about to crack. They have, more than once. Sometimes, it's the teachers.

And one time, it was even the headmaster.

7

Sonia hates Teddy's classroom. All those blank walls drive her crazy. And the fact that he won't use a smartboard is ridiculous. Just ridiculous. There's nothing she despises more than a man who wishes he lived a hundred years ago.

But most think he's good at teaching. Great, some even say.

During lunch, she finds him sitting at his desk, eating a sandwich wrapped in wax paper, along with an apple. It seems like he should be so much older than he is. Teddy is forty years old, and she knows this because the school threw him a big birthday party. Too big.

'Sonia,' he says, standing up to greet her. 'Hello.'

'Hi, Teddy. How are you?'

'I'm well, and you?'

'Very well.'

For the first time, she sees the plaque. After years of teaching at Belmont, Teddy has finally put something on the wall. Like he's been saving that spot just for his Teacher of the Year award.

Unbelievable that the board of directors chose him instead of her.

'What can I do for you?' he says.

'I understand you've given Zach Ward an extra assignment.'

Teddy stares at her, not saying a word. Not explaining anything.

'The thing is,' she says, 'Zach has an article for the *Bugle* due on Friday. You must know he is one of our best reporters.'

A curt nod from Teddy. 'I do read the *Bugle*.'

Sure he does. If there's an article about him. 'Zach says he can't possibly finish both your assignment and the article by the end of the week.'

'That's unfortunate.'

'I'm wondering if there's some way we can work this out so he can do both.'

Teddy cocks his head to one side. 'I'm not sure what you're asking.'

Sonia takes a deep breath, sucking in all her frustration. Teddy knows exactly what she's asking; he just wants her to spell it out. 'Can Zach turn in your assignment later?'

'No.'

The abruptness of his answer takes her by surprise. 'I don't understand,' she says.

'Unless I missed something, we aren't required to confer with one another about assignments to make sure they're staggered on different days.'

'Of course we don't have to do that. I'm asking for a favor so we can both get what we want.' She doesn't understand how he can disagree with that.

How dare she.

How dare this woman come into Teddy's classroom and ask him to change a due date. The nerve. The *audacity* to request something like that from a fellow educator. Teddy is more than appalled; he is sickened.

Sonia stands in front of him, her body so rigid she looks like a statue. Acting like she's done nothing wrong.

The first time he met her, a decade ago, she was a pip-squeak of a thing who looked too young to be teaching. Now she's larger, her hair is red instead of brown, she wears more makeup, more jewelry, and her breath smells like coffee.

Still irritating, though. That hasn't changed a bit.

'No,' he says. 'I can't do it.'

'What if he turns your assignment in on Monday? Wouldn't that work?' she says.

'Look, the assignment I gave Zach was a gift. A chance to improve his grade with extra work. I'm not going to give him another gift by changing the deadline.'

'But why would Zach need a gift? He's a straight-A student.'

'Students aren't perfect all the time,' he says.

Sonia draws in a breath. 'No. They aren't.'

'Why don't you move *your* deadline to Monday?' he says.

Sonia, still as unwavering as ever, says, 'Thank you for your time, Teddy.'

She turns and walks out of his classroom without another word.

Teddy feels a tiny bit bad that Courtney, the editor, will have to deal with this, but not bad enough to grant Sonia's request. Kindness has limits.

He shuts the door and locks it. With a little bit of luck, maybe he can finish his lunch before someone else wants something.

8

Sonia goes straight back to her own classroom and takes out her stress ball. Her husband gave it to her for Christmas one year, saying it might help with her snits. That's what he calls it when she gets upset.

You're working yourself up into a snit.

The gift was supposed to be his idea of a joke, but she didn't think it was very funny. She hated the word *snit* and hated the way he said it. Even if that stupid little ball with the smiley face on it turned out to be helpful.

She holds it with both hands, kneading it between her fingers, trying to work out all her anger and frustration.

It's Teddy's fault she feels this way. Not that it's always his fault, but today it is. All she wants is what's best for Zach. Maybe Teddy can see that or maybe he can't, but he's choosing to do what's best for himself.

She kneads the stress ball harder, wondering if anyone ever breaks these things. And, if so, what the substance inside is. Something gooey and messy, no doubt. Maybe once her stress is gone, she'll google it. Until then, she'll keep on kneading.

Zach shows up right after last period, and by then Sonia feels a bit more relaxed. A good thing, because it isn't Zach's fault that Teddy is such an ass.

'Sit down, sit down,' she says, motioning to one of the student desks. She sits in one right next to him.

'I'm really sorry about this,' he says, setting his backpack down on the floor. 'I made a lot of notes for the article, and I know the memorial is coming up quick. Do you think someone else – '

'Stop right there.' Sonia holds up her hand, cutting him off. 'I think I've come up with a solution.'

Zach's eyes light up. He's a good-looking kid with the kind of charisma people are attracted to. It's part of what makes him so popular. 'Really?' he says.

'Do you think you can get the article done by next Monday?'

He thinks about it for a millisecond. 'Yeah. I mean, yes, I think I can do that. But what about the editing?'

Sonia points to herself. 'I'll do it.'

'You? But I couldn't ask you to – '

'Oh, please. I don't mind. What I do mind is not having your article about the annual memorial in the *Bugle*. You know how important that day is.'

Zach nods, his brown hair flopping over one eye. 'I know.'

Everyone does.

'So, then, we're all good,' she says.

'Thank you. Really, thank you so much, Mrs B.'

'It's my pleasure.'

He smiles.

She sends a text to Courtney, letting her know everything will be okay.

I talked to Zach. We'll get his article.

You're amazing! Courtney replies.

Sonia smiles and puts the stress ball back in the top drawer. She doesn't need to use it now that everything has been fixed. Because of her.

9

Zach walks away from Mrs B feeling a little bit more relaxed. Normally, Zach would never ask for an extension on an assignment, not even for an extracurricular like the *Bugle*, but he had no choice. There wasn't a chance in hell he'd be able to get both done by Friday.

Crutcher is who he should write a paper about. Volumes could be written about that asshole, and not just by Zach. He'd heard about Crutcher before ever setting foot into his class. Everything people had said was true, and then some.

He steps outside the school, into the crisp fall air, and gets into his car. It's German, it's expensive, and it's obnoxious. It's also required driving at Belmont, at least according to his dad.

Never underestimate the power of a good first impression.

Another Ward-ism.

Zach speeds out of the parking lot, heading straight for home. If he's lucky, no one will be there and he can get some reading done. If he isn't lucky, he won't stop at all. It's crazy that in a house as big as his, he can't get any privacy, but it's true. His parents always seem to know what he's up to.

During the drive, Courtney calls. She starts talking before he even has a chance to say hello.

'Hey, Loser,' she says. 'Why the hell is your article going to be late?'

'You know already?'

'Of course. I'm the editor. And I appropriately freaked out on Mrs B about this.'

Zach rolls his eyes. 'Why do you do that to her?'

'Because it makes her think I care more than I do. So why is your story late?'

'Crutcher. Extra work,' he says.

'Sucks for you.'

'Yeah, it does.'

'You screwed up that last paper, didn't you?' she says.

'I didn't screw up. I got a B-plus because he's a dick.'

'B-plus? Yikes.'

'*You are your GPA,*' Zach says, repeating another one of his father's Ward-isms.

'You sound like my mother.'

'Ouch.'

'That's what you get for being late,' Courtney says. 'Loser.'

She hangs up.

He isn't mad about that, and he isn't mad she calls him Loser. That's always been her nickname for him, going all the way back to the fourth grade. It's a joke. Zach isn't a loser, and it's because of Courtney.

Back then, his father had been promoted and the family had moved here from Rhode Island. Zach was the new kid in school, surrounded by students who had known one another since birth. The first day, everyone ignored him. The second day, they noticed him. Particularly an asshole named Bennett. He and his friends sat down with Zach in the lunchroom and fired off a barrage of questions about who he was, where he'd come from, all while swiping most of his lunch right off his tray. Overwhelmed and afraid, he kept his mouth shut.

Courtney saved him. She walked right up to the table and

stood over Bennett. Courtney was a tiny thing, her hair already worn in a tight ponytail and her uniform as crisp as her words.

'Back off, Bennett,' she said. 'You obviously don't know who his dad is.'

She didn't, either, but Zach wasn't about to say a word. All he knew was that she must be someone important, because Bennett did back off.

'We were just messing around,' he told Courtney.

'Go do it somewhere else,' she said.

They did. Bennett and his friends got up and left without another word.

When they were gone, Courtney sat down next to Zach and introduced herself. 'Those guys think hazing is cool.' She made a face. 'And they're jerks.'

He had never been saved before – never had to be – and he had never met a girl as bold as Courtney.

'My dad's just a finance guy,' he said.

'They don't know that.'

She smiled. He smiled back.

'Thanks,' he said. 'I was starting to think I was a loser.'

'That's okay. I'm a nerd.'

And she was. Courtney was one of the most popular 'nerds' in school.

The nicknames stuck, even to this day. So did their friendship.

Zach pulls into the driveway at home and stops. The car idles. All he can think about is going back up to that grey room to read *Bleak House*. Sounds like a recipe for a suicide attempt and a bad TV movie.

Nope. Not today. The local library would be better than sitting in his room.

He drives off, imagining the scene in his mind. The library has big, comfortable chairs, the perfect place to relax and get some serious reading done. Uninterrupted reading. The only downside is he's not allowed to bring in food or drinks. A snack would make it perfect, but then when is anything ever perfect?

His mind is rambling now, like he's trying to sell himself on spending the afternoon on the extra assignment from Crutcher. It works until it doesn't.

When he stops at a red light, he texts Lucas.

Where are you?

Home, Lucas says. Why?

Got any weed?

Is that a real question?

On my way, Zach says.

Plenty of time to read later tonight. It's not like his parents allow him to have a social life, at least not during the week. Nine o'clock curfew, Sunday through Thursday, no exceptions unless it's a school function. No amount of arguing will change his father's mind. Or his mother's, for that matter. She can be even worse.

Not as bad as Courtney's mother, though. At least there's that.

10

Monday evening, when Teddy is home alone, he spends hours on social media. His user name is Natasha, she is seventeen years old, and her picture was swiped from a girl in Sweden. Natasha is an online friend of Zach's, as well as many others at Belmont, because who doesn't want to be friends with a pretty young girl?

Everybody does, boys and girls alike. And old perverted men.

Teddy has blocked dozens of them over the years. He's also gone through several profiles, including Larissa, Molly, Yasmine, and Kellie. One of the problems with pretending to be a teenager is that eventually they have to grow up. As they do, he reinvents himself.

When he first got the idea of creating a fake profile, he didn't know if he should. An older man pretending to be a high school student? If he got caught, the headline alone would destroy him.

For a long time, he resisted, telling himself how stupid it would be. Borderline self-destructive, and Teddy is anything but that.

One day, he did it anyway. The curiosity had become stronger than the fear.

Admittedly, his first attempt was horrible. He didn't know anything about creating a profile or what to say in it, nor did he know what music, movies, or bands a seventeen-year-old girl would like.

The second profile was a little better, but the third was when he really hit his stride.

Teddy scrolls through the day's messages – many of which are posted during school hours – and he tries to keep up with the conversations.

Not that he enjoys them. He couldn't care less about video games, sports, weekend plans, marijuana, alcohol, and the opposite sex. But social media is the only way to keep track of what his students are doing.

Yes, he knows who has hooked up with whom, which guy likes which girl, and who hates whom. It's not very interesting, though occasionally it's helpful.

But he isn't reading for gossip. Not really. He's looking for news about his assignment. It might be too soon, since they have several weeks to read *Moby Dick*, but eventually it'll show up online. Teddy knows his students so well, he'd bet on it.

While he continues to scroll, an email pops up on his screen.

Dear Mr Crutcher,

I want to thank you for giving Zach an extra assignment to try and improve his grade. I appreciate your time and thoughtfulness on this matter, and I know Zach does as well.

Best regards,
Pamela Ward

The words are nice enough. Kind, even. But considering the source, they somehow sound like a threat.

*

Sonia stands in front of the memorial committee, trying to smile in an upbeat yet compassionate way.

The official committee is made up of parents, faculty, and students. They've met at least once a month for the past six. Now that it's getting closer, they meet once a week.

'As you all know,' Sonia says, 'the memorial is a balance between acknowledging what happened and trying to be upbeat about our future.'

'Unlike last year,' someone says.

The room goes silent. Everyone remembers what happened last year, when all the white butterflies were supposed to be released into the air. They were kept in the box for too long. The ones that managed to stay alive sputtered out, one by one, while the rest landed on the stage in a dead heap.

Sonia hadn't chaired that event.

'No butterflies this year,' Sonia says. 'And no doves, either. Nothing live of any kind. Well, except for the people.'

'Most of them.'

The comment comes from one of the most outspoken members of the committee. Ingrid Ross is president of the Collaborative, Belmont's version of the PTA. She is also Courtney's mother.

'Yes, thank you.' Sonia turns to the admin of the group. 'Now, where are we with the food?'

'Lunch is at noon. Sharp. The buffet will be set up in the quad, weather permitting. Otherwise we'll have to be in the dining hall. Coffee, tea, and water will be available throughout the day.'

'No breakfast?' Sonia says.

Ingrid answers for the group. 'No breakfast.'

'All right. Where are we with the speakers?'

'I have them.' Ingrid clears her throat and stands up. She is tall and thin, and always looks like she just came from a Pilates class. Her straight blond hair is pulled back into a tight ponytail. 'First, the headmaster will open the ceremony, followed by a nondenominational pastor, a rabbi, and an Eastern philosopher, who will join together in a spiritual silent moment.'

'I thought we were having a Buddhist monk,' someone says.

Ingrid purses her lips. 'We voted against that on the speaker subcommittee.'

'Oh.'

'Moving on. After the moment of silence, we will have several parents speak. Including me.'

Sonia is quite proud of herself for not rolling her eyes.

'In the afternoon,' Ingrid says, 'we'll split up into smaller groups, with counselors and therapists, then come back together for the candle-lighting ceremony. A few teachers will speak, and the headmaster will close the day with some uplifting words about the future.'

'Teachers?' Sonia says. 'Which teachers are speaking?'

'The exact lineup hasn't been determined yet.'

'Then who's on the list?'

Ingrid sighs and scrolls through her tablet. 'Daniels, Jawicki, Parker, Jackson, and Timberg are being considered. And, of course, Crutcher will speak. He's Teacher of the Year.'

Yes, he is. One of the great honors of the position is speaking at every school event and fundraiser, which means Sonia will have to listen to him ad nauseum.

Perfect.

'Decorations,' she says.

This one is always a little touchy, given that it's a memorial. No one wants to feel like they're at a funeral. However, it also can't look like a party.

The head of the decorations subcommittee lists everything they're considering, from a scroll-like guest book for everyone to sign to table decorations in the shape of the school's mascot, the bobcat. For the centerpieces, they want to use cartoonish-looking bobcats dressed up in tuxedos.

'I vote no on that,' Ingrid says. 'If we must have bobcats, they should be wearing the school jersey or something of the like.'

For once, Sonia agrees with her. 'This isn't a formal event. I don't think tuxedos are necessary.'

'No tuxedos,' says the subcommittee chair. She makes a big deal of scratching that off her list. 'Anything else we want?'

'Just keep it subtle,' Ingrid says. 'Let's not embarrass ourselves.'

'Or the school,' Sonia says.

'Yes. Of course.'

The meeting ends without much fanfare, as all their meetings do. Sonia goes straight to her classroom and uses her stress ball. She knew chairing the event would be difficult. Over the past few years, the annual memorial has become a huge event at the school – and, as a result, a huge fundraiser.

No one had expected that. The first memorial was held because the last headmaster had killed himself.

He was found by the custodian in the middle of the night. Sonia shudders every time she thinks of poor old Joe, who was just doing his job when he'd found the headmaster hanging from the ceiling fan in his office.

I I

Teddy's memorial speech has been written for months. He wrote it in the summer, right after learning he was named Teacher of the Year. Every morning since, he has reviewed it, tweaked it. So far he has completely rewritten it three times.

Last year, Gabriel Stein was Teacher of the Year, and he gave a horrible speech. Too long, too sad, too much of everything. He even *cried*, for God's sake.

Teddy isn't about to repeat the same mistake.

This morning, he thinks the speech is coming along well. Eloquent without being too wordy. Compassionate without being depressing. Most of all, it sounds important. As it should, because he has a responsibility to the students and to the school. His words carry weight. They mean something. And that isn't something he takes lightly.

He walks outside, drawing in a deep breath of fresh air. The weather is perfect for fall – sunny with a light breeze. When he starts his car, the voice of his favorite talk show host fills the air.

It's a good day.

It gets even better during second period. It's his favorite class.

'All right,' he says, settling everyone down. 'It's time for our next book.'

'Do we get to vote?' someone says.

'Hand,' Teddy says.

The student raises his hand. Teddy nods at him.

'Do we get to vote?'

'No.'

'But fourth period got to vote.'

'This is second period.'

There's no requirement to do exactly the same thing in every class, as long as everything evens out by the end of the year. None of Teddy's classes read the same book at the same time. In part, it's so they can't cheat.

It's also because he hates for his students to know what's coming next.

'However,' Teddy says, 'I am willing to ask your opinion. What would you like to read next?'

Five hands go up. Two are expected. He ignores them and points to a girl in the second row. 'Amber?'

'*Lord of the Flies*,' she says.

Teddy nods and points to another hand. 'Noah.'

'*Slaughterhouse-Five*.'

'Madeline?'

'*I Know Why the Caged Bird Sings*.'

More hands go up as they get the hang of it. Funny what happens when you give them a choice.

He calls on each and every student, even the two over-eager ones.

'*The Catcher in the Rye*.'

'*The Diary of Anne Frank*.'

'*The Jungle*.'

All the short, easy-to-read classic books. Nothing with heavy, difficult language, and certainly no Russian translations. Books they've probably read before.

Teddy glances at Courtney Ross, trying to gauge her reaction. He still feels a little bad about screwing up the deadline for the paper. She shouldn't have to suffer for what Zach Ward did. Unlike him, she's not arrogant or difficult. She's never asked for an extension – never needed one – and she's always been an A student. Even by Teddy's standards.

Maybe she needs a break on this next book. Maybe something that's a little bit fun. Courtney could probably use some fun.

'What about,' Teddy says, '*The Outsiders*?'

Silence. The kids look skeptical, like they think it's a trick.

'Seriously?' someone says.

Teddy smiles. *The Outsiders* is the holy grail of books for a high school class. Easy to read, fun, interesting. Yet it also has important messages about socioeconomics and the consequences of judging anyone who is different. Plus, there's a movie with all kinds of celebrities in it.

'I'm serious,' Teddy says.

The students applaud. It's a break in decorum, but Teddy lets it go. His class knows it's a gift to be assigned that book.

They just don't know it's a gift to Courtney.

For her, he would do that. And he doesn't give out gifts very often.

If he had to be 100 percent truthful, it's not just because of Zach's article. It's because of Courtney's mother, Ingrid. As president of the Collaborative, she also has a seat on Belmont Academy's board of directors.

The same board that selects the Teacher of the Year.

Zach feels something on his arm. No. Poking his arm.

Then, a whisper in his ear.

49

'Wake up, Loser.'

His eyes fly open. Courtney is standing over him, smiling.

He's in the library, after school, and he'd fallen asleep on top of *Bleak House*. He was up almost all night reading and still isn't done.

'Hey, Nerd,' he says, lifting his head. 'I nodded off.'

'I see that.' She sits down, her backpack hitting the floor with a thump. The tables around them are all empty. Zach checks his phone. It's almost five o'clock.

'What are you doing here?' he says.

'Avoiding home.'

He nods. Gets it. 'Your mom?'

'Always.'

'What now?' he asks, rubbing his eyes.

'She's all bent about early admission. I swear, every day she finds a new way to torture me.' Courtney shakes her head as she checks her phone. 'She's sent seven texts since school got out. Three include the word "Yale." '

Again, he nods. Courtney's mom has been talking about Yale for years. As if her whole life is built around her daughter going to that school.

'You two look like you're up to something.'

Mr Maxwell, their math teacher, walks up to their table and smiles down at them. He looks more like a personal trainer than a teacher, the way he's always flexing his muscles. Like now.

Zach points to his book. 'Just studying.'

'Totally,' Courtney says.

Mr Maxwell nods, and he keeps smiling. When no one else says anything, he finally walks away.

'That was weird,' Zach whispers.

'He can be creepy,' Courtney says. 'I mean, not *creepy* like a pervert, but like he just assumes you're doing something wrong.'

'So judgy.'

'Yeah. I bet he was a bad kid and thinks we're the same.'

Zach sighs and stretches his arms. 'So much baggage. Teachers have no idea how hard they are to deal with.'

'Right?'

12

Zach is late. He was supposed to be at the memorial sub-committee meeting at 7 P.M., but he got stuck in an argument with his dad about where he was going.

Yes, it's school-related.

Yes, he swears it's school-related. He's one of the student representatives on the memorial committee, remember?

No, he won't be late for curfew. Probably. Unless maybe if the meeting runs late or he decides to escape this life and drive up to Canada or something.

Finally, Dad let him go. By the time Zach arrives at the meeting, everyone else is there.

'Sorry,' he says, rushing to sit down. A few people glance up, but at least no one gives him a dirty look. Some of the parents get pretty upset about tardiness.

The meeting is in one of the classrooms at Belmont. Ingrid Ross stands at the front, right next to the smartboard. Mrs Ross, as Zach calls her. He's known her as long as he's known Courtney.

'As I was saying, you all know how long this process has taken. The memorial statue is something that has been talked and debated about for years, but I think we've finally accomplished our goal.' She stops to smile at everyone. 'After so many attempts, so many versions we've considered and eliminated, I present to you the final statue. Or at least a picture of it.'

Mrs Ross taps the board.

A bronze rock appears.

That's all it is: a big rock. This is the end result. Most ideas were rejected because they were considered offensive or inappropriate. Angels were not inclusive. A bust of the headmaster could be misconstrued as glorifying suicide. Anything resembling a wall was too derivative. The list went on and on until someone said it should be a big bronze (plated) rock.

A symbol of strength and permanence. A symbol of Belmont.

At the bottom, a small plaque says BELMONT FOREVER. Beneath that is the name of the headmaster who killed himself, along with the year he died.

'It's lovely,' someone says.

Zach nods. He's afraid to open his mouth, because he might laugh. It's taken Belmont years to come up with a *rock*.

Mrs Ross waits for any further comments. There are none. 'The statue will be unveiled by the headmaster at the end of the ceremony, followed by the official pictures.' She smiles at the group, teeth on full display. 'It looks like we've finally done it. Thank you all for your hard work on this. I know this has been a very long road.'

A smattering of applause ripples through the room.

Next up is the pedestal for the rock, which was only slightly less controversial than the statue. The final design is very plain, and no one should have a problem with it. Zach certainly doesn't.

When the meeting is over, he fantasizes about getting out of there before anyone corners him into a conversation. Of course he won't. He never leaves without saying goodbye to everyone. It's part of the protocol.

And now, Ingrid Ross is standing right in front of him.

'Hello, Mrs Ross,' he says.

'Good evening, Zach. Am I remembering this right, or did you miss the last meeting?'

'Yes. I'm so sorry. I had an assignment to finish.' He stops, waiting for her to say something. When she doesn't, he keeps talking, to fill the air. 'This is going to be quite an event. It's great to be a part of it.'

She smiles, the skin crinkling around her eyes. 'No doubt it will look good on your college applications as well.'

It sounds like an accusation. He nods, unsure of the proper response.

'Still planning on Princeton?' she asks.

'Hope so. It's my top choice.'

'Courtney's applying for Early Action to Yale. I'm sure you know she's always wanted to go there.'

Nothing about that statement is true. Courtney wants to go out West, far away from her mother. Doesn't matter if it's Stanford or Berkeley or even UC Santa Cruz, just as long as she's on the opposite coast. 'She's mentioned it a few times,' Zach says.

'I'm sure she has.'

'It's been nice to see you, Mrs Ross. Next meeting is in a week?'

'That's right.'

Zach smiles and walks away, forcing himself to nod and smile and say goodbye to everyone. When he finally gets out of that room, he feels like collapsing. It's hard to pretend to like people you hate. Well, maybe not *hate*. But something close.

By the time he gets home, Courtney has texted.

My mom said she saw you. Princeton??

Why not, he says. It's an Ivy.

Last week you said Cornell.

Who cares? Any of them will do.

Did she talk about Yale again? Courtney asks.

Oh yes. It's your dream school.

I swear, she's driving me insane.

That's what parents do, Zach says. Must be in the manual.

Is there a manual?

Has to be.

13

Early Friday morning, before Sonia is even at school, she starts getting messages from Courtney. Deadline day for the *Bugle* is always stressful, especially for its editor.

> I'm afraid the article on the new library wing will be way too LONG!

> Still worried about the sports roundup, we won't have everything until after the weekend.

> I think we may have to redo the layout.

Sonia answers that last one: We don't have to redo the layout. We just have to make the articles fit the layout we have.

Courtney is always stressed about deadlines, but today it's even worse. The memorial issue is the one she wants to use for her college applications next year. Her anxiety is at a ten, which means Sonia's stress is at fifty-seven. Especially after a flood of emails last night about the school's test scores. The school had stellar scores last year, so of course they have to beat them this year.

'You okay?'

Sonia's husband wanders into the kitchen, fresh from his run on the treadmill. Mark is a lovely, sweet man whom she has been with since her own high school days, and she can't imagine being with anyone else. Even if he does tell her she has snits.

'Everything's fine,' she says. 'Why?'

'Because you're gripping your phone so hard, it might break.'

So she is. Sonia puts her coffee cup down in the sink and takes a deep breath. 'It's deadline day,' she says.

'Ah. You'll be working late?'

'Absolutely.'

Mark leans over and kisses her on the forehead. 'I'll leave dinner in the fridge for you.'

He runs off to the shower while she heads to the garage. Her phone pings several more times on the drive to school. Before getting out of her car, she closes her eyes and repeats her daily mantra.

Today will be a good day.
Today will be a good day.
Today will be a good day.

Ten times, and then she opens her eyes, puts a smile on her face, and gets out of the car. Three steps later, Courtney appears. Physically, she looks perfect, as always. Pressed clothes, shiny shoes, brown hair pulled back into a neat, if tight, ponytail. Just like her mom.

Panic is in her eyes. 'The library article is definitely too long.'

'It's fine. It's all fine,' Sonia says, patting her on the arm.

'But it's long by *a lot.*'

'Let's go see where we can cut it, shall we?'

She and Courtney manage to squeeze in a quick editing session before first period begins. When the bell rings, Sonia is happy to get away from her and feels a tiny bit guilty about it.

That's the part no one had told her about being a teacher. The guilt. So much guilt.

Sonia feels guilty about what she's done, what she hasn't

done, whom she has helped, and whom she hasn't. She feels guilty about the hours she works and the hours she doesn't. She feels guilty when her students don't achieve what they want to achieve or get into the college of their choice.

That kind of guilt is enough to drive anyone to drink. Not Sonia – she doesn't touch alcohol. But she knows a lot of teachers who overindulge. Parents, too.

And then there are parents who really should have a drink. Courtney's mother, for instance. If anyone needs to relax, it's Ingrid Ross.

Not that it's any of her business, except as it relates to Courtney. It's amazing the girl's head hasn't exploded from all the pressure.

During the morning break, Sonia gets her usual cup of coffee from the teachers' lounge – with sweetener, no sugar – and checks in with Courtney. A flood of messages came in after class, when Courtney was able to use her phone again. One by one, Sonia answers them. She is patient. She is kind. Today is going to be a good day.

And it is, until about an hour later, when she starts to feel a bit nauseous.

Please not today.

Any other day but deadline day. Sonia tries to will herself back to good health, convince her body that it's fine, it's all fine. Perhaps she's just nervous about deadline day.

Between classes, she goes to the vending machine and gets a Diet Sprite to soothe her stomach. Coffee doesn't even sound good anymore. The thought of all that bitterness makes her feel worse.

Sonia takes a few small sips of Sprite before her next class begins. It doesn't help.

During class, the nausea gets worse. She starts to feel a bit feverish, almost like she's coming down with the flu. Or food poisoning. *It's okay,* she tells herself. *I'll be fine, just fine.* Sonia assigns everyone to read a few pages of their current book, *Fahrenheit 451,* so they can discuss it for the remainder of the class.

She takes another sip of her Sprite and draws in her breath, steadying herself against her desk. With the back of a hand, she wipes her forehead, hoping the students don't see her perspire.

The one thing she won't do is walk out in the middle of class, no matter how bad she feels. A lot of teachers would, but not her. She is here to do her job, and do it to the best of her ability.

A few minutes later, she's unable to control it. Sonia tries to make it to the wastebasket but doesn't. She vomits all over her desk.

14

By the time Zach gets out of third period, his phone is exploding with messages about Mrs B. They range from concern to graphic descriptions of projectile vomiting all over the classroom. Someone even posts a picture of the aftermath.

Could be the 'rona, Lucas says. Or she's pregnant.

You're an idiot. It's probably the stomach flu, Zach texts back.

He also makes a note to get Mrs B a get-well-soon card. It's one of the reasons the teachers love him so much – he always remembers their birthdays, he gives them all Christmas gifts, and if they get sick, he sends a card. So easy, so simple, and so many benefits.

Well, except with Crutcher. Zach emailed his *Bleak House* paper first thing this morning, earlier than necessary, and hasn't heard a word back. Certainly not a thank-you. Not that Zach had expected one.

From the first day, Crutcher had it out for him. Zach had no idea why, or what he had done, but he knew. All he did was walk into class, shelve his phone, and sit down. That was it.

'Excuse me,' Mr Crutcher had said. 'What's your name?'

'Zach Ward, sir.'

'Well, Zach Ward, before you get too comfortable, perhaps you would like to check the seating chart. I've left copies of it at the front of the room, but it seems you've ignored them, because the person who is supposed to be in that seat is Siobhan Drexler.'

Zach glanced up at the front, where a stack of papers sat on top of a chair. 'I'm sorry,' he said, standing up.

As it turned out, the seating chart was only for the first week of class, until Crutcher learned their names. After that, they were allowed to sit wherever they wanted. Zach took his original seat, in the center of class.

Ever since then, Crutcher has hated him. Okay, maybe because of what had happened on the first day, it was wrong of Zach to take the same seat again, but he likes sitting in the middle of the room. Not too close, not too far, a view of the window and of the door. It's perfect, and so that's where he sat. Crutcher didn't have to punish him for it.

Never underestimate the power of a good first impression.

Maybe that Ward-ism is right. Maybe Zach had screwed up from the beginning.

Teddy doesn't hear about Sonia until lunchtime. His students may or may not have been talking about it after his last class, but he wasn't really listening. He was too busy reading Zach's paper. It had arrived in his inbox first thing this morning.

To prepare for the paper, Teddy had watched the entire *Bleak House* TV series. Two episodes a night, every night, for the past week. Just in case Zach's paper was based on that instead of the book. There are far more characters in the novel than there are in the series, and he thought it would be interesting to see if Zach mentions anyone who didn't make the TV cut.

Given this preoccupation, he doesn't know what's going on when he walks into the teachers' lounge at lunch. The conversation is animated and loud, words like *vomit* and *upchuck* are being thrown around, like it's fine to talk about such things while people are eating.

Frank is the one who finally explains the whole story, starting in Sonia's classroom and ending in the ladies' room on the first floor.

'And, no, it's not COVID,' he says to Teddy. 'Contrary to the rumors.'

'COVID? Good God.'

Frank purses his lips, but at least he doesn't mention taking the Lord's name in vain. 'And don't believe what they're saying about an ambulance, either,' he says. 'Her husband picked her up.'

No, there was definitely no ambulance. Teddy would have heard the sirens if an emergency vehicle had come to the school.

'So she just got sick in class?' he says.

'Yes,' Frank says. 'All over her desk.'

'How horrible.'

'Horrible for Joe,' Frank says. 'He's the one who has to clean it up.'

Teddy nods, but he's not thinking about the school custodian. He's thinking about Sonia becoming so ill. 'I wonder if it's food poisoning,' he says.

'That or the stomach flu, I bet.'

Teddy doesn't get a cup of coffee. Instead, he goes back downstairs and walks by Sonia's classroom. The door is shut, but he peeks in. Everything has been cleaned, the window on the far side of the room is open, and he can smell the bleach.

He goes back to his own classroom to eat his usual lunch: bologna on white bread and an apple. While eating, he returns to Zach's paper. The topic Zach chose is about the legal system, which isn't a surprise. His mother, Pamela, is a lawyer. Teddy learned that when he looked her up online.

But he didn't just get a paper. Zach also sent along a letter, thanking him profusely for giving him a chance to improve his grade. A lesser teacher would've bought into it.

Not Teddy. Sucking up is desperate, and he has no respect for students who try it.

He continues reading the paper until lunch ends. Sonia and the events of the morning are long gone. He doesn't think about them again until Frank pops his head in at the end of the day.

'Sonia's husband called,' he says. 'Looks like she's got a bug. Probably the stomach flu.'

'Good to know,' Teddy says.

In the evening, when he's alone at home, he heads into the basement. Three test tubes are on his worktable, each one half-filled and capped. He picks up the first, which has a sticker with an *S* on it. For *Sonia*.

The substance he put in Sonia's coffee was a new formula, something he's been researching and playing around with for a while. Having never tested it before, he wasn't sure if the amount was correct or what it would do, but he had to find out sometime. With a green pen, he marks the tube with a plus sign.

That done, he goes upstairs to pour himself an ice-cold glass of milk.

I 5

Wrapped in blankets, her head sunken into the pillows, Sonia feels like she wants to die. In the moments when she doesn't want to die, she is very pissed off.

Sick is one thing, bedridden is another. And at the worst time possible.

For the rest of the day, she feels nauseous every time she moves. She feels nauseous when she reads Courtney's texts. She feels nauseous when she looks at her computer or the TV. All she can do is lie in bed, with the shades drawn, and take a tiny sip of water every hour or so. Late Friday night, she finally drifts off to sleep, cursing her body, the day, and her whole life.

She wakes up covered in sweat, the sheet wrapped around her legs and the blankets kicked off the bed. It's light outside, so she made it through the night without dying. After remaining still for a few minutes, she reaches for her phone. Her stomach starts to roll when she sees twenty-four messages from Courtney.

As Sonia curls up into a tight ball, she realizes there is a silver lining to being so sick. *Everything has a silver lining if you look hard enough.* That's what her mother used to say. Turns out she was right. Again.

Another day or two of this flu, and Sonia will be able to fit back into her red dress. Just in time for her ten-year anniversary at Belmont.

*

Teddy has read Zach's paper three times. First, for the overall flow. Second, to check characters and story details. Third, for grammar.

It's a damn good paper.

Too good, perhaps. Teddy wonders if Zach did read the book and write the paper – with a little legal help from his mother – or if he paid someone to do it.

Given the one-week deadline, Teddy would bet it's the latter.

During the weekend, he spends a lot of time online, checking on Zach and what he's saying.

Teddy does find a conversation about a movie night. It seems a few kids from his class are planning to watch *Moby Dick* together. Not surprising. Also not surprising that Zach isn't on the list of students attending. If he wants to watch *Moby Dick*, he'll do it in his own theater room.

Teddy looked at the aerial view of Zach's house on Google: A place that big must have a theater room.

By Sunday night, Teddy is sure Zach paid someone to write the paper. His social media posts show someone who is too active, too available, for him to have read such a long book and written a paper over the course of the week. Teddy just can't prove it.

If his wife were around, Teddy would discuss it with her. Allison is one of the most ethical people he has ever met. She would understand his disgust toward Zach.

Instead, he goes to the basement.

At one time, Allison had planned to build the basement out into a rec room for the kids. But they never had kids.

Now it's used for storage, with the exception of one

corner. Teddy has set up a workstation that looks a bit like a laboratory. Beakers, test tubes, and even a Bunsen burner are lined up on the table. The shelves behind it hold coffee pods.

It's been years since Teddy tried his first pod. The pods were terrible at first, and he much preferred his French press coffee.

But as the pods became more popular, he decided to give them another go. Better, but he still wasn't convinced – not until he found Prime Bold. Now, he can't imagine his day without it. After a while, he even threw out his French press.

His wife was rather upset about that.

Allison went right out and bought another, placing it on the kitchen counter next to his new one-cup machine. Every morning, Teddy listened to her French press gurgling away as he enjoyed his first coffee. She had to wait for hers. He never said a word, though. Her body, her choice, and all that.

On one morning, when he was in the house alone, a coffee pod malfunctioned and leaked. He wanted to figure out why. He pulled it apart, carefully looking at each part of the pod, and finally spotted an extra hole where the grounds were seeping out.

That's when it first occurred to him that not only did coffee come out of the pod, but something could be put *into* it as well.

So he tried it.

Using a syringe, he punctured a tiny hole just under the lip of the pod. The first time, he injected a bit of alcohol right into the filter of coffee. Just to see if it would work, and if he could taste it.

He did.

After that, the possibilities were endless.

All it took was a little observation. Who drank coffee in the break room? Who brought their own pods to work? Which flavors did each of them drink?

Again, he performed an experiment. He slipped a Gold Roast into his pocket, took it home, and injected it with half a Valium diluted with water. The tiny hole made by the syringe was invisible unless someone carefully inspected it before brewing.

Mindy did not. She drank up that horrible flavor of coffee, and for a few hours, she wasn't quite as high-strung. She wasn't happy necessarily, but she wasn't huffing and puffing about anything.

So he tried it again. And again. And again.

He mixed up all sorts of things – Valium, sleeping pills, even over-the-counter meds. The things he did were good: People who kept sniffling and coughing got cold medicine so they'd keep their germs to themselves. The ones who didn't get enough sleep got woken up a little.

And high-strung people got to relax. They needed to, or else they'd have a heart attack. Like the current headmaster, who had one last year.

Teddy is just helping everyone. Doing what's best for them.

Well, except for Sonia.

16

On Monday morning, Sonia feels fine, just fine. By yesterday, her stomach had felt a lot better, and she was able to review the work Courtney had done on the *Bugle*. Sonia doesn't know why she was ever worried. Courtney had done a spectacular job without her, getting most of the edits done and a large portion of the layout. After going through it several times, she had just one thought:

I should have more confidence in myself.

Sonia was, and is, a good teacher. Maybe she isn't a college professor like her husband, but she is a great teacher. Courtney knew exactly what to do because Sonia had taught her how to do it.

That was the second silver lining of her little stomach flu. It reminded Sonia that she's good at what she does.

With a smile on her face, she heads into the school and straight to the *Bugle* office. Courtney is already at her desk, looking almost as stressed as she did on Friday.

'Mrs B! How are you?' she says, getting up from her chair. 'How are you feeling?'

'Oh, I'm fine. Just fine. It was only a little bug. Well, maybe more than a little bug, but I powered through.'

Courtney smiles. 'Good.'

'Now, let's see where we are.' Sonia moves past her, to the computer, and bends down. Back in her element now. 'Courtney, this issue looks even better than it did last night.'

'Really?'

'Absolutely. You've done an incredible job.'

Courtney smiles so big it's blinding. 'Thanks, Mrs B.'

'I'll let you know as soon as I get Zach's article,' Sonia says.

It's still a bit early, so Sonia heads to the far end of the school. The custodian's room is deep in the corner of the south wing, far away from the classrooms. Joe has been at the school much longer than Sonia. Twenty years at least.

No doubt he was the one who had to clean up her mess on Friday, and what a mess it was.

His door is shut, so she knocks, but he doesn't answer. Sonia is a little relieved, and embarrassed, so she is fine with writing him a little thank-you note and slipping it under his door.

Next stop before class: the teachers' lounge. The room is crowded – everyone is getting their coffee before first period, and they all ask her how she is doing.

'Oh, I'm fine. Just fine.' She smiles. 'I'm not dead yet, anyway.'

'Great, great,' they all say. 'So glad you're better.'

'Me too.'

She gets her coffee and leaves, getting the feeling that they had been talking about her before she walked in. They couldn't still be talking about Friday. By now, that must be old gossip. Nothing lasts more than a day around here.

So maybe they had been planning her ten-year anniversary party. It's just four days away.

One of the reasons Teddy despises giving extra assignments to students is that he has no recourse. From the beginning, the terms are set. Do this assignment, and your grade will go up. Unless the extra assignment is abominable, the deal has been fulfilled. Which means Teddy is stuck raising Zach's current grade up to an A.

Minus.

For all the extra trouble.

Zach knows it, too. In class, he smiles and looks relaxed. Jokes with his friends and flirts with a girl like he's got all the time in the world.

Too bad the students don't drink coffee from the lounge.

All of this puts Teddy in a bad mood, which doesn't get any better when he sees Sonia. She is back at work and getting lots of attention, due to her dramatic upchuck on Friday. He expected this. He just didn't expect her to be even more pompous than usual.

They run into each other outside the teachers' lounge before school has started. Today, her dress is green. Puke green.

'So happy to see you back,' he says. 'We were all worried about you.'

'Oh, that's so kind. I certainly appreciate all the well-wishes, but I'm fine now. Just fine.'

'Good to hear.'

'And,' she says, 'the *Bugle* will be out on Wednesday, as scheduled, *with* Zach's article.'

Teddy is a little surprised at this but doesn't show it. 'Wonderful,' he says.

'I think so, too.'

With one last self-satisfied smile, she goes into the lounge. Teddy does not. Instead, he heads back toward the stairs. Along the way, he passes through the Hall of Fame. That's what they call it, this area that houses portraits of the

Belmont founder, all the headmasters, including the current one, and the board of directors.

Beyond that are portraits of the teachers and staff. But not all of them.

The teachers who 'make the wall' – as it's called – are the teachers who don't just work at Belmont; they also attended the school. Former students who return to teach or work at the school are considered special. Better, even. Belmont, they say, is their home.

Teddy is not one of them.

Sonia is.

17

With the distraction of Sonia out of the way, Teddy can go back to doing what he's supposed to do: teach.

Although his second-period class was assigned to read *The Outsiders* less than a week ago, they are already burning through it. He knows this from some of the online talk. Many of the students have read it before, which he expected, but for some it's the first time.

'I know you've all just started on this book,' he says to the class. 'So I just want to talk a little about your first impressions.'

Danielle is the first to raise her hand. Always.

'Yes?' Teddy says.

'In general, the book's about the socioeconomic differences between the Socs and the Greasers, and the differences in how they're treated. The Greasers are treated horribly because they are poor, and everyone assumes they have to be criminals.'

'Kind of like today,' says Alex, another student. He is not a scholarship student – in fact, his family is very wealthy – but online Alex claims to be quite 'woke.'

'Would you agree,' Teddy says, 'that if you lived in the world of *The Outsiders,* the majority of you would be considered Socs?'

'Yes.'

'Yes.'

'Yes.'

'Probably yes,' Danielle says. 'Except they didn't have the internet. Things are different now.'

'No, they aren't,' Alex says.

'Of course they are,' Danielle says.

Teddy looks at Courtney, who is staring at her desk. She doesn't raise her hand to say anything. Unusual for her. Must be all that work on the *Bugle*, which comes out in just two days, because it certainly isn't the book.

'I know some of you have probably read this before,' Teddy says. 'So without giving anything away, what else has struck you about this book?'

'The nicknames,' someone says. 'Ponyboy, Sodapop, Two-Bit. It's weird.'

'Is it? Don't some of you have nicknames?'

A few students nod.

'So maybe the names themselves are odd, but not the idea of having a nickname,' Teddy says. 'What else?'

'The division is so clear, even in the first chapter,' Danielle says. 'There are the Socs and Greasers. It's like the middle class doesn't exist for Ponyboy.'

'Because it doesn't.'

Courtney.

Finally.

'What do you mean by that?' Teddy says.

'The middle class doesn't pick on the Greasers. The Socs do – they beat them up. That's why it's important.'

'Excellent,' Teddy says. 'And why do you think the Socs beat up the Greasers?'

'They think they're better,' Alex says. 'Because they're rich.'

'But bullying isn't like it used to be. It's not like any of *us* bully kids who don't have money,' Danielle says.

Most of the students nod, including Courtney.

Granted, the students at Belmont aren't violent, and there aren't many fights at the school. Still, Teddy wants them to realize how hypocritical they are about the way they treat those who are less fortunate. Like the scholarship kids. They're always pariahs.

There's one in his class right now. Katherine, one of the Invisibles, who sit in the back. She says nothing during this conversation. Teddy would call on her but doesn't want to embarrass the poor girl.

He remembers what it was like to be that kid. What it was like to be looked down on. It's not so different now, as an adult. His picture isn't on the wall because he couldn't afford to attend Belmont.

Always the outsider. Just like in the book.

The same book Allison was reading when he met her.

She was sitting in front of a grocery store. Teddy almost passed right by her on his way in. Someone was always gathering donations for one organization or another, and usually the tables were manned by a group of children and parents. He'd never stopped.

Not until he saw Allison.

She sat behind a fold-out table, book in hand, and she twirled a strand of dark hair around her finger. The hand-printed sign on the table read:

Memorial Hospital Fundraiser
The Children's Wing needs toys!
Can you help make a sick child smile?

The sign was decorated with a bunch of stick figures resembling kids with big smiles on their faces. Teddy stopped and stared at it a second too long.

'You don't like my drawing?' she said.

'Oh, no. I think it's great. Are you an artist?'

She smiled. A real smile. Not like the ones he saw later, when she was angry. 'Funny,' she said. 'I'm a nurse.'

'I didn't know nurses raised funds like this.'

'I didn't, either. But it's my first year, and apparently we all have to do it the first year. Well, we don't *have* to, I guess, but it's recommended.'

'Like extracurricular activities in school,' he said.

'Just like that.'

'I'm a teacher.'

'I'm Allison.'

He laughed. Teddy didn't laugh a whole lot, certainly not while he was working, but it took this woman less than a minute to crack through that wall.

'I don't mind it, though,' Allison said. 'The children really do need new toys. The ones they have are just sad.'

He reached for his wallet and pulled out what little cash he had. 'I have a twenty. Will that buy some toys?'

She snatched the bill out of his hands. 'Of course it will. I'll write you a receipt for your taxes. It should save you a whole twenty-five cents.'

Again, he laughed. Probably much harder than he would have if she hadn't been so cute. He started thinking maybe she was what he needed. Someone who made him laugh. He couldn't remember dating anyone who could do that.

Teddy nodded toward her book. 'I teach that book in class,' he said.

'Really? First time I've read it.'

'What do you think?'

She shrugged, tearing off a receipt from the book and handing it to him. 'It's not bad. The Socs are real assholes, though.'

That's when he knew for sure. She was exactly what he needed.

18

Right after the last bell, Teddy leaves the school and heads home. It's not often he does this. Usually, he has meetings to attend or someone to see, but today his schedule is clear. He treats himself by taking off as soon as he can.

The house looks the same when he gets home. Same overgrown garden and weeds, same dilapidated porch, same weathered siding that needs to be painted. Nothing out of order.

Until he walks inside.

It's the scent. Fresh and clean, like laundry right out of the dryer. So familiar, and so wonderful.

'Allison?' he calls.

No answer.

'Allison, are you here?'

When he still doesn't get an answer, he runs up the stairs to the bedroom.

It's empty. The bed is unmade, just as he left it, and his pajamas are still thrown over a chair. On the nightstand: a stack of books, several empty glasses, a blinking alarm clock he never reset after a power outage.

The scent is stronger here.

'Honey?' he says.

No answer, no movement. No sound of anyone other than himself.

But she's been here.

He goes to the closet – her closet. The house is so old, it wasn't built with a lot of storage. They never did get around to building a walk-in. Instead, there are two tiny closets in their bedroom, one for each, and the rest of their things are stored in other rooms. Each season, the clothes are rotated.

Her closet door is closed, just as it was this morning. He hesitates before flinging it open.

Empty.

Hangers with no clothes, a shelf with no shoes. Even up high, where Allison kept sweaters and handbags, there's nothing.

Yesterday, there was. The closet was at least half-full, if not a little more. She hadn't taken everything when she left.

Four months ago, in the dead of summer, Teddy and Allison had gone to bed at around the same time they always did. Both had read a bit before turning out the lights, though it wasn't easy to get to sleep. There was air-conditioning, but it wasn't enough. The heat came in through the cracks in the old doors and windows, even up from the floor. Allison hated it.

When he woke up, she was gone. Along with some of her clothes, her toiletries, and her computer.

After thirteen years of marriage, she just quit. The only thing she left behind was a bill. Right on the kitchen table. No note. Not even a Post-it. Just a bill mistakenly addressed to her instead of him.

That was the day Teddy started picking at his cuticles again. Whenever he thought about contacting her, he did that instead.

One more day before the *Bugle* goes live, and Courtney is finally starting to calm down.

'See?' Sonia says, pointing to the computer screen. 'It looks fantastic.'

Courtney nods, maybe listening or maybe not. When she isn't staring at the screen, she's fielding text messages from her mother. But the next time her phone lights up, she turns it over.

'Everything okay at home?' Sonia says.

'Just the usual.'

Sonia doesn't answer. But, yes, she knows how Ingrid is. When she's not pushing the board or the Collaborative into action, she's pushing her daughter to excel. Not that Courtney needs it. She's hardly a wayward child.

Courtney flips back to the first page of the paper and starts going through it. Again.

'It looks great,' Sonia says.

'I'm submitting this issue with my applications. It has to be perfect.'

'All right.' Sonia pauses, letting the tension deflate a little. 'Why don't you run out and get some food. Let me go over it. Fresh eyes, you know?'

Courtney almost argues, but then she nods. 'Yeah. Fresh eyes are good.'

'Get some air. Come back in an hour or so. That'll give me time to go through it.'

'I'll be back in thirty minutes.'

Once Courtney is gone, Sonia goes through the *Bugle*, as she said she would, but she starts with the article about herself. She flips through the pages on the screen until it pops up on page three. It's after Zach's article, after the lacrosse spotlight, but before the article about the new library wing. Not a bad placement at all.

MRS. BENJAMIN CELEBRATES 10-YEAR
ANNIVERSARY THIS WEEK

English teacher Sonia Benjamin will celebrate her 10-year anniversary this Friday. Benjamin attended Belmont Academy (class of 2001) and went on to attend Brown University. She received her master's from St John's University and then went overseas as a volunteer for Teachers Without Borders. When she returned to the States, she came back to Belmont, which she considers her 'home away from home.'

During her time here, she has been active in the Belmont community, serving on a number of committees throughout the years. She is currently a liaison to the Collaborative and faculty advisor to the *Belmont Bugle*.

On Friday, the school will have a day-long celebration in her honor in the Stafford Room, next to the dining hall. At noon, the anniversary ceremony will commence, and it is open to all.

Overall, Sonia is satisfied with the article, though she does wish it introduced her as 'Beloved English teacher Sonia Benjamin.' It would have been more accurate.

19

Early Wednesday evening, Teddy maneuvers his way around the back of his house. It's dusk, making everything look grey. He can't decide if that makes the garden look better or not.

Using his phone, he takes pictures of every plant, weed, bush, and tree. Back inside, at his computer, he runs each picture through a search to identify it and double-checks the information in a real book. No one knows better than he does how fake everything can be on the internet.

What a lucky state of affairs that he'd never cleaned up that garden. It's filled with so many good things.

He stares at the pictures and taxonomic names until he gets a headache. The pain is right above his eyes, beneath the brows, and it feels like his nerves are exploding.

Closing his eyes, he sits back in the chair. Not his chair – it's Allison's. He has moved into her office to work, only recently realizing that she had the better space. A better chair, too. It belongs to him now.

But he's not thinking about Allison for long. In his mind, he sees the *Bugle*.

The issue came out today at noon, as always, so everyone could read it at lunchtime. Teddy did. He sat in his classroom, first reading Zach's article about the memorial. He read it three times, searching for similarities to the essays Zach had turned in.

If he were 100 percent honest, he'd have to say the styles

were similar. Thankfully, though, no one was putting him under oath, so he didn't have to be honest. Not even to himself.

And Zach did mention Teddy's name, because he'll be speaking at the memorial.

Sucking up again.

He's always been an ass-kisser — that's how he gets away with being so cocky. Like the way he gives all of his teachers a Christmas gift. Teddy hasn't received one yet, because this is his first semester with Zach, but one will be coming his way in December. Last year, Zach gave each one of his teachers a Montblanc pen engraved with their name.

Teddy saw them in the lounge. He specifically remembers Sonia mentioning that it was the nicest, most thoughtful gift she had received from a student. And that was saying something. Belmont students aren't cheap.

Unlike Sonia, he isn't moved by this kind of thing. Whatever Zach gives this year won't improve Teddy's opinion of him.

There's also an article in the *Bugle* about Sonia. Her ten-year anniversary party has become so elaborate, a special committee has been set up just to organize everything.

With his eyes still closed, Teddy scoffs out loud.

It wasn't that long ago that he had his own ten-year anniversary at Belmont. The only party they'd had for him was in the teachers' lounge, where someone had hung up a cheap CONGRATULATIONS banner and set out a plastic container of cupcakes from the grocery store. Teddy's ten-year pin showed up in his department mailbox.

But Sonia is different. As a former Belmont student, she's part of the family.

And she's rich, too. She doesn't even have to work, but she does, which makes it even worse.

Teddy opens his eyes, massaging his temples to try and get rid of the pain. He goes back to work identifying the plants in his yard. Earlier in the week, he'd used the sap from creeping juniper, which is what made Sonia so sick.

But there are so many other possibilities.

The dress fits.

Sonia doesn't try it on until Friday, just in case the extra day makes a difference in her size. But when she slips it on first thing in the morning, it fits almost like it did when she first bought it. Sure, it's a little tight around the hips and it rides up a little on her legs, but it fits.

'You look nice.'

Mark has just come out of the bathroom. He's wearing no shirt with his pajama bottoms. They're pulled down low because of his tummy. She's not the only one who has gained weight over the years.

'Thank you,' she says, slipping into a pair of spiky heels. Not shoes she would normally wear to school, but today isn't a normal day.

'Ready for the big party?' he says.

'Absolutely.'

'You sure you don't want me there?'

No. No, she does not. This day belongs to her, and her alone. Not to Dr Mark Benjamin, PhD and professor at Stanhope University. The same Dr Benjamin who publishes an academic paper once a year. Yes, she loves him and, yes, she is proud of him, but in a roomful of educators, he is always the star.

Not today.

'Oh, spouses don't usually come to these things,' she says. 'It's a school thing.'

'All right.' He leans forward to kiss her, but she moves, not wanting him to mess up her lipstick. He kisses her on the top of her head. 'Congratulations. You deserve this party after all your hard work.'

Yes. Yes, she does.

She walks down the stairs, taking her time so as not to twist her ankle wearing those high heels, and goes straight to her car. No breakfast this morning – there will be plenty of food at the party. No, the *soiree*.

On the way to school, Sonia smiles as she thinks about that word. Sure, it's a daytime party and not an evening affair, but it's still a soiree. And she's the guest of honor.

She parks and gets right out of her car, not bothering to repeat her mantra. Of course today will be a good day.

20

It's very early, at least thirty minutes before Sonia usually arrives. Frank, the math teacher, walks toward the front door. He's always here before everyone else, because it's quiet and he can get his work done. Since he has a toddler at home, she can understand why.

Ingrid Ross's SUV is parked by the side door, the back of it still open. Ingrid comes out of the building wearing her usual yoga pants, and Sonia feels a pang of jealousy. Ingrid gave birth to a child and still looks better than Sonia ever has.

She takes a deep breath, reminding herself that Ingrid is setting up a party for *her*.

Her intention is to go straight to her classroom. The official pin ceremony isn't until lunch. She walks down the hall, pausing just briefly outside the dining hall. The Stafford Room is on the other side of it.

No. She's not going to check on things. It's not her place.

Sonia continues to her classroom, puts all her things down, and heads for the teachers' lounge to get her coffee.

Instead, she ends up at the door to the dining hall. Maybe it would be okay to take a quick peek, since it's so early.

As soon as she walks into the Stafford Room, Ingrid sees her.

'Sonia! Congratulations on your big day.' She walks over and gives Sonia a brief hug. Their bodies barely touch. 'We're still setting up.'

Sonia nods, smiling as she looks around. A long table has been covered with a linen cloth and topped with a series of tiny roses inside glass bowls. Two of the other moms are hanging a large CONGRATULATIONS banner above it. Although the room is only half-decorated, it already looks amazing. Sonia should have known it would; Ingrid never does anything halfway. 'This is lovely. Really, thank you so much,' she says.

'Oh, of course. It's our pleasure.'

'I just wanted to stop by and thank you,' she says. 'I'll leave you to it and get ready for class.'

'Absolutely. We'll see you soon.'

Sonia takes one more look around before turning to the door. She opens it and finds a woman standing there with her arms full.

The woman looks startled at first and then says, 'Sonia! Congratulations!'

Sonia recognizes her as Connor's mother. 'Thank you so much. I'll see you later.' She holds the door open for her to enter. She has a coffee machine in one hand and a jumbled box of coffee pods in the other.

Zach takes his time after fourth period. He doesn't rush to put away his things or grab his phone, and he stops in the hallway to scroll through his messages. While everyone else heads to the dining hall for lunch, he lags behind, waiting for the hallways to clear.

On a normal day, the teachers would still be around, working in their classrooms or heading up to the lounge. Today, they're all going to Mrs B's anniversary party. All Zach has to do is wait for everyone to clear out.

Once they have, he heads straight to Crutcher's classroom.

The desk has been cleared off, and there's no sign of his laptop. Zach knew it wouldn't be here, because Crutcher is the type who would lock it up. Like anyone would steal that ancient computer.

He's more interested in what Crutcher keeps in his desk.

Between the *Bleak House* paper and the letter he sent with it, he should've been removed from Crutcher's shit list. Any other teacher would've done it, but not this one. Zach didn't even get a thank-you email. Nothing, just nothing.

Which pissed Zach off. If he couldn't get Crutcher to like him by working hard, he'd find another way.

Even if it meant a little snooping. Some might call it an invasion of privacy. His dad wouldn't.

Know your enemy better than he knows himself.

Zach shuts the door to the classroom and sits down at Crutcher's desk, pulling open the center drawer. First impression: It's a lot messier than he'd expected. Pens, Post-its, and scraps of paper are all jumbled together. He has a collection of odd erasers, including a pink butterfly and a bumblebee, which were probably left behind by students. Zach rummages around, finding two calculators, three pencil sharpeners, and highlighters in every color. Nothing of interest.

He moves to the drawer on the right. This one is filled with books – *Moby Dick*, *The Outsiders*, *The Scarlet Letter*. Zach flips through them, looking for notes, and finds nothing. Underneath the books, copies of the syllabuses for all of Crutcher's classes. Nothing good in those.

Zach isn't looking for something specific. He's looking for anything he can use to get on Crutcher's good side.

87

He moves to the drawer on the left. A stack of takeout menus – mostly Chinese food and delis. Underneath those, he finds another book:

Local Flora & Fauna: A Field Guide

Gardening.

Zach wouldn't have guessed Crutcher was the gardening type, but at least it's something. The first thing he's learned about Crutcher's personal life.

A business card is stuck in the book, maybe as a bookmark. Zach reads the name on the front:

DR. LEO TOBIN

FERTILITY SPECIALIST

And that's the second thing he has learned about Crutcher: He and his wife are trying to have a baby.

21

The Stafford Room looks ridiculous.

Teddy hadn't gone down there all day, on purpose, because he was already tired of hearing Sonia's name. But he wouldn't miss the lunchtime ceremony for anything.

He stands just inside the door, taking it all in.

The room has been decorated from corner to corner, from the huge CONGRATULATIONS banner to the roses on the tables. Not to mention the toy bobcats. Those little creatures are everywhere.

Most of the teachers are already here, along with a number of parents from the Collaborative. Ingrid Ross is front and center, right where she should be.

A number of students are also in attendance, mostly those who work on the paper, including Courtney. She and her mother are on opposite sides of the room.

'This is quite a shindig,' Frank says, walking up next to Teddy. The math teacher looks both wired and pumped, like he was just doing push-ups out in the hall.

'Yes, everything looks nice,' Teddy says.

'Try the sandwiches.' He holds one up. 'Salmon, I think.'

'Salmon? Really?'

'Tastes like it.'

Salmon. Teddy wants to scoff, but he holds it in. He certainly didn't get salmon at his party.

From where he stands, he can see the giant cake. Three

tiers, almost like a wedding cake, and personalized just for Sonia. It's as over-the-top as everything else in the room, and Teddy feels a strong urge to run his finger through the icing.

When Ms Marsha enters the room, the room quiets down. She is the gatekeeper, the one who controls who sees – or doesn't see – the headmaster. Her appearance means he is on his way.

Even Teddy straightens up when he walks in the door. A few others do the same. He's not a tall man, but he is imposing. It's the posture, no doubt. Ex-military.

After greeting Sonia, the headmaster turns to the group. 'First, let me thank the Collaborative for organizing this fine event.' The headmaster's voice is deep. Commanding. When he speaks, there's no doubt he is in charge.

Or so he thinks. Teddy smiles. This really might be his favorite day ever at Belmont.

'Now to the reason we are all here,' says the headmaster. He turns to Sonia, who looks so excited, she might spin off into another galaxy. 'As you all know, Sonia Benjamin attended Belmont – '

Bang! The table of food shakes, and people rush to steady it. Everyone turns to see what happened.

Ingrid.

She is standing at one end of the table, looking a bit embarrassed. Her face is red, her eyes wide. She bends over and picks up a plastic bottle filled with something green. Tea, probably. All the yoga moms drink green tea.

'Sorry,' she whispers. 'I dropped it.'

Courtney is on the other side of the room, and she looks like she wants to die.

Teddy isn't sure whom he pities more, Courtney or her mother, but it sure as hell isn't Sonia. She looks a bit angry.

The headmaster starts up again. 'As I was saying, Sonia Benjamin attended Belmont Academy and then went on to . . .'

He drones on, listing her whole résumé, and Teddy tunes it all out. Instead, he watches Sonia, looking for signs of his latest experiment. So far, she looks happy and fine – and not sick at all.

Disappointing. Very disappointing. Perhaps he shouldn't have tried something new *today* of all days. Maybe it takes too long to work. Or perhaps he didn't use enough.

With a sigh, he looks over at Ingrid. Her face is still pink with embarrassment, and it makes Teddy smile. He looks down at her hands, which are gripping the table.

The table.

For the first time, he notices the coffee cup. No, the coffee *cups*.

They're everywhere.

One is right in front of Ingrid. It's almost empty.

The others are scattered about: on the table, in people's hands, on the counter. Right next to a one-cup coffee maker. A box of coffee pods is next to it.

Must be a new box. It's not as if these mothers would take pods from upstairs. They certainly can afford to buy them.

Teddy turns his attention back to the headmaster, who is still going on and on.

'And after earning her master's degree, she went on to work with . . .'

He can't help but look back over at the counter. That box of coffee pods is calling to him, because it isn't right. Boxes are stacked tight with pods, all fitted in to maximize the space. This one looks different.

The pods appear to be thrown in, all jumbled and disorganized. As if someone threw them in after gathering them from . . . somewhere else.

No. No, no, it's not possible. Teddy shakes his head, telling himself not to be ridiculous. He's just making things up because the headmaster's speech is so boring.

But he can't shake that sick feeling in his stomach, and it's not from coffee.

'And I am very proud and honored to congratulate Sonia on her ten-year anniversary. It is an incredible achievement.' The headmaster turns toward Ms Marsha, who hands him a small velvet box. The pin. The all-important pin.

Teddy is wearing his.

The headmaster opens the box, revealing the pin, and Teddy checks his watch. *This is taking so –*

A scream interrupts that thought.

It comes from over on the right, where Ingrid is standing. *Was* standing.

She has collapsed on the floor.

22

Teddy can't move. Everything in front of him is still moving, but he has frozen. Almost like he's watching a thriller on a life-size screen:

Ingrid, completely unconscious, a trickle of blood on her forehead from the fall. Surrounded by people, none of whom know what to do.

Ms Marsha, calling 911.

Sonia, in that too-tight red dress. She looks thunderstruck.

All because of Teddy. He isn't sure if he should laugh or cry, so he does neither as it all plays out in front of him.

'Ambulance is on the way,' Ms Marsha says. She motions to the Collaborative members, telling them to get all the food off the table. 'It may be contaminated.'

It isn't. Teddy knows that. But he also now has a reason to move, because he's got to get rid of that coffee.

He walks toward Ingrid, where everyone is freaking out. No one pays attention when he picks up Ingrid's cup, along with a few others, and maneuvers through the crowd toward the sink.

One of the mothers is already there, reaching out to take the cups from him. 'I've got it,' she says.

Teddy has no choice but to hand them over. He keeps his eye on Ingrid's cup as the other woman puts it on the counter.

Outside, a fire truck pulls up, along with a police car. It's a small town that doesn't have much crime, so he wouldn't be surprised if the whole department shows up.

The firefighters, officers, and EMTs distract the mother who took Ingrid's cup. She moves like a cat, almost leaping toward them, then forges a path through the crowd so they can reach Ingrid. Teddy takes the opportunity to get to the counter and dump out Ingrid's cup.

Just in case.

'What happened?'

Zach, eyes bugging out of his head. He just walked in the door.

'Mrs Ross collapsed,' Teddy says.

'Oh my God.' Zach rushes off, toward the center of the chaos.

Teddy takes a step and almost runs into Sonia, who looks as frozen as he was a few minutes ago.

'I don't . . . understand,' she says.

'No one does.'

She shakes her head. He backs away.

'Teddy, move.'

It's Ms Marsha, trying to make a smooth path for them to get Ingrid out. She's on a stretcher, an oxygen mask over her face, and they rush her past him and out the door, Ms Marsha leading the way.

Teddy follows, but not to go to the hospital. He walks through the dining hall and heads upstairs, to the teachers' lounge.

Maybe he didn't have to empty Ingrid's cup. Maybe the coffee came from someone's house, not the lounge. Maybe he's just being ridiculous.

That must be it. Conscience can be such a terrible thing.

The chance that Ingrid drank the coffee meant for Sonia is . . .

One hundred percent.

There's only one coffee maker in the lounge, which means the one downstairs came from here. So did the coffee pods.

Oops.

By the time Teddy returns to the Stafford Room, almost everyone is gone. Two policemen are still hanging around, talking to a few of the mothers.

He scans the room, looking for a garbage can.

The pod. He has to get the pod.

One garbage bin is near the table, which has now been cleared of all the food. Only the decorations remain. The miniature roses are in tatters, and at least one of the vases has tipped over.

The second garbage bin is over by the counter, close to the coffee maker. And the officers. He has no idea how he can manage this, but he's got to try. As he takes a step forward, he feels a hand on his arm.

'Teddy.'

Ms Marsha's veiny hand holds him back.

'Oh, Ms Marsha,' he says. 'Any word on Mrs Ross?'

'Nothing yet. But we've got to clear the room.' She leads him back through the door, away from the garbage bin. 'The headmaster has decided it would be best to cancel classes for the rest of the day, given how traumatic this event might be for the students.'

'Yes. Yes, that's a good idea.'

Ms Marsha is preparing to close the door on him. The

kids who were hanging around, trying to see what's happening, scatter when they hear school is out for the day.

'Thank you,' she says. 'The headmaster will send out a notice if we hear anything.'

She shuts the door, leaving Teddy standing by himself.

Ruined. Totally ruined.

Sonia stomps around her empty classroom, stress ball in hand, and it's not working. She hurls it against the wall. It makes an unsatisfying sound when it hits. Not a *bang*. A *whomp*.

Not that she isn't worried about Ingrid. Of course she is. Of course she feels horrible Ingrid was taken away in an ambulance, even if it was due to not eating enough. Probably. Because the woman is so damn thin.

Ruined.

Sonia does have her pin. It's right on her red dress. She'd had to retrieve it from the *floor* after the headmaster dropped it in all the chaos. That's what her ceremony had come down to. Scurrying around on the floor to get her ten-year pin.

Picking up the stress ball, she almost hurls it against the wall a second time.

But she stops. Takes a deep breath. Reminds herself it could've been worse. *She* could've collapsed at her own ceremony.

Actually, at least then everyone would still be paying attention to her.

She throws the stress ball again.

23

A mistake. It was all a horrible mistake.

Teddy is alone in his classroom, sitting at his desk, picking at his cuticles. It helps him think. He replays everything in his mind, step by step, leading right up to what had happened a few hours ago.

He also thinks about the possible outcomes.

A woman collapsed. That's all. She didn't have a seizure or go into convulsions. She just . . . fainted.

That may or may not be enough to warrant testing everything in the room. To be safe, he assumes it is. He assumes Ms Marsha will demand it. After all, Ingrid Ross isn't just a board member; she's a parent who helps pay the bills. The headmaster will want to get to the bottom of this. The board will demand it.

Which means the police will test everything, including the pods in the garbage. But do they even have tests for the particular plant Teddy used? Would they be able to find the cardiogenic toxins found in *Actaea pachypoda*?

Again, to be safe, he assumes they can and they do. That the police discover a pod has been tampered with. Not that Ingrid had been *poisoned*, for God's sake. Teddy wasn't trying to poison anyone. He'd just . . . *manipulated* a pod. A little bit.

But would they know it's him? Maybe. He could've left fingerprints on it.

Teddy picks at the cuticle of his thumb so hard, it begins to bleed.

Ridiculous. This is all ridiculous, because Ingrid will be fine. She'll wake up, and everyone will think she fainted, and it will all be over. The police department isn't going to waste all that time and money testing every edible thing at the party, and they certainly aren't going to test every coffee pod in the garbage. It's absurd.

And it wasn't intentional. He wasn't trying to hurt anyone. Certainly not Ingrid Ross, whom he personally likes. She is on the board, after all.

He just wanted . . . He just wanted Sonia to stop being so smug. And to stop telling him what to do, especially about his own students. Perhaps he even meant to ruin her party. Just a little.

Ultimately, that was his goal. To bring her down a peg or two by having her faint at her own party. That's all he'd wanted.

Totally harmless.

Then everything had exploded, into police and EMTs, and it became . . . unbelievable, just unbelievable.

Although, on the upside, it did work. He had never used that plant before, but it did what it was supposed to. Something to be said for that, especially since he's not a scientist. He's just Teacher of the Year.

And it's not his fault the wrong person drank it. If those moms hadn't brought the pods downstairs, it would've been perfect.

So in a way, he did succeed.

He looks out the window. The last police car is pulling away. That's what he's been waiting for. He leaves his class, briefcase in hand. If anyone sees him, it will just look like he's leaving for the day. Normal, totally normal.

The dining hall is empty. Even the workers there have left. The door to the Stafford Room is closed but not locked. He walks right in like he's supposed to be there.

The room is not empty. Damn it.

Frank, the math teacher, is on the floor looking underneath a table. 'Oh Jesus, you scared me.' He stands up, brushing off his khaki pants. 'I didn't know anyone was still here.'

'I didn't, either.'

'Yeah, I lost my pen earlier. My good pen.' Frank looks around the room, arms spread wide. 'Still can't find it.'

'That's a shame.'

'Who knows, maybe one of the kids took it,' he says. 'What about you? What are you doing here?'

Teddy does his best not to look toward the counter, where the garbage is. Unfortunately, the room looks like it's been cleaned. The decorations are all gone, there's no sign of the food, and the coffee machine has been removed. 'I was just checking to see if anyone was still around. For any news.'

Frank shrugs, his muscular arms twitching. 'Nothing yet.' He moves toward the door to leave.

Teddy has no choice but to leave as well, having no reasonable excuse to stay. They walk through the empty dining hall, and Frank says, 'Weird day.'

'To say the least.'

'They'll probably have counselors available on Monday.'

'Yes, I expect they will.'

'Probably should have a clergy member here, too,' Frank says. 'In case someone needs it.'

Teddy doesn't answer that.

Outside, very few cars are left in the parking lot. No one wants to be at Belmont now, not after what happened. Teddy turns to Frank to say goodbye, and as he does, Frank's phone dings. Frank pulls it off the phone clip on his belt.

Teddy's phone vibrates. The message is from the headmaster.

Colleagues and friends,

It is with deep sorrow that I announce the untimely death of Mrs Ingrid Ross. She passed away at the hospital this afternoon.

Our thoughts and prayers go out to her family.

24

Frank Maxwell can't believe what he's reading. Ingrid Ross is dead.

Dead.

'My God,' Teddy says.

'Unbelievable,' Frank says.

They stand there for a minute, staring at their phones, until Teddy slips his phone back into his pocket. 'Well,' he says. 'I suddenly feel an urge to go home and see my wife.'

'Me too,' Frank says.

Teddy walks off toward his ridiculous old Saab, and Frank goes to his Jeep. He walks normally, or what he thinks is normally, but he can't tell, because his adrenaline is surging.

His hand goes to his chest, gripping the cross underneath his shirt.

Home. He should go home. His wife is there, along with his son.

They live in a modest but nice home, with a freshly mowed lawn and a fantastic old oak tree right in front. Frank doesn't make a lot of money, but his wife was creative with the decorating. To him, it looks like something out of a magazine. But it's comfortable. Home is a good, safe place to be.

He just doesn't want to go there.

Instead, he starts driving around. He likes to drive around when he needs to think, a habit that started way back when he got his driver's license – if eleven years can be considered way back. To him, it is. Feels like a million years ago when he first drove a car by himself. It was a crappy car, too, maybe older than Teddy's, but that didn't matter. Between the loud music and the ability to go wherever he wanted, Frank had gotten his first taste of freedom. He loved it.

So he drives. But it doesn't feel the same now – maybe because he is anything but free. With a wife, a child, a mortgage, and a job, nothing about his current life is free. He doesn't even buy groceries, because his wife is so particular.

And that's on a normal day. Today is anything but.

Frank drives away from the school and down the interstate, away from his home, his family, his wife. The music is loud, the windows are down, and the Jeep bounces down the road like he's got nowhere to be.

None of it helps. He feels worse than ever, trapped in a straitjacket with a chain pulling him back where he should be.

If he could, he'd go to the gym, but he's still nursing a shoulder injury. He forces himself not to work out and turns back toward home.

Missy's car is in the driveway, right where it should be. Before going inside, he takes a few deep breaths, says a quick prayer, and checks the mirror to make sure he has a normal expression on his face.

And here comes Missy. He has barely opened the door when she appears.

'I just heard what happened at the school,' she says. 'Are you okay?'

'Oh, I'm fine.'

'I swear I just picked up the phone to call you. Are you sure you're okay?'

Frank wraps both arms around his wife, willing her to shut

up. 'I'm fine. I barely saw anything.' He feels her relax against him.

'Good. Oh, that poor woman. Ingrid something? Russ?' She pulls back and walks him toward the kitchen. He can smell chicken cooking. They eat chicken a lot.

'Something like that,' he says, sitting down on a stool. The smell of the food relaxes him. 'Where's Frankie?'

Missy points to the family room. 'Watching cartoons.'

Frank takes a shower before dinner. By the time he gets out, his two-year-old son has moved to the kitchen. Frankie is hungry but doesn't want to sit still, and Missy explains to him that they all have to sit at the table to eat. This conversation plays out almost every evening, and it always ends with Missy bribing their son to sit still.

Frank welcomes the familiarity. Everything at home feels normal – the dinner, the cleanup, giving Frankie a bath. When Frank goes into his son's room and reads to him before bed, it feels like today was just a dream. A waking nightmare.

But it all comes back later, after Frankie and Missy are asleep. Frank opens up the Belmont website, and the news is right there, reminding him that it did happen. It wasn't a nightmare.

The same message the headmaster sent earlier is posted on the home page. Beneath it, scores of parents, teachers, and students have expressed their condolences. Frank adds his own.

My deepest sympathies to the Ross family.

He deletes it. Types it again. Deletes it again. Maybe it's best not to say anything. Maybe it would be worse not to.

Ingrid.

Goddamn Ingrid.

The guilt for that thought hits quickly.

His hand goes to his chest again, to his cross. He wears it every day, all day. Never takes it off.

For the rest of the night, he keeps his hand on it. And he wonders who is going to show up first: Ingrid's husband or the police.

Teddy doesn't go home. He doesn't even leave the Belmont parking lot. After watching Frank drive away, he gets out of his car and goes straight back to the Stafford Room. Because he has to be sure.

The trash is gone. Both bins have brand-new liners, not a single coffee pod to be found. Not on the counter or in the cabinets. He can't tell if the police took the garbage or not. After Ms Marsha threw him out of the room, he has no idea what happened.

With a sigh, he heads toward the back of the school. To the dumpsters.

25

Today will be a good day.
  Today will be a good day.
  Today will be a good day.
  Monday morning, Sonia sits in her car and repeats her mantra, bracing herself for what lies ahead. The weekend was terrible, with a slew of messages passed back and forth about the annual memorial. What should they say about Ingrid? Should the focus change?
  And what if it was something Ingrid ate?
  Could something have been spoiled?
  Where did those pastries come from?
  What about the milk in the coffee? Does she use milk, does anyone even know?
  Endless, absolutely endless. And not a single word about her ten-year anniversary, not even a congratulations.
  Sonia has to remind herself that a woman is dead. That's what she's competing with here: a dead woman. Impossible. It's not like she can run around saying *What about me?* and expect to get any sympathy. Or any congratulations, for that matter.
  So she puts a concerned-yet-pleasant look on her face and gets out of the car. The kids need her. Someone *died* on campus, for God's sake. They need her now more than ever.
  Let the day begin.

*

Frank pulls up to the school, still on edge. He's been that way the whole weekend, jumping at every knock at the door, every ring of the phone. Like he's standing at the top of a building, waiting for the push.

It's a terrible thing knowing your life is about to implode.

But it hasn't yet. Maybe it's all the praying he's been doing. He hopes it is.

He gets out of his car and heads into the school. No police, no angry husbands, no pitchforks. An auspicious start to the day.

As soon as he walks inside the building, Ingrid Ross stares him in the face.

A tribute has already been erected, no doubt by the Collaborative, and it features a large framed portrait of her. It's perched on a table, with flowers around the bottom, which makes Frank feel bad he didn't bring anything. Didn't even think about it.

The picture of her is one he hasn't seen before. Her hair is longer, and she isn't wearing any makeup. She's outside, with a big tree behind her, and she's smiling like she's truly happy. The Ingrid he knew wasn't happy. Determined, yes. Focused, absolutely. But happy? No, he wouldn't say that. Then again, neither was he. Not completely, anyway.

She knew that. Saw it in him, zeroed in on it, and made her move. Like a . . . one of those Greek things. He can't think of the name – he's a math teacher, not a mythology teacher – but eventually it comes to him.

A Siren.

Is that it? No, no. A succubus. Ingrid Ross was a succubus.

Just thinking about her makes him furious again.

He grabs his cross, outlining it with his finger through his shirt. Sometimes he thinks he's going to spontaneously combust for the things that go through his mind. Actually, he *should* spontaneously combust for what he has done.

For some reason, it doesn't happen. Instead, he is left with the guilt. That might be worse.

He walks away, not wanting to be caught staring at Ingrid's picture. Down the hall, he takes a right, away from his classroom, and heads to the Porter Room. Over the weekend, the school sent out a notice about a faculty meeting before first period.

The room is half-full when he arrives. Unlike the Stafford Room, this room isn't open to students. It requires a key card, and it's at the end of the south hall — too far away for any kids to hear what's happening.

Ms Marsha stands at the front and starts the meeting precisely at 7:40. Her tweed suit is as crisp as her voice.

'I'll be brief, as I know you all need to get to your first class,' she says. She holds a clipboard in her hand, because, like many of the old guard, she eschews technology. Even things that would make her job easier. 'You have all heard about the passing of Ingrid Ross. Rest assured, we are in constant contact with the police and the family about what happened to her. We are waiting for autopsy results to confirm the cause of death.'

News of an autopsy doesn't make Frank feel better. Not one bit.

'The family, as you might imagine, is devastated,' Ms Marsha says. 'We've placed an area at the school's entrance for anyone to express their condolences with flowers or notes. All of them will be passed to the family. In addition, we have extra counselors on staff today for the students and faculty. Please don't hesitate to refer someone there if they need help. That's what the counselors are for.' She stops and looks up from her clipboard. 'Questions?'

Someone else asks if attendance will be excused due to seeing a counselor. Another asks about Ingrid's funeral.

The funeral. Frank hadn't even thought about that.

God help him if it's held in a church. No way could he sit through that.

'We'll give you more information as we receive it,' Ms Marsha says. 'That's all for now.'

Eight minutes. That's how long the meeting took, and yet Frank's blood pressure feels even higher. He is standing near Sonia when Ms Marsha approaches her.

'Teddy Crutcher is out sick today. We're bringing in a substitute, but can you . . .'

Sonia nods, and Frank walks away, missing the rest of the conversation. He's too busy thinking about that autopsy.

He should have stayed away from her bottle of green tea.

That's what he had been looking for in the Stafford Room. Not his pen.

26

For the first time in who knows how many years, Teddy stands on his back porch – still worn, still dilapidated – and looks out over his backyard. It's been cleared of every single plant, bush, and shrub. The only thing left is the trees that were too large to cut down.

It's Tuesday evening, right around dusk, and Teddy hasn't been to work since Friday. He isn't sick and can't remember the last time he was. He's been too busy to go to work.

But he wasn't at first. Although he'd never admit it to anyone, he almost gave up. In fact, for a little while he did. Friday evening, after going through the school dumpster and coming up with nothing, he went home and got into bed. No food, nothing to drink. Certainly not milk – he didn't deserve that. He didn't deserve anything. Not after what he had done.

It was so horrible.

An idea that started as something so innocent had spiraled so far out of control that someone had died.

He was an awful man. Someone who focused on petty disagreements with his fellow educators. Someone who wanted to punish them for being so annoying. Someone who poisoned their coffee.

Well, maybe not poisoned. *Fiddled* with. He *fiddled* with their coffee. Lightly fiddled.

What he should've been doing was concentrating on his students. That was his job, his purpose, his *mission*.

He had screwed it all up.

The feeling inside him had started slowly. A tingle, like a mosquito was crawling around. No, a worm. Definitely a worm.

One that replicated.

The longer he stayed in bed, the more worms there were. It felt awful, as if his insides had been replaced with those slimy, slithering creatures. By Saturday evening, he was consumed with them.

The feeling was not new.

Teddy had felt it once before, after Allison left. When she'd left that bill on the table.

The feeling was so much worse than regret, which was just a nagging thought in the brain. Remorse was having your insides replaced by worms.

None of this would've happened if she were still here. She had a way of making everything better.

Whenever he was in a particularly bad mood, they would watch a movie together. She always picked the stupidest comedies. Allison hated dramas, hated anything serious or depressing. At first, he thought her movies were silly and not worth his time.

'It's worth it if you laugh,' she said. 'Even once.'

She was right. Those stupid movies did make him laugh, sometimes more than once, because he was with her. Allison had the most infectious laugh – it was a beautiful sound. One time, he told her it was like listening to poetry. She laughed at that, too.

Now he doesn't watch those movies. Not without her.

He barely laughs at all, and that's what started all of this: when he stopped laughing and started noticing how irritating his coworkers really were. He started fiddling with their coffee because they annoyed him no end.

Thinking about that, and about Allison, made him feel even worse.

He stayed in bed until the worms tired out, fell dormant. The pain began to subside as they wore themselves out. On Sunday morning, he finally crawled out of his hole, his sense of purpose renewed. He had to get back to his students, had to keep trying to teach them not to be selfish, entitled little bastards.

First, though, he had to get rid of all his wrongdoing, starting with the basement. Teddy got rid of all the pods, the test tubes, all of his experiments. The pills, the research, everything. It was all just a terrible distraction from what was really important.

Next, he had to tackle the garden, starting with the *Actaea pachypoda*.

The plant had immediately caught his attention. It was impossible to miss those berries – white with a black dot. That's why it was also called doll's-eyes. Those little berries looked just like tiny eyeballs, and they were filled with toxins that lower blood pressure. Too much would cause a heart attack. Just a little could make someone lose consciousness.

All he'd wanted to do was make Sonia pass out, preferably in the middle of her ceremony. He had been very careful not to extract too much juice from the berry when he injected it into the coffee pod. Death wasn't the goal. Not for anyone.

Wearing gloves, he pulled that plant first and wrapped it up tight. Then he moved on to all the others. It didn't matter if they were poisonous or not – they all had to go. It took

111

two days of atrocious, grueling work. Returning to school wasn't an option, not until the yard had been cleared.

Then he had to dispose of everything. That was the difficult part. As much as he wanted to pay someone to haul it away, he couldn't let anyone know what he was doing. No choice but to bag it all up and drive it to a yard-waste disposal facility himself. It took five trips, all to different facilities in different towns. He gave all of them a fake name.

Now, standing on his porch on Tuesday night, his body is sore from all the manual labor. Yet inside, he feels great, like he's been given a new start. No, he's given *himself* a new start.

A fresh glass of milk ends the day. It signals the end of penance.

He has cleansed himself of all the bad things he did, all the ways he was distracted from his true mission: the students.

He's ready to start over. Again.

27

The morning is glorious. Sun shining, birds chirping, Teddy wouldn't be surprised if a butterfly landed on his shoulder as he walks to his car. One doesn't, of course. He checks.

He pulls up to the school early, before most have arrived. The only car he recognizes is Frank's. Not surprising. Frank always arrives early. Teddy passes by his classroom, tempted to stop and say hello, but instead he goes straight to the teachers' lounge.

Everything looks the same, even the coffee pods. He smiles as he makes himself a cup.

Coffee pods. What a stupid idea that was.

He never found the pods in the dumpster, either. Didn't find anything of interest, but he did embarrass himself. Joe, the custodian, saw him climbing out of the dumpster. Neither of them said anything, which made it even worse. Joe's not likely to forget it, either.

Teddy goes down to his classroom, opens his laptop, and checks his email for the first time since Friday. He scans quickly, reading the flagged messages first. Ingrid is still dead and not yet buried. The word *autopsy* makes him freeze for a second, but he moves on. No time for the worms today.

Fallon distracts him. His former student continues to tell him how angry she is.

Hey, asshole, me again.

Just so you know, you aren't going to keep me from succeeding.
I'm graduating early and have already been accepted into a master's
program. It won't be long before I'm making more money than you.

Later.

Teddy smiles, as he always does when Fallon writes. She
still doesn't get it.

He's not the enemy. Never was. His goal for her, for all his
students, is to transform them from selfish brats into something better.

Fallon may not get it now, but he hasn't lost hope. Not yet.
Not for any of his students. He hasn't given up on her just like
he hasn't given up on Zach. One day, they just might get it.

And if they do, it will be because of him.

Death. Belmont is surrounded by death.

Sonia walks through the hall thinking about death because
it's everywhere. Ingrid's funeral will be on Friday and, not
long after that, the annual memorial.

'Good morning, good morning,' she says, nodding to the
students, looking each one in the eye. Reassuring them that
everything is A-OK, even though it's not. Yesterday, just
when everything had started to calm down a bit, an article
appeared in the local paper.

DEATH AT BELMONT ACADEMY?

That was the headline, question mark and all. Yes, there
was death at Belmont. So much death.

However, since Sonia is still alive and still the faculty advisor to the *Bugle*, she needs to find a new editor. Courtney isn't coming back to school anytime soon, if at all. Can't blame her for that, given that her mother died here.

There's that death again. Always sneaks up when it's least expected.

Sonia shakes it off and searches the main hall until she finds whom she's looking for.

'Zach,' she says.

He smiles at her, looking as normal as ever. 'Hey, Mrs B.'

'Have you spoken to Courtney? How is she doing?'

'I haven't talked to her since . . . well, since Friday,' he says.

'She's grieving. Give her time.'

'Yeah,' he says.

'She'll call you when she's ready.' Sonia pats him on the hand, offering her most reassuring look. 'I wanted to ask you something else. About the *Bugle*.'

'Another article? Already?'

'Not exactly.'

Zach stares at her, his face so open and trusting. 'What's up?'

She motions for him to follow, leading him around the corner, where the hallway isn't as busy. It's morning break, which lasts exactly sixteen minutes.

'It's about the editor position.'

'Oh,' he says. His eyes widen even further as he gets it. '*Oh.*'

'Yes,' she says, with the appropriate amount of seriousness. 'We don't have an editor at the moment.'

'But Courtney's coming back,' Zach says.

'Of course, of course. It's just for right now, while she's out. I'm sure she needs time with her family.'

Zach nods and keeps nodding. Sonia can almost see him weighing his options.

'Why don't you think about it overnight?' she says. 'Obviously, it's a big decision.'

'That's a good idea. I'll think about it.'

'Whatever you decide is fine. Either way, your participation at the *Bugle* will look good on your college applications,' she says. 'Even as just a reporter.'

He continues nodding as she walks away, leaving him to think about that.

The students are looking at Frank, but he doesn't really see them. They're just a blur of sleepy eyes, chins propped up by hands, and lots of blank stares. For him, seeing them like that is unusual. Most of the time, he watches them with care, waiting for one of them to act up. To do something wrong.

The devil and his minions can be anywhere, anytime. Always trying to lure these kids to the dark side. Frank is usually on guard for that, trying to help them resist the urge.

Today, not so much.

It's fourth-period calculus, and no one wants to be here. Not the students and not Frank. If he had his way, he'd be at the gym. Working out all his nervousness, which is a constant state at this point.

Or at church, praying out all his guilt. He was there last night, and the night before, and it hasn't worked yet. He hasn't heard a peep from anyone – not the police, not Ingrid's husband – and it's driving him insane.

A hand shoots up in the middle of the class.

'Yes, Stella?'

'If *a* plus *b* is the inverse function of *f*, then wouldn't the intersection point be *a* equals 1 over *a* plus *b* minus 1?'

Frank looks at the problem, working through what she'd said. It takes him longer than it should. 'Yes,' he finally says. 'Yes, you're right.' He swipes the smartboard and makes the whole problem disappear. How easy math can be.

Another problem appears on the board, and he asks the class to solve it. He uses the time to open his desk drawer and check his phone.

One text from his wife, telling him to get the oil changed in his car.

Relief, at first, but the angst comes back quickly. Two words express how he's feeling: *If only*.

If only he hadn't met up with Ingrid at that fundraiser.

If only Missy had come with him instead of staying at home with Frankie.

If only he hadn't had so much to drink. It always gets him in trouble.

If only he hadn't left with Ingrid instead of going home alone.

28

The day has been splendid, just splendid. Teddy loves that word. It might even be in his top ten, although that changes. Sometimes, he comes across a word he hasn't seen in a while, and then that word goes onto his mental list. But *splendid* is an all-time favorite.

His second-period class is largely done reading *The Outsiders*, so now they have to write their papers. Fourth period is a bit slower, reading *Moby Dick*, but that's to be expected.

By the time school is over, Teddy thinks about having a big glass of milk, even though he had one last night. Normally, he doesn't drink milk two days in a row, but if he can't celebrate the successes in life, then what's the point?

On the way home, he stops at the corner store. One of the many downsides of being a teacher is not being able to shop at the nice grocery stores. On this matter, Teddy made his peace long ago. He's even become friends with Hector, the owner and full-time cashier of Fourth Avenue Liquors.

They first met several years ago, when he discovered Hector's store had cheaper prices for milk than the discount grocery stores. Hector was also amenable to special orders. That's a good business owner, one who's willing to cater to his customers. Teddy has been loyal to him ever since.

'More milk today?' Hector says.

Teddy smiles as he walks toward the back, nodding his head.

'Have to keep an eye on you,' Hector says. 'That much milk can't be good for the body.' He laughs at his own joke, drowning out the TV stationed above the register.

Teddy grabs his milk from the refrigerator. Hector carries the brand just for him. Teddy only drinks milk from a glass bottle. Not that plastic or carton nonsense.

'Now tell me,' Hector says. 'What the hell is going on at your school?'

Teddy has to think for a minute. 'Oh, yes. It's just such a tragedy. That poor woman.'

'I'll say.'

'No one really knows what happened. She just . . . collapsed.'

'You haven't heard?' Hector says.

'Heard what?'

'Wow, I thought you guys would've known first.' Hector picks up the remote and changes the channel on the TV. It flips from a soccer game to the local news. 'I saw it a little while ago.' Using the remote as a pointer, he gestures to the screen. 'What the hell are you teaching those kids?'

The banner at the bottom of the screen doesn't make sense. Teddy reads it over and over, trying to understand.

17-YEAR-OLD BELMONT
STUDENT ARRESTED, ACCUSED
OF KILLING MOTHER

PART TWO

29

The first snow is always the most magical. It comes late this year – not until January. Blanketed in white, Belmont Academy looks like it belongs in a Dickens novel.

If not for the chain-link fence around the perimeter.

Two and a half months have passed since Courtney was arrested. Her trial is still a few weeks away, but the media has already set up camp outside the school. Their equipment is protected by tents, mini-heaters keep them warm, and a vendor sells hot coffee out of a van while someone else hands out flyers for a local business.

This is just the beginning, Sonia realizes.

The security guard waves her through, and she restrains herself from flipping off the reporters while passing by. She parks and gets out of her car, not bothering with her mantra. Even if she repeated it a thousand times, today would not be a good day.

Just inside the front door, the counseling room has been set up. Sonia walks past it and goes straight to the teachers' lounge. Frank is the only one there, which is surprising. The parking lot is at least half-full.

'Oh,' Frank says. 'Hey.'

'Good morning,' she says.

He sits in the corner, watching her as she puts her lunch in the refrigerator and makes a cup of coffee. He looks even worse than last week, if that's possible. Pale skin, dark circles under his eyes. Even his muscles look like they've shrunk.

'Everybody's in the Porter Room,' Frank says.

'Is there a meeting? I didn't get a notice – '

'No meeting. They set up a TV down there.'

Sonia purses her lips. School was the one place she'd expected to escape the madness, but apparently not. With a sigh, she puts sweetener in her coffee and leaves the lounge with every intention of going back to her classroom. Instead, she ends up in the Porter Room.

It's wall-to-wall packed with faculty and staff, all of whom are staring at a giant screen. The reporter on TV is a woman with platinum hair and so much makeup.

'*. . . awaiting the arrival of the assistant district attorney and the defense lawyer. Courtney Ross is not expected in court today for the first pretrial motion, or during jury selection. We don't expect to see her until the trial begins.*'

When they cut to a commercial, the talking starts.

'Are those reporters going to be outside for the whole thing?'

'Shouldn't they be at the courthouse?'

'They are. They're everywhere.'

'Jesus Christ.'

Sonia seconds that. After the holiday break, just as everyone had started settling into the new semester, it had all exploded again. The case, the trial, the media. It's even worse than when Courtney was arrested.

Jesus Christ, indeed.

A furniture commercial is playing when the TV goes silent. Ms Marsha steps in front of the screen, the rustle of her tweed skirt echoing through the room.

'If I can have your attention for a minute,' she says. 'This will not be an easy time for our students. The school will be under a spotlight until this . . . event is finally over, and many reporters will try to interview both you and the students. We prefer that you do not speak to them, though of course that choice is yours to make.' She pauses to look around the room, making a threat with her eyes. 'Downstairs, the counseling room is still fully staffed for anyone who needs it. It will be open until six every evening, and on Saturday mornings.'

Someone coughs. Behind Ms Marsha, the reporter is back on TV, but no one can hear her.

'Last but not least, please refrain from discussing the trial during class. Students will be checking their phones through-out the day and, no doubt, will be talking about it. Let's keep class time limited to your regular agenda.' Ms Marsha takes a deep breath. Sonia notices how tired she looks. Everyone who works at Belmont appears to have aged ten years over the past couple of months. 'Does anyone have questions?' Ms Marsha says.

No one does.

The first bell rings. At least one thing hasn't changed. Ms Marsha still has impeccable timing.

Sonia's first class goes about as well as expected. Belmont enrollment is down by at least 10 percent – no one knows the real number, and no one in admissions is talking, but all the classes feel smaller.

As directed, she doesn't mention the trial, or Courtney, during class. But the students do, both before and after. Throughout the day, she hears snippets about what's been on the news, what the pundits predict will happen, and what the kids think.

'She did it.'

'Totally.'

'No way. Courtney would *never.*'

'Did you ever meet her mother?'

By the time the day is over, Sonia feels so heavy. And she *is* heavy. None of her clothes fit; some are even too tight to wear. Stress eating. That's what her husband called it as he handed her another stress ball. She has three now: one at work, one at home, and another in her car.

They haven't helped much.

Also, she prefers to eat.

At home, she doesn't turn on the TV. She has no desire to hear – again – what happened today at the courthouse. She doesn't want to hear about the charges against Courtney, or how they suspect she killed her mother. Maybe intentionally, maybe not. It depends on which reporter is talking. Some say she drugged Ingrid Ross, others say she poisoned her, and a few describe what Courtney is accused of doing as 'tampering.'

And everybody's read the text messages – at least the ones that have leaked. Courtney repeatedly saying her mother was driving her insane convinced a lot of people she's guilty.

Sonia doesn't believe a word of it. Not. One. Single. Word.

While dinner is in the oven, she slices up some cheese and takes out a few crackers for a little snack before her meal. She almost has the first bite in her mouth when the phone rings. She recognizes the number but doesn't answer.

Before listening to the voicemail, she eats two crackers with cheese. Newly fortified, she plays the message.

'Mrs Benjamin, I'm calling for Jeffrey Brewster. Mr Brewster has finalized the witness list, and your name is on it. Once the trial begins, we will let you know what day you will be needed to testify. I'll give you

a call soon to review your testimony. Please let me know if you have any questions.'

Sonia hits DELETE.

Half the teachers at Belmont were put on the preliminary witness list. That was normal, they were told. The list always has more names than are needed. Everyone was preinterviewed and prepped, just in case. But now, Sonia will have to get up on that stand, swear on the Bible, and testify.

For the prosecution.

30

Frank doesn't want to see the news, hear the news, or even talk about the news, but when he gets home from work, his wife is watching it on TV.

'That poor girl,' she says.

'Yeah.' He drops his bag and heads into the bathroom, where he shuts the door and turns on the water. It's the only place he can't hear the TV.

A minute later, Missy knocks on the door. 'Honey?'

'Yeah?'

'We're having spaghetti tonight. It'll be done in about half an hour.'

He already smelled the sauce. The onions, tomatoes, and garlic made his stomach flip-flop as soon as he walked in the door. 'Great. Be out in a minute.'

When he returns to the family room, little Frankie is playing on the floor with plastic cars, crashing them together, over and over and over again. The noise is maddening.

'Stop that,' he says to Frankie.

Frankie does. For a minute.

The news is still on, and Courtney's picture stares back at him. It's the same one they've been showing on all the TV stations. The picture, taken from her social media account, shows her outside with friends, but they've been cut out. It's just Courtney, posing for the camera, her hip stuck out and her skirt just short enough to raise a few eyebrows.

Horrible. It's all so horrible.

For the rest of the evening, he stumbles through the motions. Eat the spaghetti, give Frankie a bath, put him to bed, go back out to the family room for quality time with Missy. Tonight, it revolves around an episode of *Bosch*, followed by more news.

'Coming to bed?' Missy says.

'Soon.'

'Okay.'

'You know what?' he says. 'I think I'm going out for a drive.'

'A drive? Now?'

'It's all this stuff about the school.' He waves his hand toward the TV. 'It's just ... I just need to get out for a minute.'

Missy gives him a sad look, and it's almost more than he can bear. 'Okay. I understand.'

She always understands. It makes everything so much worse.

Frank does get in his car and drive. He goes straight to church.

The Unity of Life Church is where he goes for answers. When he was trying to decide if he should ask Missy to marry him, he came here to pray for guidance. When she was pregnant, he came here to pray for a safe delivery and a healthy child. When he recently hurt his shoulder, he came here to pray for a speedy recovery.

The praying always made him feel better. Always made him feel like he'd come to the right place.

Now it doesn't.

He shouldn't be here, shouldn't be talking to God. He

should be talking to the police, starting by telling them what Ingrid did to him.

Or at least what he remembers. It isn't much.

At the fundraiser, where he saw Ingrid, she was wearing a sleek black dress that showed off her curves. Their conversation was normal at first. Nothing out of the ordinary for a teacher and a board member. The bar came next, and a drink.

'I'd really like to discuss the math curriculum with you in more detail,' she said. Her lips were a deep shade of red. Painted-on color that didn't smear on the edge of her glass.

'I'd like that,' he said.

'And I'm not just saying that. I really do mean it.'

'So do I.'

'Then let's go,' she said. 'Right now. Let's go around the corner to Mona's. We can have a drink and discuss it.'

He went. Because when the president of the Collaborative requests your company, you show up.

And when she keeps ordering cocktails, you drink.

They talked about math, about Belmont, maybe even some gossip. Nothing too bad, nothing harmful. Although by then, the night had become a little hazy.

She ordered two more drinks.

It never occurred to him that she might not be drinking them, that maybe she was emptying her glass into the planter behind them. He didn't think about that until later.

He remembers, sort of, when they got up to leave. She took him by the arm and led him out the door. A burst of cool air hit him, although he didn't shiver, didn't feel too cold.

That's the last thing he can recall.

He woke up alone in a hotel room.

31

The mall, or what's left of it, is an atrocious place. Sonia walks past the empty retail spaces, heading into the only decent store left. She has nothing to wear to court. Nothing that fits, anyway. And that won't do, not at all, because she's going to be on TV.

No way around it, as far as she can tell. The trial itself won't be televised, but everyone is filmed walking in and out of the courtroom. She'll be identified, too. Everything will be on the record and public.

The idea that she, Sonia Benjamin, a representative of Belmont Academy, is being forced to testify against one of their own is abominable. It makes her want to scream.

Instead, she grabs a piece of hard candy out of her bag and shoves it into her mouth.

She already knows what they're going to ask. They went through it in the preliminary interview, and again this afternoon, when one of the DA's assistants had called. The woman sounded as young as Sonia's students.

Her questions were the same as last time. As much as Sonia wanted to lie, she didn't. Couldn't. And she can't stop thinking about how her answers will sound in court.

Did you ever see Courtney Ross with her mother?
Yes.
Once? More than once?
Several times.

Did you ever see them argue?

Yes.

More than once?

Yes.

What did they argue about?

I didn't eavesdrop. I walked away to give them privacy.

Did Courtney ever talk to you about her mother?

Yes.

What did she say?

That her mother was rather demanding.

What was her mother demanding about?

Her grades, her activities. She texted Courtney quite a bit, asking where she was and what she was doing. Courtney said she didn't like that. It made her feel like a child.

Did she say she loved her mother?

No.

Did she say she hated her mother?

Yes.

More than once?

Yes.

You've been a teacher for over a decade, and you've seen many students and their parents. In your opinion, was Ingrid Ross's behavior unreasonable?

At times, yes.

Can you describe how?

She was insistent about Courtney attending Yale, and only Yale.

Did you ever see Ingrid hit her daughter?

Not hit her, no.

Did you ever see her lay a hand on Courtney at all?

I saw Ingrid slap her.

*

It had happened in the fall, a few weeks after the first semester started. The first issue of the *Bugle* was twenty-four hours away from publication, and Sonia was at the school, working late with Courtney.

Ingrid was already angry when she showed up. Courtney looked horrified to see her.

'Why didn't you answer my texts?' Ingrid said.

'Because I'm working.'

'Since when do you ignore your phone when you're doing schoolwork?'

'I wasn't ignoring it. I just don't sit around all day with nothing to do, like some people.'

If venom had a voice, it would sound like Courtney's.

Ingrid smacked her so fast, Sonia almost couldn't believe it had happened. Courtney's whole face turned red, and for a second, Sonia thought she would hit her mother back. Instead, she ran out of the room.

'Ingrid,' Sonia said.

'I'm sorry, I'm sorry.' Ingrid threw up her hands, palms forward. 'She was just so disrespectful.'

Sonia wanted to tell her that she was the one being disrespectful, but she kept her mouth shut. It wasn't her place, even if they were on school grounds. Sonia was well aware of the laws regarding children and corporal punishment by parents. An open-handed slap is legal in every single state. As far as the law is concerned, there was no reportable action.

The next time Sonia was alone with Courtney, she'd tried to get her to talk about it. But Courtney shut her down, refusing to answer any questions.

Now, she would have to tell the story in court and it wouldn't help Courtney one bit. It would only make things worse. She knew what the prosecution wanted, could see the story they were planning to tell. Courtney had an aggressive, overbearing mother who'd pushed her to the breaking point.

That's motive.

An understandable one, too. They weren't going to make Courtney out to be the devil in a schoolgirl uniform. She was just a kid who'd had enough. It wasn't self-defense, either. Ingrid didn't die in the middle of an argument or a fight. Courtney poisoned her mother. Or so they say.

In the store dressing room, Sonia cringes when she thinks about the final question. The worst one of all.

Did you tell anyone you saw Ingrid slap Courtney?

No.

Sonia hadn't done a thing.

Never told anyone, never mentioned it to the school officials.

Because Ingrid Ross was a parent. Without parents to pay the bills, Belmont wouldn't exist.

32

It's getting irritating how often Zach's father is right. Yet another one of his sayings has turned out to be true.

Money can open doors.

He's right: It does open doors. Even jail cells.

It's the middle of the night, long past Zach's curfew. Doesn't matter. This is the only time he can see Courtney, so he has to sneak out.

When he arrives at the side door, he sends a text to the night guard. The woman who opens the door is almost sixty years old, with short white hair and a nervous twitch in her eye. She also has a mortgage she can't afford because her deadbeat ex-husband doesn't pay alimony and doesn't show up for his court dates.

The internet can be a beautiful thing.

Zach didn't think twice before contacting this guard, whose name is Kay. Yes, it was illegal. Yes, she could've reported him. He knew that and did it anyway.

Because it was Courtney. She was there for him when no one else was. She'd saved him from what could've been years of being bullied. Of course he would do this for her. No question.

'Come in, come in,' Kay says, almost pulling him inside. She slams the door and locks it behind him.

'I really appreciate this,' Zach says, pulling an envelope out of his pocket. 'Thank you again.'

She looks in the envelope before answering. 'This never happened.'

'What never happened?' He smiles at her. Winks.

Kay smiles and leads him down a hallway. The whole place is dark, with cement floors and dark green walls. It's not like anywhere Zach has ever been or would want to be. But Courtney was here even at Christmas.

As the district attorney had said – loudly and in front of the cameras – accused murderers don't get out on bail, no matter how much money they have. He is also running for reelection this year.

Kay leads Zach to a small room with one door, no windows, a plastic table, and two chairs. She tells him to put both hands on the table and pats him down. It's more than a little weird when she gets to his groin.

After confiscating his phone and keys, she leads him out of the room and down another dark hallway. They pass two empty jail cells before getting to Courtney.

She looks worse than Zach imagined. Pale, tired, and so very thin. She looks like she hasn't had a decent meal in months. Probably hasn't.

Courtney gasps when she sees Zach. 'How – '

'Doesn't matter how,' Kay says, unlocking the door to the cell. She motions for Zach to enter. 'You've got fifteen minutes.'

Zach steps inside the cell and gives Courtney a hug. 'Hey, Nerd.'

'That's enough touching,' Kay says.

'Sorry,' Zach says.

Kay nods at both of them and closes the door. The metal-on-metal sound is horrible. So final.

Zach waits until Kay walks away, then points to Courtney's outfit. It looks like hospital scrubs, except grey. 'I'm pretty disappointed you aren't wearing an orange jumpsuit.'

'Me too. I was kinda looking forward to that.'

She smiles. He smiles back.

'Have a seat,' she says, pointing to a metal chair bolted to the floor. She sits on the bunk. 'I can't believe you found a way in.'

'I can be pretty persuasive when I want to be.'

Courtney rubs her fingers together, the international gesture for cash. Zach nods.

'I should have thought of this earlier,' he says.

'Yeah, you should've. Loser.'

He smiles. 'Is it stupid to ask how you are?'

'I'm exactly as bad as you think I am.'

'How are they treating you?'

'They're pretty nice, actually. Sometimes, the guards play cards with me. Through the bars, I mean.' She stops, clears her throat. 'They're the only ones I have to talk to. Other than my lawyer and my dad.'

'I guess that's good,' Zach says, though he doesn't think it is. None of this is good.

'But I don't want to talk about here,' Courtney says. 'Tell me what's going on at school. Distract me.'

What's going on at school is her. It's all Courtney, all the time, especially now that the trial is so close and everyone is divided about what's going to happen. What should happen.

'Connor broke up with Siobhan,' he finally says.

'Seriously?'

'Truth.'

'Tell me.'

Zach gives her the details, stretching the story out to be as dramatic as possible. Anything to avoid talking about the trial or Courtney's mother.

'I knew they'd never make it,' she says. 'What else?'

He tells her all the gossip he can remember, even the small stuff. She smiles and laughs, and even squeals a few times, but it sounds forced. Like she's trying to enjoy the things that used to make her happy.

Kay appears in front of the cell door, looks inside, and then disappears.

Finally, Courtney gets around to asking the question Zach knew was coming: 'Does everyone think I did it?'

'No.'

'But some do.'

He shrugs.

'Truth,' she says.

'Yeah, some do. The assholes.'

She shifts in her seat, leaning forward toward Zach. 'What are they saying on TV?'

He hesitates.

'Come *on*. No one will tell me,' she says.

He takes a deep breath and tells her the truth. 'They're saying you cracked under the pressure to get into a good college.'

Courtney sits back and stares at him, shaking her head. 'Wow.'

'Yeah.'

'That's messed up.'

'But on the upside,' Zach says, 'you're the poster child for why parents need to back off.'

Her eyes widen. 'I'm a poster child?'

Kay appears in the doorway. 'Hank's break is almost over. He'll be back soon, so wrap it up.'

Zach nods. Courtney stares at the one window in the cell. It's small and narrow, with bars on it. She looks much older now, though he isn't sure why.

'It'll be okay,' he says. 'This will all be over soon.'

She turns to him. 'I didn't hate her,' she says. 'I mean, yeah, I said that, but I didn't really. She was my mom.'

'I know.'

'You get that, right?'

'Of course.'

Courtney sighs, her body slumping. She looks so defeated. 'You remember when we were like eleven years old and our families went to the lake? We all stayed in that house together?'

He nods. 'Sure.'

'We had that blow-up raft with the clear window in it, so you could see the water below. We lay on it facedown to watch the fish.'

Zach smiles. 'And floated out too far. We had to take turns paddling back.'

'But remember when we first looked up?' she says. 'And we saw how far the dock was?'

'Yeah.'

'Everyone had gone inside or something. No one heard us when we yelled.'

'I remember.'

'That's how it feels in here,' she says, looking at him with hollow eyes. 'The same way it felt on that raft.'

33

All Frank wants is for everyone to shut up. They won't.

Before class, during class, after class, at breaks, at lunch, after school, at home. Yesterday, he stopped at the CVS after work and a reporter tried to talk to him. The asshole had followed him from Belmont, then walked right up behind him in line and asked him a question about Courtney.

'No comment,' Frank said.

'Look, I get it,' the reporter said. His breath smelled like cigarettes. 'A lot of reporters out here are just looking for a juicy story. A byline. I'm looking for the truth.'

'No comment.'

'I won't use your name.'

'No comment.'

The reporter had tried three or four more times before giving up and walking away.

This morning, as Frank drove into school, he saw that same reporter standing outside the fence. It wasn't snowing, but the temperature was below freezing and Frank hoped that reporter was cold.

A second later, he scolded himself for thinking such a thing.

He could imagine what that reporter would say if he knew the truth about Frank.

If he saw that picture.

The first time Frank saw it was a week after he got drunk with Ingrid. She'd called, saying she wanted to continue their conversation. He'd said yes. In part because he was embarrassed, but also because he couldn't say no. Not to a board member.

The bar was out-of-the-way, dark, and quiet. Ingrid looked good. Then again, she always looked good. But that night, especially so. At first, the conversation was mundane – work, school, the change in weather. Then she brought up Courtney.

'I understand she's been having some trouble in your class.'

Frank shrugged, not wanting to talk about Ingrid's daughter at that moment. 'It's AP Calculus. Most students have trouble with it.' And Courtney wasn't doing that badly, though she was usually a straight-A student. In his class, she was averaging a B+, but there was plenty of time left in the semester.

He didn't say any of that to her mother.

'Is there anything you can do to help her?' Ingrid asked.

'Like tutoring?' he said. 'I can give you some names, if that's what you mean. There are several good math tutors that Belmont recommends.'

'That's not what I meant.'

Frank's hand froze midair, his drink suspended between the table and his lips. Something in her tone was different. Not so flirty anymore. In fact, not flirty at all. 'I'm not sure what you mean,' he said.

'I think you do.'

He smiled a little, trying to bring back the lightness. 'Do I?'

'Don't be stupid, Frank.' Ingrid took out her phone. She swiped it open, clicked a few times, and slid it across the table.

The photo, clearly a selfie, taken by her, was of him. And of Ingrid, though her face couldn't be seen; it was covered by her hair. His was visible, though. His eyes were closed, they were in bed, and from the waist up, they were naked.

He didn't remember that at all. He didn't even remember taking off his shirt.

'What is – '

'I assume you don't want anyone to see that,' Ingrid said.

'No, I – '

Ingrid snatched the phone away from him. 'Then my daughter better get an A.'

He stared at her, at first confused. The realization came slowly and, with it, the agonizing pain of how bad this was. 'But we never did anything,' he said. 'I *couldn't* have done anything.'

Ingrid smiled. 'Try explaining that to your wife.'

Revenge wasn't something Frank had ever thought about. He was taught to turn the other cheek, so that's what he had always done.

Until he saw Ingrid on the day of Sonia's party.

Frank was at school early, like always, because it was quiet there and he could work.

And there she was.

Ingrid. In the parking lot, her arms filled with boxes full of party supplies, and she was taking them into the school. She was wearing yoga pants and her Collaborative jacket, her hair pulled back into a neat bun. Ingrid looked so normal, just like all the other parents. She didn't look like a succubus.

Frank pulled in behind another car, blocking her view of him, but he could see her car from his side mirror. He didn't move.

Not yet.

The back of her SUV was open, which meant she would return.

As he sat in his car, waiting for her, he imagined that picture on her phone. What she had done was worse than horrific. It was . . . unconscionable.

And Frank was embarrassed, even more so because today he would have to see her at the party.

He imagined her staring at him, a silent threat in her eyes.

He stopped feeling embarrassed and started feeling angry. That's when the idea hit.

The water bottle.

She always had it with her, and inevitably it was filled with green tea. She loved that stuff, had even told him about her love for it when they were drinking alcohol.

Her car was open, the doors were unlocked, and no one was around. The water bottle was right in the cup holder next to her seat. So easy. It would be just so easy.

All he wanted was for her to go away for a while. To spend half the day in the restroom and miss the party. So he wouldn't have to look at her.

Not so she would die. He'd never wanted that.

His gym bag was in the car, always, even though he hadn't been working out recently. And one thing he always kept in his bag was diuretics. How was he supposed to know his real weight if he was bloated with water? Impossible. When he wanted to check his weight and body fat, he used a diuretic a few hours before. It wasn't that big of a deal to spend more time in the bathroom.

So when he had the chance, he slipped some into Ingrid's tea.

It wasn't until much later that he googled the potential effects of the drug. One of them is heart failure.

34

At lunchtime, Frank makes the mistake of going to the lounge. He assumed it would be empty and everyone would be in the Porter Room, watching TV, but the room is packed. Everyone is grabbing their lunch out of the fridge or heating it up in the microwave. And everyone's talking about who will be testifying. More specifically, who they are testifying for.

'I can't believe they called me,' Sonia says. 'The fact that any of us have to testify against one of our students is just . . . abhorrent.' She's dressed in black, again, just like she has been since Courtney was arrested. Some say it's because she's in mourning. Others say it's because she's been gaining so much weight.

Frank doesn't care. He just wants her to shut up.

'I heard they're going to call Nari, too,' someone says. Nari is a history teacher, and like Sonia, she's a faculty liaison to the Collaborative.

'I bet a lot of parents will be testifying, too,' another teacher says.

'What about the students?' Sonia says. 'Some of them must be testifying for the defense.'

'I certainly hope so,' says Louella Mason. She's an art teacher with a self-proclaimed old soul. On more than one occasion, Louella has burst into huge, wracking sobs while talking about Courtney. This is one of those occasions.

Everyone has something to say. A lot to say, actually.

Except God. He isn't talking to Frank anymore.

'I'm going back to my classroom,' Frank says to Teddy. 'Get some work done.'

'I don't blame you.'

Back at his desk, Frank checks his phone. There's a message from his wife, asking him to pick up a cheese grater on his way home from work. The request is so mundane, so normal, it makes him feel a little bit better.

He reads the Bible on his phone until his fifth-period class starts.

1 John 1:9. *But if we confess our sins to him, he is faithful and just to forgive us our sins and to cleanse us from all wickedness.*

Frank doesn't feel the forgiveness. He reads the passage over and over again but still feels nothing.

AP Calculus. The same one Courtney used to be in. Her desk still sits empty. He tried to move it once, but a student asked him not to. She said Courtney would be back soon and he should leave it, so he did.

The empty desk bothers him. When he stands at the front of the class, he sees it out of the corner of his eye.

Today, he sees Courtney sitting there. Right where she should be.

When he looks directly, the desk is empty.

A few minutes later, he sees her again out of the corner of his eye. She sits up tall and straight, her hair pulled back tight, her shirt crisp and ironed. When he looks straight at the desk, she disappears.

He sees her three more times before class ends. Once, Frank almost speaks to her before she vanishes.

As the students leave, he slumps in his chair, exhausted.

His eyes are just playing tricks on him – that's all. Those weren't hallucinations. He refuses to call them that.

Sonia bought fourteen possible outfits to wear in court. She tries each one on, takes a selfie, and loads the photos onto the computer. One by one, she goes through them, trying to decide which outfit makes her serious but not somber, intelligent but not unstylish. And thin. Or at least thinner than she is. It's so unfortunate real life doesn't have filters.

'I think I have to go shopping again,' she says.

'Again?' her husband says.

She looks up, surprised he answered. Surprised to see Mark sitting beside her on the couch. She hadn't realized he was even there.

Eating ice cream.

'Can you do that in the kitchen?' she says.

'What? Eat?'

'Yes.'

He shrugs. 'I won't spill any.'

She grits her teeth, keeps her mouth closed.

'Let me see,' he says, leaning toward the screen.

Sonia closes her laptop, not wanting him to see that she was googling 'How much weight can I lose in one week?'

'It doesn't matter,' she says, standing up.

'Sure it does. Sit back down and let's talk about this.'

She hesitates. It *would* be nice to talk about all of this.

Mark reaches out and coaxes her back down to the couch. 'I know how nervous you are about testifying. So talk to me.'

With a sigh, she sits down and leans into him. He offers her a spoonful of ice cream, and she eats it. 'I just can't believe any of this is happening,' she says. 'This might be the worst thing that's ever happened at Belmont.'

'Worse than when the headmaster committed suicide?'

'Yes. Much worse than that. *So* much worse.' She sits up to look at him. 'Do you know we have *students* testifying?'

'That's not surprising.'

'I'm not half as worried about me as I am about them. Imagine being a teenager and having to testify in a *murder* trial.' She accepts another spoonful of ice cream before getting up off the couch. 'That's enough for me. I've got to make my lunch for tomorrow.'

She walks away, rather proud of herself for not staying on the couch, helping her husband finish off that pint of ice cream. While cutting up carrots and celery into bite-size pieces, she also finds herself proud of all the things she didn't share with him. Like eating candy in the store dressing room. The last thing she needs is to be told she's in a snit.

She isn't. She is just very worried about testifying.

Today was the worst so far. Up until everyone started talking about who was testifying and who wasn't, the faculty and staff had tiptoed around the topic of Courtney. Specifically about whether she was guilty or innocent. The students talked about it, yes, but not the staff. Not until today.

It wouldn't surprise me if she did it. Ingrid could be a nightmare.

What are you saying? You really think that girl could kill *someone?*

I think it's possible.

Impossible.

Think about how much pressure she was under. Her mother was relentless.

Lots of parents are relentless. That doesn't mean Courtney killed her.

Regardless, we have to prepare for a guilty verdict.

148

All day. The conversations went on all day.

Sonia had tried to stop going into the Porter Room, where everyone watched the news during breaks, but she couldn't. The least she could do was make her view known: There was simply no chance Courtney had killed her mother. Sonia made that point very loud and very clear.

Despite the text messages Courtney had sent to her friends, wishing her mother was dead. Despite the poison – whatever it was – supposedly found on their property. Despite how much pressure Ingrid had put on Courtney.

Despite all of that, Sonia refuses to believe it. The idea that anyone thinks otherwise is enough to make her go back out to the couch and get another spoonful of ice cream.

35

In the morning, Frank stumbles into school. His head feels like it's going to explode, in part because he didn't get any sleep. Not after he saw Courtney standing at the foot of his bed.

He had just drifted off when he jerked awake. There she was, standing over him, wearing her school uniform. She had a notebook in one hand and a pen in the other, poised and ready to start taking notes. Just how she used to look in class.

Frank bolted upright so fast, he woke Missy.

By then, Courtney was gone.

He knew it wasn't real, that she wasn't in his house and never had been, but he still couldn't get back to sleep. For the rest of the night, he wondered if it was possible she was haunting him. While he had never heard of a living person haunting someone, he started to think it was possible.

The person who should be haunting him is Ingrid, but he hasn't seen her yet.

A week ago, he didn't believe in ghosts at all. Or hauntings. Now, he might.

He avoids the Porter Room and the lounge, staying in his classroom even during the breaks. Sleep still doesn't come, not even when he puts his feet up on the desk. Out of the corner of his eye, Courtney is there. Watching him. Waiting to take notes.

With no other option, he starts googling 'haunted by

living person.' All that does is give him a bunch of sites about stalking.

If only it were that easy.

During his last class, he tells the students to work on the problem on the board, then he leaves the room. In theory, to use the restroom. In reality, to escape Courtney. Some of his other students are starting to look like her.

Sleep. He really needs sleep.

He strolls down the empty hallway. Paces up and down it, actually. Thinks about going to the police.

That fantasy is interrupted by Sonia.

She's at the end of the hallway, standing still, not moving. He waves and walks toward her.

She doesn't wave back.

As Frank gets closer, he sees how pale she looks. Sonia places her hand on the wall as if to steady herself.

'Hey,' he says, walking a little faster. 'Are you okay?'

Sonia looks up at him, her eyes glassy, and she shakes her head no.

Now, he can see the sweat on her face and her neck. As he reaches out to her, because she looks like she's about to faint, her whole body starts jerking around – arms, torso, head. Almost like she's doing a strange sort of dance.

He's trying to grab her arm when her body jerks again and she falls to the floor.

A seizure. She's having some sort of seizure. Her body continues to convulse, and Frank puts his hand under her head to stop her from banging it against the floor.

His first thought: *She's possessed.*

Especially when her eyes roll back into her head.

But then she stops breathing.

36

As far as Teddy is concerned, there are two types of people in the world. The first are those who say 'Think of the children.' They say it loud, they say it often, and they post it all over social media.

The second are those who *actually* think of the children and then *do* something to help them. Not many go the extra mile to make sure kids are protected.

He does.

And given that he's sitting in a room filled with people who educate children, it's disappointing so few are like him.

It's late in the evening, well after dark, and the headmaster has called an emergency meeting at the school about Sonia Benjamin.

The late Sonia Benjamin.

'Her sudden death is a great shock to everyone. Most of all the students,' the headmaster says, shaking his head after every phrase. 'Given her age, the medical examiner has already said he will perform an autopsy.'

Perfect. That's exactly what needs to happen. Exactly what Teddy had expected.

While the headmaster drones on about counseling, Teddy tunes him out. He glances around at his colleagues, counting how many are crying. Trying to figure out which ones are faking it.

Not that it's difficult. He's sure his wife used to do the same thing.

Or ex-wife, he should say. If he ever signs the papers.

They'd arrived from her lawyer the day after Christmas. She'd planned it that way, no doubt. For maximum pain.

Allison doesn't want anything. Not half the house, half the retirement funds, half the bank accounts. All she wants is a divorce. One day, perhaps, he will grant it. But for now, the papers sit on his desk – formerly her desk – and that's where they'll stay.

After more headshaking and so many tears, fake and real, the meeting finally ends. Several of the teachers plan to go get a drink before heading home, and they ask Teddy to join them. Any other time, he would have said no. This evening he says yes.

They end up at a sad little place with bad lighting and scuffed tables. Teddy orders a tonic and lime, even though it's disgustingly bitter, but it makes everyone think he's drinking.

Neither Ms Marsha nor the headmaster is present, so Nari Tam assumes the leadership position. She isn't the oldest or the longest-serving faculty member, but she did go to Belmont. She's part of the family. And one of the few who isn't white. Belmont is a distinctly pale school.

'To Sonia,' she says, standing up and raising her glass. She's wearing black, her dark eyes looking a bit teary. 'She was our colleague and our friend, and may she rest in peace.'

'To Sonia,' everyone repeats, clinking glasses all around.

'The first day I met her,' someone says, starting the memory portion of the evening, 'she gave me a tour of the school, and what I remember most is how everything came back to the students. That was her whole focus.'

'She loved the kids so much. I think that's why she didn't have any,' Nari says. 'She considered her students to be her kids.'

Lots of nodding.

'She said that once,' someone else says. 'That she didn't need to have kids because she already had enough.'

A few people laugh. A few others cry.

Teddy listens to his coworkers rewrite history, the way people do when someone dies. He even chimes in with his own story. 'When I picture Sonia, I always see her carrying that coffee cup,' he says. 'That big red coffee cup.'

Someone laughs. 'Yes! It says "Teaching Is My Superpower."'

'I think a student gave that to her,' Nari says.

'I'm sure,' Teddy says, although he doesn't believe that. Sonia was the type who would buy that cup for herself.

After an hour of reminiscing, the group starts to break up. It's only then that they get around to talking about the way she died. As if it would've been insensitive to start with that topic.

'It has to be something natural, right?' someone says.

'Absolutely,' says Nari. 'There's no way we've had two murders at Belmont.'

Everyone nods, but they don't look sure.

Good.

On the way out of the bar, Frank stops him in the parking lot. He was so quiet all night that Teddy forgot he was there.

'Are you okay?' Teddy asks. Everyone knows Frank is the one who found Sonia in the hallway.

'No.' Frank shakes his head back and forth with a bit too much violence. 'I'm not okay.'

Teddy waits.

'Something wasn't right about Sonia,' Frank finally says. 'That wasn't . . . It wasn't like a heart attack. She was, I don't know, convulsing. Or having a seizure.'

'A seizure? Like an epileptic seizure?'

'I don't know. The paramedic asked me the same thing, and I told them it just didn't look right. I don't know how else to explain it.'

Teddy places his hand on Frank's shoulder. 'Go home to your family and get some rest. You've had an awful day.'

'Yeah, you're right,' Frank says. He walks away, shoulders slumped, head hanging low.

Teddy drives home feeling a little bad about Frank. It was unfortunate he was the one who found Sonia, especially given how hard he was taking Courtney's arrest, but Teddy couldn't help that. Someone had to find her.

He also feels a little bit bad about Sonia. It's not remorse. Not even regret. Teddy did what had needed to be done, and he can't regret that. What he's doing is fixing his mistake, the one that put Courtney in jail.

And now Sonia won't be testifying against her.

As far as Teddy could tell, this was the only way. Plus, he got away with killing someone the first time. Why not a second?

37

The only sound at the table is the clink of silverware. Zach takes a bite of his almond-crusted salmon and washes it down with bubbly water.

His mom sits across from him, his dad next to him. This is the first family dinner they've had in months. The food was brought in from Arendale, his mother's favorite restaurant. No one in the Ward house cooks.

'I thought it would be good for us to spend some time together,' Mom says. 'Given what happened today at school.'

'It's unbelievably tragic,' Dad says. 'Sonia Benjamin was a fine woman.'

Zach nods. He's still a little dazed about what happened. It was at the end of the day when he heard the sirens. His first thought was that the police had come to arrest someone for killing Ingrid. Someone other than Courtney.

Instead, someone else was dead. No one knows why, or what happened, but a bunch of rumors are already making the rounds online.

'She was a good teacher,' Zach says.

'Yes, she was.' Dad pauses to take a sip of water. No one drinks alcohol in the Ward home, not unless there are guests. Too much work and no time for fun. 'I spoke to her many times and always found her to be a reasonable, intelligent woman.'

Zach doesn't add that Mrs B always did what Dad wanted her to do. That's why he liked her so much.

'There's just been so many traumatic events over the past months,' Mom says. 'First Ingrid, then Courtney. And now, this . . .' She reaches across the table but can't quite reach Zach's hand. The table is too big. 'How are you doing, Zach? Really, how are you?'

Even if Zach knew how to answer that question, he wouldn't. Not with both of his parents staring at him.

'I'm still processing it,' he says. They like those kinds of words. Processing is something they understand.

Dad nods. 'It will just take some time.'

'And, of course, if you want to talk to someone, I can arrange that,' Mom says. 'A partner at my firm is married to one of the finest psychologists in the area. Shall I make an appointment?'

'I don't think so.'

'Well, you just let me know,' she says.

'Okay,' he says.

The silverware starts clinking again as they fall back into silence. Zach senses that something is coming, but he isn't sure what.

His parents wait until they're done eating. The business way of doing things. People don't talk about the difficult things at the start of a meal, because if everything goes sideways, you still have to eat together. No one wants to do that when they're angry. Zach's father taught him well.

'Given everything that's been happening at Belmont,' Dad says, 'your mother and I have been wondering if it's the best place for you.'

'You want me to change schools?' Zach says, unable to control himself. '*Now?*'

His parents exchange a look, and Mom takes over. 'It's just something we're discussing. There is a very good school I'm looking at in Vermont.'

'*Vermont?*'

'Zach,' Dad says. 'Belmont's reputation has taken a huge hit. This trial is turning into a circus. And now, with this unfortunate event today . . .'

'We just want what's best for you,' Mom says.

Zach stares down at his sautéed spinach. A month ago, a year ago, two years ago, he would've jumped at the chance to go to a boarding school in Vermont. To get out of this house, out of his cloudy room.

But not right now. Not with Courtney in jail and about to go on trial for murder. He can't leave her.

'Do I have a say in this?' Zach says.

'Well,' Dad says, 'if you hadn't gotten an A-minus in English last semester, maybe you would have a say.'

Zach goes straight up to his room to get away from his parents. He's on the verge of saying something he'll regret. In his dad's eyes, a lack of self-restraint is a sign of immaturity.

A man who cannot control himself will never be successful.

As soon as he's alone, he wants to throw something. Anything. Instead, he screams into his pillow.

That A-minus.

No matter how hard Zach had worked or how many hours he'd spent on his final essay, Crutcher still gave him an A-minus. And, given how much the teacher hated him, Zach had accepted it. At least it wasn't a B-plus.

Besides, he'd had too much on his mind after Courtney

was arrested. He'd also had too much to do. The *Bugle* took up an extraordinary amount of time.

None of that mattered to Dad, who still hadn't let up about that grade.

At one time, Zach had planned to get on Crutcher's good side. The idea had been put off and then abandoned. He'd never thought it would come back to bite him in the shape of Vermont.

Ignoring all of social media – especially the rumors about Mrs B – Zach turns to Google.

Theodore Crutcher, Belmont Academy

Within minutes, he knows where Crutcher went to school, how long he has been teaching, where he lives, and how much he paid for his house. He also learns that Crutcher's wedding anniversary is August 11 and his wife's name is Allison.

Zach remembers the card he found in Crutcher's desk, the one for the fertility doctor. He wonders if Allison ever got pregnant.

Allison Crutcher

A picture of her pops up on the screen, surprising Zach. He knows her.

38

The only light in the room comes from Teddy's laptop. It's long past his usual bedtime, and he's drinking coffee, not milk. All the students are online tonight, and they're talking about Sonia's death.

Using his Natasha profile, Teddy maneuvers around, checking in on every conversation. Usually, their talk is rather banal, even boring, but tonight they're letting loose.

> Mrs B was getting pretty heavy, wouldn't be surprised if she had a heart attack.
>
> Drugs, has to be drugs. I bet half the teachers use them.
>
> I saw her eating a cheeseburger last week. Her diet was shit.
>
> Agree with heart attack. She was totally unhealthy.
>
> I liked her. I'm sorry she's gone.
>
> OMG this is SO SAD. WHAT IS HAPPENING?
>
> Calm down, people die every day.
>
> At our school, they do.

Those are the students who think Sonia's death was natural. Another group is convinced it wasn't. Teddy participates in this conversation.

Is it possible we've had TWO murders at Belmont?

I mean, what if someone did kill her?

If it's poison, it has to be arsenic or cyanide.

Um, there's like a million poisons in the world. Not two.

WHY WOULD ANYONE POISON MRS B?

Right?? I can think of at least ten other teachers that would be murdered before her.

But what if it is? My parents are gonna lose it.

We'll know soon if we're right.

If it's a murder, the media is going to blow up.

Is this going to affect my college applications?

Oh shit, I didn't even think of that.

My parents will totally sue if it hurts my college chances.

You can't sue for that.

How do you know?

My dad is a judge.

If you didn't commit the murder, it's not going to hurt your chances.

Jesus Christ, let's all calm down until we know for sure.

Teddy scrolls through the comments, adding his own to egg them on. It doesn't take long for one of them to see the obvious.

Guys, what if she was poisoned? Like with the same thing that killed Courtney's mom?

Boom goes the dynamite.

The coffee pods were the flaw in Teddy's original plan. He'd realized that after a lot of reflection and a hard, honest look at what had happened. It was all about the pods.

The faculty all had their favorite flavors, so on a normal day it was almost guaranteed the right person would drink the right pod. The day of Sonia's party wasn't normal, though, which ruined everything. Coffee pods were just too impersonal.

When he began working on his plan to save Courtney, he was forced to rethink the method. Trying to put something in the coffee after it was brewed seemed impossible. No way to do that without getting caught. He also couldn't put it in the sweetener, the sugar, or the milk without potentially affecting the wrong person.

A real conundrum. A puzzle. And Teddy likes puzzles. Good ones, at least. Not the kind that insult his intelligence.

He let this float around in his head for a few days, dismissing one idea after another. Either they were too risky or they were imprecise. None worked for what he needed.

One morning, while making his usual sandwich for lunch, it hit him. Lunch.

It was so obvious, he laughed.

Faculty members put their lunches in the refrigerator located in the teachers' lounge. While there had been a few instances over the years of people eating each other's food, it hadn't happened in a while.

Once he'd heard Sonia was called as a witness for the prosecution, the plan came together like it was meant to be. She had been talking about losing weight and had started bringing salad for lunch.

So perfect. So easy.

At first, anyway. Then he remembered he had cleared his yard. Teddy had nothing to work with. No doll's-eyes plant or berries. And it was winter.

He also had no time to grow anything, so he had to get creative. Walking around trying to find the plant was useless while everything was covered in snow. He started visiting nurseries, asking about flowers and herbs and vegetables. It might be winter, but he said he was planning for spring.

'Smart,' one of the nursery employees said. 'Most people wait until spring, and they've got no plan at all.'

'Oh, I've always been a planner,' Teddy said.

He walked around the nurseries, pointing out plants he already knew about, testing the employees to see how much they knew. That was just for fun, though. Something to keep himself occupied as he searched for the plant he needed.

In the midst of all those meaningless conversations, he'd managed to locate what he needed and break off a few sprigs of doll's-eyes. They disappeared into his pocket fast, like he was a magician.

He'd made sure to buy plenty of seeds and bulbs to make up for that indiscretion. Including tulips, Allison's favorite. Maybe he'll even plant them. In the spring, the entire back-yard could be a field of tulips. She would love that.

But first, the doll's-eyes.

Back at home, Teddy had filled a syringe with the juice from the berries. Far more than what he'd used in the coffee.

Ten times more, to be exact, and more than enough to kill an adult. But he had berries left over for another round or two, just in case it didn't work the first time.

If anyone else had been arrested, he never would've gone to so much trouble. But this was Courtney. Not only did he kill her mother – an *accident*, albeit a horrible one – but Ingrid Ross was, at least in part, responsible for his Teacher of the Year award. He owed her. And since she was dead, he owed her daughter.

During third period today, his free period, Teddy had gone up to the lounge. Someone was there, but it didn't matter. He opened the refrigerator and pretended to rummage around for his own lunch, all while holding a conversation about the weather. It only took a second to plunge the syringe through Sonia's plastic container, empty it into her salad, and shake it up.

A few hours later, she was dead.

Too bad there wasn't an award for that.

39

The memorial service at Belmont is huge. It's held outdoors, on the football field, and it looks like the whole school has shown up. Maybe the whole town. Luckily it's an unseasonably warm day so nobody will freeze to death.

Teddy stands in the bleachers with the rest of the faculty, wondering if this many people would show up for him. Then again, it's not like Sonia is around to see this. Hard to enjoy the turnout when you're dead.

'This is lovely,' Louella says. She's dressed in head-to-toe black, including lots of black beads around her neck. 'I'm so happy to see everyone here celebrating Sonia's life.' The art teacher thinks everything should be a celebration.

'I thought this was to mourn her death,' Teddy says.

Louella's burgundy-tinted lips morph into a scowl.

Frank shakes his head, saying nothing. He hasn't looked well since finding Sonia, but that's not Teddy's fault. Just bad luck for Frank.

Down on the stage below, Sonia's husband is talking. Teddy has met him several times at school functions over the years. He's the type of man who fills the room — because he's big, both tall and wide, and because he's a prominent professor. Sonia may have been the one with the money, but she definitely married up.

When he's done blubbering through his speech, the

headmaster takes over. He is a calm force in a sea of emotion. The way a leader should be.

Not like the old headmaster, the one who killed himself.

Teddy can't help but sigh out loud when he thinks of that sniveling little pip-squeak. He truly was a pip-squeak, too. Otherwise, he wouldn't have been able to hang himself in a room with such low ceilings.

'Are you bored?'

It's Nari. She's wearing a hat with a veil, like this is a funeral, and her straight black hair is in a tight bun at the nape of her neck. Her eyes are obscured by the lace, but Teddy can still feel the daggers.

'No, I'm not bored. I'm frustrated by all these deaths at Belmont.' He is careful not to say *murders* instead of *deaths*. Another day or two, and everyone will know. That's how long it took with Ingrid, and Sonia had so much more poison in her system.

'This is horrible,' Frank says. 'It's all so horrible.'

'Death is a part of life,' Louella says.

'Shh,' Nari says.

'We should pray,' Frank says. His voice sounds raspy, like he can barely get the words out.

No one answers him.

Teddy looks out across the field, toward the full parking lot. So many expensive cars. A lot of parents have shown up in the middle of a workday, like they have nowhere else to be. The amount of money here just in clothes, jewelry, and handbags must be in the millions. Not to mention the wristwatches. The only acceptable jewelry for a man is a wedding ring and a wristwatch. Teddy always checks out both.

It's too bad he doesn't have binoculars. Bet there are some extraordinary watches here today.

The headmaster introduces the school band, which is set to play 'one of Sonia's favorite songs.' The band bleats out a pathetic rendition of 'Lean on Me.'

When the crowd starts to sing along, Teddy excuses himself.

Behind the football field is the school's state-of-the-art concession stand, which even has an app to let people know how long the line will take. Today, the stand is closed. The only people around are a few parents who just had to use their phones.

One of them is James Ward.

Teddy can smell him from ten feet away. The stench of entitlement is that strong.

James sees him while he's still on the phone, and he holds up his finger, as if telling Teddy to wait. He does. Not because James told him to, but because he wants to know what James is going to say.

'Teddy,' James says, reaching out to shake his hand. 'I'd say nice to see you again, but under these circumstances it seems inappropriate.'

Teddy nods.

'It's unbelievable, really,' James says. 'Two deaths in just a few months.'

'Yes. It's so tragic.'

James looks at him, his head slightly cocked to the side. 'And they still have no idea what happened to her, do they?'

'Not that I'm aware of.'

'How odd.'

Teddy doesn't answer that.

'I never thanked you, by the way,' James says. 'For giving Zach a chance to improve his grade on that paper.'

'Of course.'

'It's unfortunate his final grade wasn't better.'

Teddy almost smiles. Zach was never going to get anything better than an A-minus in his class. Never. 'Yes. Very unfortunate,' he says.

They are interrupted by Pamela, Zach's mom, who is dressed in a dark suit. Going back to work soon, perhaps.

'I wondered where you were,' she says. 'I thought you were still on the phone.' Pamela turns to Teddy. She's wearing the same plum-colored lipstick he saw before, in the school parking lot. 'Mr Crutcher, nice to see you again.'

'Nice to see you, even at a time like this.'

'Yes, well,' she says. 'There's been too much tragedy around this school, hasn't there?'

'We were just talking about it,' James says, glancing down at his phone.

'Well,' Teddy says. 'At least there hasn't been a school shooting. I guess there's that.'

The silence that follows is long and uncomfortable, and Teddy enjoys every second of it.

'I hope we see you again soon under more pleasant circumstances,' Pamela finally says.

Teddy watches them leave. The Wards walk in step together, Pamela's high heels making her almost the same height as James. They really are a handsome couple. It's unfortunate they're such horrible people.

As Teddy starts to walk away, he catches a glimpse of someone. The profile of a girl as she passes by.

No, not a girl. A woman. Dark hair, pert nose, ruby lips.

He shakes his head, laughing at himself. Because it can't be her.

About halfway through the memorial service, it hits Zach. Up until Mrs B's husband starts talking about her, he hadn't felt much of anything about her death. Like he didn't believe it was real.

Now he does, and the sadness is bigger and heavier than he'd expected. Mrs B was a nice woman, a good teacher, and she was young. Not even forty. Whatever happened to her, it wasn't fair. Just like it wasn't fair that Courtney was sitting in jail right now.

Too much. It's all too much.

Enough to make Zach leave the memorial before it ends. Any place would be better, including the hospital.

Zach drives straight there and walks in through the emergency room door. It smells the same, even looks the same, as far as he can tell. The last time he was here was when he broke his arm two years ago.

The ER is nothing like it is on TV. There are no gurneys rushing by with bleeding patients being wheeled into surgery. No one is screaming for a crash cart, and not a single person says 'Stat.' The only one in the waiting area is an older woman who is watching a talk show while knitting.

Zach smiles and waves to the receptionist, and he keeps walking, right into the hall where the patients are. The receptionist doesn't say anything, doesn't stop him. Not surprising. Being white and clean-cut gets Zach into a lot of places.

And out of them, if need be.

He wanders down the hall, past drawn curtains and

swinging doors, glancing around at everything. A woman asks if she can help him.

'Oh,' he says, a smile spreading across his face. 'A friend of mine texted me and said he was here. I'm just trying to find him.'

'Go to the desk and give them his name,' she says. She's a stern-looking woman, the kind who would make a scary teacher. 'They can help you.'

'Thanks.' Another smile.

She walks away, and he doubles back, making another loop around the emergency area. It's not that big in a town this size. Not too many emergencies around here.

Finally, he finds her.

She looks exactly as he remembers. Same curly hair, all tied up in an unruly mess. Same rosy cheeks. Even the same pinkish lips. A sweet woman. She took good care of him until his parents arrived.

And she's not pregnant, or at least she doesn't look it. Maybe those fertility treatments aren't working.

'Aren't you . . . ?' he says, stepping toward her. 'You were here when I broke my arm. I remember, you're the one who wrapped it.'

She blinks at him. 'Oh, I . . . Wait, wait. Yes, I remember. Zeke?'

'Zach,' he says. 'Zach Ward.'

'Close.' She smiles at him. He remembers she smiles a lot. 'I'm Allison Crutcher.'

Perfect. 'Crutcher? Wait, you aren't . . . ? Sorry. I mean, I have a teacher named Crutcher. Over at Belmont.'

The change in her face is instantaneous. Smile gone, eyes dull. Like he had just brought up someone who was dead.

'I'm sorry to hear that.' Her hand flies to her mouth, as if she didn't mean to say that. 'Oh, that sounded terrible, didn't it?'

'Um . . . sort of.'

'I apologize. Your teacher is my ex-husband.'

Zach is so surprised, he isn't sure what to say. 'Oh.'

'Well, almost-ex-husband. Close enough,' she says.

Zach nods. 'Okay.'

She laughs a little. 'Sorry. I'm boring you with my personal life. How are you? Are you sick, or . . . ?'

'Oh no. It's not me. I was just here visiting someone.' Even as he talks, his mind spins. Talking to Allison isn't going to help him at all.

'It was nice to see you again,' Allison says to him. 'Hope your friend will be okay.'

'Thanks. So do I.'

He walks away, looping around and exiting through a different door. Zach no longer thinks about getting on Crutcher's good side.

He thinks about the wedding ring Crutcher still wears.

And he thinks about yesterday, when he overheard Crutcher talking to another teacher about Sonia's memorial. He said his wife couldn't make it because she had to work.

Zach also thinks about another one of his father's favorite sayings.

Knowledge isn't just powerful; it's valuable. Know when to use it and when to shut up.

40

When Frank gets to school the next morning, something is different. More reporters are out front. A lot more. Which doesn't make any sense, because the trial still hasn't started. They haven't even picked out the jury yet. But as soon as he starts driving through the gate, everything becomes clear.

The police. They're everywhere. Cars all over the parking lot.

Frank stops right in front of the security guard.

'Little crazy here this morning, eh?' the guard says.

'Yeah. Just a little.' All these police. They must be here for him.

No one to blame but himself, and he deserves it. He deserves everything, including having to watch Sonia die. A punishment for killing Ingrid. It's all connected. Always is. Always has been.

God makes sure of that.

'Everything okay, Mr Maxwell?' the guard says.

'No,' Frank says, shaking his head. Whatever is coming next, he's not ready for it. 'I just realized I forgot something at home.'

He backs up into the street and drives away.

If Teddy had to describe the detective in three words, it would be old, tired, and worn-out. Like a used couch.

Bates is his name, though his first name is not Norman. Unfortunate, because that would've made everything perfect.

They are sitting in the Windsor Room. Normally, it's used for the headmaster's meetings, but today it's used for questioning. Bates has a notebook and a sad little pencil, chewed at the end. One by one, he wants to speak with every staff and faculty member of Belmont.

Everyone, Teddy assumes, who had access to the refrigerator in the lounge. No doubt they've found the salad bowl right now. Teddy didn't even try to get hold of that, and for good reason. He'd wanted them to find it.

'Do you remember seeing Sonia Benjamin the day she died?' Bates says.

'I saw her every day at some point, either in the lounge or the hallways. Sometimes the parking lot.'

'But on that day,' Bates says. He sighs as he speaks, like he'd rather be anywhere but here. 'Do you remember seeing her? Talking to her?'

'I'm sure I said hello, at the very least. A lot of the teachers have been in the Porter Room recently – they've set up a TV in there, because of the upcoming trial – but I ate lunch at my desk. I've been trying to avoid the media coverage. It's all a bit much.'

Bates nods. He has a bulbous nose and wears thick reading glasses. 'So you didn't see her eating lunch?'

'Oh, well, I've certainly seen her eat lunch many times. But that day, no. I ate alone,' Teddy says.

The detective writes that down. 'Would you say you and Sonia were close?'

'We were colleagues, and we worked together a long time. But if you're asking if we socialized outside of school, then no. Sonia and I were never *that* close.'

'You're Teacher of the Year, aren't you?'

'I am.'

'I bet people are jealous. Your coworkers, I mean.'

Teddy takes a deep breath. 'It's an honor to work at Belmont. This is one of the most competitive schools in the Northeast, not only for the students, but also the teachers. I think everyone is just happy to work here.'

Bates chuckles. His breath smells like coffee. 'That's interesting. I've never been in a place where *everyone* is happy to work.'

'Well, I can't speak for every single person here. But overall, yes,' Teddy says. 'Teachers are very happy to work here.'

'Can you think of anyone who didn't like Sonia?'

'Wait,' Teddy says, leaning forward in his chair. He's been waiting for this question. 'Are you thinking that someone *killed* Sonia? Right here at school?'

'I didn't say that.'

'But you asked if anyone disliked her.'

'I did. I'm just gathering information.'

Sure he is. That's why the parking lot is flanked with cops scouring for evidence. 'I assume you are asking if anyone on the faculty disliked her?'

Bates shrugs. 'Sure. Faculty, staff, students . . . anyone who didn't like her.'

'There isn't anyone who hated her. Not that I know of, anyway.' Teddy pauses, pretending to think. 'Actually, I don't think the school's custodian liked her very much.'

'The custodian?'

'His name is Joe. Joseph Apple. He's been with the school for at least twenty years . . . Getting older now, but still good at his job.'

Bates writes this down. 'And he didn't like Sonia?'

'Well, I don't know how *he* felt about *her*, but I don't think *she* liked *him* very much.' Teddy shrugs a little, like he's trying to decide how much to say. 'Sonia was wealthy, as I'm sure you know. And people like Joe are just . . . the help. I'm not sure she treated him very well.'

'Gotcha,' Bates says, still writing. 'And you don't think Joe appreciated that.'

'As I said, I can't speak for him.'

But since Joe saw him rooting through the dumpster out back, he's the first one who comes to Teddy's mind. Someone has to get blamed for this.

41

By the time Zach checks his phone after third period, he feels a bit dazed. The rumors are all over the place, making it impossible to know what's true and what isn't. Except for the fact that Mrs B was murdered.

Up until now, he didn't think she was. Sure, everyone was talking about it, but *two* murders at Belmont? Not possible. Especially not Mrs B, because no one hated her. She was harmless.

You still here?

It's Lucas, sending him a text between classes.
Yeah, Zach says. I doubt my parents know what's going on.

Come over after school.

Ever since the news got out about Sonia, some of the parents had picked up their kids, taking them out of school – now known online as Homicide High. Belmont's new nickname is all over social media.

The news hasn't stopped there, either. Now there's some rumor about Mr Maxwell's wife showing up at the school, looking for her husband. She made some kind of scene near the office, and someone recorded it on their phone.

All Zach can see is a woman who looks hysterical. She keeps saying, 'Frank left for work this morning, and so he

176

has to be here,' and she doesn't understand why they called the house looking for him.

Anyone seen Maxwell? Zach asks Lucas.

Nope.

Now, security guards are everywhere. Unlike this morning, when there were no adults around, a fleet of rent-a-cops is all over school. Zach passes by a tall, skinny one with a plastic badge on his way into English. He almost runs right into Crutcher.

He's standing at the door, like he's been waiting for Zach.

'Hi, Mr Crutcher.'

'You're almost late,' he says.

Zach is about to answer when the final bell rings. Now, he *is* late. Only because his teacher stopped him from walking in the door, but he keeps his mouth shut and sits down.

Throughout the class, he stares at the wedding ring on Crutcher's finger. Maybe he should ask him how his wife is doing.

No. That would defeat the purpose.

But it's fun to think about.

Yet again, Zach realizes his dad is right about something else. *Life isn't fair. Not by a long shot,* he always says.

He's right. If life were fair, Mrs B would still be around and Crutcher wouldn't.

Frank sits in church, but not his own. He left Belmont, drove right by Unity of Life, and kept going, looking for something. A feeling. Solace. Forgiveness. Escape.

Thirty miles out, he stopped at Touchpoint Ministry. A megachurch, the only one in the area, with a massive building built like an arena. Frank sits halfway up the stadium seating. The stage below is empty, as are most of the seats. On the wall behind the stage, a floor-to-ceiling screen displays biblical scenes. The picture changes every fifteen seconds.

It's mesmerizing.

Frank recognizes every story. The Bible has been a part of his life for as long as he can remember. At first, the pictures are a trip down memory lane. He thinks of his childhood church, a place of so many good memories. Social gatherings, bake sales, church plays. The services were just a prelude to the fun.

For a long time, he stays in that nostalgic place, when life was simpler and he hadn't killed anyone.

Zacchaeus changes everything.

Frank recognizes him immediately. Zacchaeus was a corrupt tax collector, who cheated, lied, and stole. But the guilt caught up to him.

The picture shows him on the top of a sycamore tree, waiting for Jesus. Waiting to repent for his sins. Jesus did not disappoint.

Frank finally gets it.

Missy and his son may not forgive him, and the police certainly won't, but God will. God always forgives.

With a heart that feels a bit lighter, Frank leaves Touchpoint Ministry. He drives the thirty miles back, windows open, rock music blasting, and he doesn't stop until he reaches the police station.

He sends a text to his wife as he gets out of his car.

I will love you and Frankie forever

He walks right into the station. No hesitation, no deep

178

breath, no gathering of courage. Speaking the truth feels like the easiest thing he has ever done.

'I killed Ingrid Ross,' he says.

Detective Oliver looks like a nice man. A little soft around the middle – obviously, he doesn't work out enough – but he seems experienced. Maybe even wise. Frank just doesn't understand why he's still sitting in an interrogation room instead of in a jail cell.

'Tell me again how it happened,' Oliver says.

Frank sighs. He's been through it three times already. It's not like confessing to murder is an easy thing. 'I saw Ingrid outside the school. When she brought in a load of boxes, I went over to her car and put a diuretic in her green tea. It's MaxFit 2000.'

'And you just happened to have this in your car?'

'Well, yeah,' Frank says. 'For my weigh-ins.'

Oliver nods and writes that down.

'Like I said, I didn't mean to kill her. That was the day of the party, and she was an organizer, and I . . .' Frank's voice trails off. It's hard to admit this part once, let alone four times. 'I wanted to embarrass her, I guess. So she'd be in the bathroom the whole time and would miss the party.'

'Why?'

Frank takes a deep breath and goes through it all over again. The drunken night. The staged picture. The blackmail for Courtney's grade in AP Calculus. After saying it so many times, he's beyond the point of humiliation. Almost.

'I didn't even know I killed her,' Frank says. 'Not until I googled diuretics and found out they cause heart failure. Obviously, it's my fault, and that's why I'm here. So you can arrest me now. I'm not going to fight it.'

Oliver listens, not moving, his glasses perched at the end of his nose. 'Give me a minute. I'll be right back.'

He walks out, leaving Frank alone. He is absolutely positive Oliver will return with a couple of uniformed cops, who will place him under arrest.

Instead, the detective comes back by himself. The only thing he has brought with him is a file folder.

'Mr Maxwell,' Oliver says.

'Frank.'

'Okay, Frank.' He sits down and opens the folder. 'I understand what you're saying. And I understand that you believe you inadvertently killed Ingrid Ross.'

'I did.'

Oliver doesn't answer. He flips through the file and pulls out a single sheet of paper, waving it in the air in front of Frank.

'This is a report on Ingrid Ross's cell phone,' he says. 'There was no . . . revealing photo on her phone. Not of any kind.'

'Then she deleted it. Or moved it to the cloud or something.' Frank thinks for a minute and snaps his fingers. 'She's rich. She might have her own cloud.'

Oliver pulls out another piece of paper and holds it up. 'I also have this.'

Frank squints to see it but has no idea what any of the words mean. He shrugs.

'This is a lab report with the contents of Ingrid Ross's stomach when she died,' Oliver says. 'She never *drank* the green tea.'

42

Four o'clock in the afternoon, and Zach is high. So very, very high.

He and Lucas are in Lucas's theater room, watching a Marvel movie. Zach isn't sure if he's seen this one before or not, but it doesn't matter. He watches it anyway. Lucas's parents aren't home, and even if they were, they wouldn't give a shit. Not as long as Lucas stays on track to be Belmont's valedictorian.

'What I want to know,' Zach says, pausing to exhale, 'is who did you pay to avoid Crutcher? You haven't had him for a single class.'

'Oh, screw Crutcher. My brother told me about him. I bribed one of those women in the office to switch me.'

'With money?' Zach says.

'Nah. With charm.'

'Dick.'

Lucas shrugs. 'Why? You on his shit list?'

'Yep.'

'Sucks for you.'

Yes. Yes, it does.

They stop talking long enough to watch a battle in the movie. Zach and Lucas have seen dozens of superhero movies. They've been friends ever since they were twelve, when Lucas told Zach his parents were assholes. Zach could relate.

They pass the bong back and forth, alternating between checking their phones and watching the movie.

'Holy shit,' Lucas says. He struggles to sit up in the recliner. 'Did you see this?'

Zach glances over, seeing the glow of Lucas's phone. It's so very bright. 'See what?'

'The hashtag "HomicideHigh" is trending.'

'Shut up.'

'Seriously. Just around here. Not nationwide,' Lucas says. 'Not yet, at least.'

Zach pulls it up on his phone and scrolls through the messages. Most are stupid. Still, he reads them, because he can't not read them. He scrolls until the screen is just a blur.

'They still haven't found Mr Maxwell,' Lucas says. 'There's a rumor he's dead, too.'

Zach groans and sinks deeper into his chair, trying to hide from this news. If someone else is dead, he's definitely getting sent to Vermont.

An hour later, Frank is still at the police station. He hasn't been arrested, nor have the uniformed cops shown up. But his wife has.

Missy is angry and crying at the same time. It's the worst combination, though hardly surprising. Tough to find out your husband is a murderer.

The door to the interrogation room is open, and Frank watches Missy talking to Oliver. She gestures with her hands, often pushing back her hair. She does that when she's frustrated. Her eyes flick back and forth between her husband and the detective.

Frank knows she must be mad. Must be disappointed, hurt,

and confused. All the bad things. But she'd also know that he had to tell the truth. Missy is a huge advocate for the truth.

When she walks toward him, he sits up a little. Braces himself.

'Frank,' she says. Her voice isn't angry. It sounds a little weird, like she's talking to their son.

'Hi,' he says.

She pulls the other chair around the table, next to him, and sits down. 'I'm not sure what's going on with you, but we're going to get you some help.'

'Help? I don't need help. I need to be arrested.'

Missy nods and smiles. She reaches over and pats his hand. 'I know you think that.'

'Why does everyone keep saying that? I know what I did.'

'Of course you do.'

Frank frowns. It doesn't sound like she believes him.

The detective walks into the room. He's smiling – like everything is fine, just fine. 'Here's the thing, Frank. It's illegal to spike a drink with anything, even a diuretic. So, yes, we could arrest you for that. But the thing is, we don't have any proof you did it. That bottle of green tea is long gone.'

'You don't keep evidence?' Frank says.

'Once we determined she never drank the tea, it wasn't evidence anymore.'

'So . . . you aren't going to arrest me?'

'No,' Oliver says. 'But we are going to get you some help. Because if you did what you say – '

'I *did*,' Frank says.

'All right. We all just want to make sure you don't do it again. You don't want to do it again, do you?'

Frank shakes his head no. 'But I don't need help.'

Oliver doesn't answer that.

Missy is giving him that patronizing smile again.

Frank is confused. And disappointed. He should be locked up and punished, or else he'll never be forgiven.

From his bedroom window, Zach watches his parents drive up to the house. Separate cars. They both went straight from work to the big meeting at school.

He's sitting at his desk, working on his math homework while eating Chinese takeout. Zach is an expert on all the Chinese restaurants in town. The problem is, one has the best Mongolian beef but another has the best noodles. It's always so hard to decide.

He flips over to social media, checking the #Homicide-High tag. Tonight, Belmont held a meeting for all the parents to 'clear up any rumors and misunderstandings.' The reports are already coming in, and Zach is reading them when he gets a text from his dad.

Come downstairs please.

They're waiting in the living room. Zach sits, but they don't, which is never a good thing. His mom also hasn't taken off her shoes. She's still wearing those high heels.

'That meeting was a madhouse,' Dad says. 'Total chaos.'

This isn't what Zach heard online. Not surprising. James Ward has his own version of reality.

'Here's where we are,' Mom says, getting back to the facts. 'Sonia Benjamin was, in fact, murdered at the school. I'm sure you already know that.'

She's using her lawyer voice. Zach nods.

'Good. As for Frank Maxwell, he disappeared today but is

not dead. He apparently had some kind of breakdown. Everyone seems to think it was because he saw Mrs Benjamin die, but no one really knows.' She pauses to gauge Zach's reaction. He doesn't have one. 'He'll be out on medical leave for the time being.'

'Unbelievable,' Dad says, pacing back and forth in front of the sectional couch. 'All your mother and I wanted was to give you the best education. "Belmont," everyone said. "Send him to Belmont." And now' – he waves his arms around in the air, as if trying to capture the words – '*this* happens.' In the middle of his rant, he stops and takes out his phone. 'Have to take this,' he now says, walking out of the room.

Zach would sigh if he dared.

Mom sits down next to him. Her face softens when she stops being a lawyer.

'You know we just want what's best for you,' she says.

'That's not Vermont.'

'I know you want to stay here with your friends. And I know this whole thing with Courtney has been very difficult for you, but you have to understand that we're afraid. God forbid anything should happen to you.' She pauses. 'Or any of the students.'

'You're acting like there's some serial killer at Belmont,' he says. 'No one's wandering around with a machete butchering people.'

'No, they're poisoning people.'

Before Zach can answer, Dad walks back into the room. 'Sorry,' he says. 'What did I miss?'

'I was just telling Zach how worried we are about him,' his mom says.

'Well, of course we are.'

'Understood,' Zach says. 'Can I go now?'

Mom says nothing. Dad glances at his phone. 'It's getting late, and I'm sure you have work to finish,' he says. 'Let's plan on discussing this further on Sunday. Dinner?' He says it like they're setting up a business meeting.

'And from now on, don't eat or drink anything at school,' Mom says. 'Bring your lunch.'

'Sure, I can do that,' Zach says, having no intention of doing that. He leaves the room before they say anything else.

Back upstairs, Zach's computer is still open on his desk, but there are now hundreds of new messages with the #HomicideHigh tag. Weird, since he was only away for twenty minutes or so.

It doesn't take him long to understand why.

43

In a perfect world, the judicial system would work as it's supposed to. In the real world, Teddy knows it needs a little help. A nudge, so to speak. So that's what he did. He nudged.

By the time he wakes up in the morning, the news is everywhere. As he'd expected.

TWO MURDERS, ONE POISON?

Sources say that Ingrid Ross, 45, and Sonia Benjamin, 38, were killed with the same substance. Neither the police nor the district attorney's office have publicly disclosed the name of the substance that killed Ingrid Ross, but the new information is making some wonder about the arrest of Courtney Ross, who stands charged with her mother's murder.

'It doesn't make sense,' says Robby Herald, the proprietor of Nature's Food, a gourmet grocery store downtown, and a lifetime resident of the area. 'If they caught the murderer, how could someone else be killed the same way?'

He's not the only one asking that question, yet the ones who can answer it – the police and the DA's office – aren't talking.

Teddy smiles. All it took was an email.

If he had never created all those fake social media profiles online, he wouldn't have known anything about sending anonymous emails or how to route them through Eastern Europe so they couldn't be traced.

And if he hadn't gone to the trouble to learn all of that, he wouldn't have known how to send an email looking like he'd *tried* to hide it but failed. The way a normal, unknowledgeable person would do.

So that's how he sent it. Just a tip from an anonymous source.

And when the police get around to tracing that email back to who sent it, the trail will lead right to someone who knows everything that happens at Belmont. Someone who hates the parents and teachers who look down on him. Like he's barely a human being.

Someone like Joe, the custodian.

It's truly remarkable how good Teddy is at this. And he didn't even know it until now.

When he arrives at school, the crowd of reporters out front is much larger than yesterday. More food trucks as well. Teddy drives by without looking at them.

The security guard at the gate waves, then motions for him to roll down his window.

'Be careful out there,' the guard says. 'Some of these reporters have been rushing up to people, trying to get a comment.'

Teddy refrains from smiling.

Inside the school, a security company is setting up cameras over the doors and in the hallways. Last night at the parents' meeting, the headmaster had said this would happen. He'd said Belmont would be the most secure school on either side of the Mississippi River. Some of the parents even looked like they believed it.

Not that any of it matters. Teddy has no intention of killing anyone else.

This morning, he doesn't go to the teachers' lounge.

Instead, he goes straight to his classroom, gets settled, and starts working on today's assignments. Last night, he spent so much time fixing the justice system, he didn't have time for his own work.

When his first-period students arrive, they're all talking about the news. Two classes later, they're talking about the killer at Belmont.

'He needs a name.'

'The Belmont Butcher?'

'But he doesn't butcher people.'

'Why are we assuming it's a "he"?'

'How about the School Slayer?'

'There's no slaying. It's poison.'

'The Exterminator.'

'You guys are sick.'

Zach Ward. He walks into the room and doesn't look happy about the conversation. 'Courtney's still in jail, you know,' he says to a group of students. 'If someone is killing people here, the police need to admit they were wrong and let her go.'

For the first time he can remember, Teddy agrees with Zach. Maybe his selfish student is finally learning something.

During class, Teddy even starts to think maybe Zach isn't so bad. Still has that smirk, of course, and he's still one of the most arrogant kids at the school. But he is smart. Teddy has to give him that. Teddy also has to give himself credit, because he never stops trying to make his students better. There's always a way.

At lunchtime, Teddy goes up to the lounge to see what the teachers are saying. At least, that was his plan. As soon as he steps out of his classroom, he runs into Ms Marsha.

'Teddy,' she says. 'I'm so glad I caught you.'

Ms Marsha looks more tired than usual. The bags under her eyes are quite dark. 'Good afternoon,' he says. 'You're looking well today.'

'Thank you for saying that, but I'm afraid I didn't get much sleep last night.'

'How is it going?' he says.

'Busy, as you can imagine.'

Right across from them, someone is on a ladder installing a camera. Busy day, indeed.

'However,' she says, 'we do have a temporary replacement for Sonia. She'll be teaching her classes for the rest of the semester.'

'Wonderful,' Teddy says. 'You do work fast.'

Ms Marsha almost smiles. 'Actually, we got lucky. She volunteered to help us out.' She glances behind him, making Teddy turn around.

When he sees who it is, his heart stops.

Same shiny dark hair, same pert nose. No longer a girl, either. She's the woman he saw at Sonia's memorial service.

Fallon Knight.

His former student. The one who didn't get into a top school because of him. The one who calls him an asshole in her emails.

Fallon turns to him and smiles.

44

The look on Teddy's face is glorious. Fallon stares at it for a second before reaching out to shake his hand.

'Teddy. How nice to see you again.'

Shock delays his answer. Maybe it's the shock of seeing her. Maybe it's because she called him by his first name. He's not Mr Crutcher anymore.

'Fallon,' he finally says. 'Welcome back.'

'Thank you.'

'Let me show you where Sonia's classroom is,' Ms Marsha says, leading Fallon away. 'You can get settled and review her lesson plans. Teddy, we'll speak later.'

As they walk down the hall, Fallon has a strong urge to look back at her old English teacher to see if he has recovered. She doesn't, though, because it would make her look weak.

Ms Marsha, still as old as dirt, leads her to Mrs B's classroom.

No. *Her* classroom.

It's been a few years since Fallon graduated from Belmont. With the exception of the security guards in the hallways and the chain-link fence outside, the school looks exactly the same. But it feels different.

Everyone looks a little dazed, like they were playing video games for too long and have just reentered the real world. Even the students seem different. Not quite scared, but not nearly as confident.

'I had Sonia's lesson plans printed out for you,' Ms Marsha says, pointing to a file on top of the desk. 'I'll have her student list and their current grades emailed to you.'

'Thank you,' Fallon says.

'A substitute will finish out her classes today if you want to sit in. I expect you'll start tomorrow?'

'Yes. Absolutely.'

'Perfect.' Ms Marsha pats her on the shoulder. 'Good to see you again, dear. Now, I've got to run.'

Fallon wonders if she calls any other teachers 'dear.' Not likely. Although that's not a battle she's willing to fight. Just like when she'd volunteered to come help out, the headmaster had offered her a salary far below what a starting teacher should make. She didn't argue then, either.

She's going to need all the friends she can get at this school. The Teacher of the Year is a big enemy to have.

The last time she and Teddy spoke face-to-face was the day she graduated from Belmont. By then, she had been turned down at every college she had applied to. No Ivy would touch her. Neither would Bennington, Amherst, or Georgetown. No one would even talk to her, let alone explain why. It felt as if there were an incriminating video of her on the internet that everyone had seen except her.

Graduation day was the worst. Her friends were all going to their favorite schools, or close to it, while her parents were angry. They showed up at the ceremony out of spite, convinced their daughter had a secret life that was preventing her from getting into a better school.

There she was, lost in a sea of blue gowns and gold sashes, feeling like the pariah she had become. Her parents posed for one picture with her before leaving altogether.

As she watched them go, she heard Crutcher's voice.

'Fallon,' he said. 'Congratulations.'

He stood before her, wearing his stupid tweed jacket with the elbow patches. At the time, she had no idea it was all his fault. He was just the arrogant English teacher she never had to see again.

'Thanks, Mr Crutcher,' she said.

'I heard you didn't get admitted to your top choice.'

She shook her head, not telling him she didn't get into any of her choices.

'It will all work out,' he said. 'This is the kind of thing that makes you a better person.'

'I doubt that.'

'It's true. You'll see.' He smiled and walked off to congratulate someone else.

Fallon has spent a lot of time thinking about that conversation, replaying it again and again. Because she still can't believe how cruel it was.

Back at Belmont now, she sits through the afternoon classes, watching the students more than the substitute. It's surprisingly easy to read their personalities. While she was in college at State, her parents had refused to give her spending money, so she worked part-time as a waitress and bartender. That experience in the service industry was coming in handy.

When the last class ends, she stays behind, trying to get comfortable sitting at Sonia's desk. The room looks different from this perspective. She imagines all those teenage eyes staring at her. Waiting for her to mess up. Waiting to make fun of her. Waiting for a weakness they can take advantage of.

Just like she used to.

Not an easy job. Not a desirable one, either. She would

rather be in grad school, on her way to getting her master's and then her PhD. College is where she always wanted to teach.

At the end of the day, she drives through the gate. The road is empty, the reporters gone. Fallon drives across town, as far away from Belmont as she can get and still be in the same county. To the wrong side of town, the wrong side of everything – as her parents used to say. They don't pay her bills anymore. They don't pay for anything.

Her apartment is a box, a studio with a kitchenette and a bathroom. Empty except for an inflatable bed, a suitcase, and a single lamp. Almost like she just moved in.

She didn't.

Although there are no pictures on her wall, she has a lot on her computer. Most are of Teddy, and they're all organized in separate files: Home. School. His regular corner store.

She's been watching Teddy for a while.

45

If it's not one thing, it's another. Teddy is wise enough to know that. He doesn't expect life to be good every day, or for only good things to happen.

But if he could reap the rewards of his hard work for a day or two, that would be great.

He's on the brink of saving Courtney. The media is going nuts, the police and the DA are under pressure, and, no doubt, Courtney's high-priced lawyer is right in their face, demanding answers about what's going on. Anytime now, they'll drop the charges. They have to. Just days before the trial is due to start, the tide has turned. The jury pool has been tainted. No one likes to try a case they're going to lose, and the DA knows he will.

Because of Teddy. He had to save Courtney, and that's exactly what he did.

But does he get to enjoy this?

No. No, he does not.

Tonight, he planned to drink some milk, watch the news, and celebrate his good deeds.

Ruined.

Instead, he sits in front of the TV, and the news is on, but he can't enjoy it at all. He poured himself a glass of milk, but it's been sitting too long. Not cold anymore.

Ruined because of Fallon. She had to come back now.

In just a few years, she's aged quite a bit – and not in a

good way. Sometimes, those things can't be helped, though. It's all in the genes.

The last time he saw her was the day after she graduated from Belmont. He was heading into Hector's store when she drove up and stopped at the light. Fallon drove a Mercedes SUV, all black, and she was talking on her phone, gesturing wildly, not paying attention to anything but her call. Despite how unhappy she looked at the graduation ceremony, he didn't regret what he had done. She was so self-absorbed, so vain. So clueless.

She's still angry at him. He knows this from her emails, and from the petulant, bratty look on her face today. Fallon hasn't changed a bit. Hasn't learned a thing.

If only people understood how difficult it is to teach these students to be better people. He tries and tries and tries, and yet sometimes, even he can't help them.

Not that he's going to give up. He never gives up.

It's for their own good.

Money can't buy everything.

Another Ward-ism, and it's true. No matter how much Zach offers Kay, the jail guard isn't willing to let Zach see Courtney again. Too many people paying attention, she says. The day has been crazy with news and media and a stream of lawyers coming in to see Courtney. Yes, she needs the money, but she also needs her job.

He has to try another way. There's always a way.

Another Ward-ism: *Even cement walls have cracks.*

'A phone call,' he says to Kay. 'What if I call you, and you give Courtney the phone?'

They're in the parking lot of a bank, now closed for the

day. Both are still in their vehicles, like they're undercover police. Kay's car looks like it's from the eighties. Zach's looks and smells like it belongs to an ostentatious prick.

An ostentatious prick with cash.

'I'll give you the same amount.' He holds up a fresh stack of bills straight from the ATM. 'For just a phone call.'

Kay is quiet. The radio is on in her car, turned down low, playing a country song. Zach almost breaks the silence to say how much he likes that song, which is true, but then she speaks.

'I'll call you at one o'clock in the morning. Hank will be on his break.'

'Perfect.'

Zach stays awake, afraid to miss the call, and keeps himself busy with homework, the news, and social media. The #HomicideHigh messages have multiplied again, and now everyone thinks Courtney is innocent.

Imagine that.

But it makes him wonder what he would think if he didn't know Courtney. Maybe he would've believed she was guilty before deciding she was innocent. Yes, most likely he would've, and that disappoints him. Something to talk about with the school therapist, if he feels like it. Or think about when he's high.

At exactly one in the morning, his phone buzzes.

'Hello?'

'You have eight minutes,' Kay says.

Zach starts to answer, but she's already gone.

'Hey,' Courtney says. She sounds half-asleep.

'Hey, how are you?'

'I can't believe Mrs B is dead.'

Right. Zach forgot he hasn't talked to her since that happened. The sadness comes back when he remembers. 'I know. It sucks.' He keeps his eye on the clock. Seven minutes. 'You've heard what's happening in the news?'

'My lawyer told me today. He thinks they have to let me go.'

'They better.'

'But I kind of liked being a poster child,' she says. 'Now I'll just be normal again.'

Zach smiles. Now she sounds like Courtney. 'Then you have to be the poster child of something else.'

'Like what?'

'I don't know. You should be the poster child of high school newspapers.' Four minutes. 'I took over editing the paper while you've been out, and that's a horrible job.'

'You screwed it up, didn't you?' she says. 'You screwed up my paper.'

'Probably.'

'Loser.'

It's good to hear her say that.

'Hey,' he says, 'are you really coming back to Belmont? Like, after your . . . after what happened to your mom here?'

'Hell, yes. How else am I going to find out what happened to her?'

A minute and a half left. 'Can I ask you something? About the case, I mean,' Zach says.

'Sure.'

'Do you know what was used? I mean, to . . . kill them?'

'Yeah. They had to tell my lawyer. It's just not public.'

'Was it really a poison?'

Pause. 'Yes. And they think I put it in her coffee.'

46

Fallon arrives at school early, but not before the reporters. They've already congregated outside the gate, along with a coffee-and-pastry food truck. She stops only to introduce herself to the guard.

The reporters don't interest her, and neither does the trial. The murders are horrible, yes. Especially the murder of Sonia Benjamin, who was a good teacher. Not the best she ever had, but she did treat her students with respect. Teddy could have learned a lot from her if his head wasn't stuck so far up his own ass.

Fallon's car is just as crappy as her apartment. Probably the worst one in the parking lot. She doesn't care about that, either. Or her clothes, which are secondhand, from a thrift shop in the ritzy area of town. It's possible she is wearing a skirt and blouse donated by a student's parents.

Doesn't matter.

The security company workers are still on-site, installing the new camera system. They're the only people around this early in the morning. Fallon parks and goes inside, heading straight to the teachers' lounge.

Before yesterday, she had never seen it. The kids had always wondered what it was like inside, speculating that the lounge was a private dining room with menus and waiters and golden carafes filled with coffee.

Wrong.

It really is just a lounge, albeit a nice one with comfortable furniture, a decent kitchen area, and an extraordinary amount of coffee choices. They do have real cups and plates and silverware, though it's nothing fancy. A portrait of the school's founder hangs on the wall, right next to a framed poster that declares EDUCATION IS THE KEY TO FREEDOM.

Fallon makes herself a cup of Prime Bold and heads back down to her classroom. Taking advantage of the quiet, she sits down at her desk to prepare for the day.

She's reviewed Sonia's lesson plans three times. Now that she's here, working at the school, she feels nervous about teaching. She has no idea how to do it.

'Good morning.'

The headmaster stands in the doorway, briefcase in one hand and a travel mug in the other. Fallon is a little stunned. Though she briefly saw him during her initial interview, they didn't really speak.

'Good morning,' she says, rising from her chair. 'What a surprise.'

He smiles a little. 'It's not often anyone arrives before I do. When I saw you in here, I had to say hello. And welcome back.'

'Thank you. I appreciate that.'

'The circumstances aren't ideal, of course,' he says. The headmaster takes a deep breath and glances away, into the hall. 'But it's always nice to have a former student return. Belmont students are usually our best teachers.'

He leaves her feeling even more nervous.

Maybe this was a mistake.

When she volunteered to be a teacher, it sounded easy enough in her head. Now that she's sitting in a real classroom, it doesn't.

Coming back to town was one thing. First, because she had nowhere else to go. She'd never be able to get a job teaching anywhere else. This is the only place that will take her at her word, because she's part of the Belmont family.

Contrary to what she'd emailed to Teddy and what she'd told the school, Fallon had never graduated from college.

Two o'clock in the afternoon. The first thing Teddy hears on the radio, while driving to work, is that the DA will be holding a press conference at two o'clock in the afternoon.

What an obscure time of day. Nestled right in between lunch and the evening news.

The news must be bad, though not for Courtney. For the DA.

Teddy smiles all the way to Belmont, and he continues to smile until he remembers Fallon.

Always another problem to solve.

He goes straight to his classroom, avoiding the teachers' lounge. Plenty of time for Fallon later. Right now, he needs to prepare for class. Last night, even as her return weighed heavily on his mind, he still had a brilliant idea for his students.

It's a perfect time to have them read a book about someone falsely accused of a crime.

For the sophomores, it's the classic novel *A Lesson Before Dying*. But for the juniors, he has prepared a special treat. It isn't often he assigns a modern novel. Not when there are so many classics to read. And how many of these students will read classic literature once they're out of school? Not many. They'll be too busy making money.

However, last night he decided a modern novel is just

what his class needs. *Atonement* by Ian McEwan will be their next book. A bit of a cheat, since it's set during World War II, but it's the first book written in the twenty-first century that he's ever assigned.

All in anticipation of Courtney's potential return.

At least he hopes she returns to Belmont. This would certainly clear up some of the dark clouds hanging over the school.

The door to his room is shut, but he can hear the students in the hall, starting to arrive. A familiar feeling of anticipation creeps in. The kind he gets when he's excited about a class or an assignment. Students don't understand that part of being a teacher. Sometimes, teachers *like* to see their students happy.

Or at least Teddy does. One day, maybe he should tell them all of this. Perhaps in the speech he still is due to give at the annual memorial. Whenever that will be.

But then, as Teacher of the Year, he will also give a speech at commencement. Maybe that would be a good time to explain to the students what teaching is really like. Yes, he should do that. He only has a year to take advantage of the position, though his name will be etched into the master plaque in the main hallway of the school. Teacher of the Year is a title that never really goes away.

It's always there, even after his official year is over. A title to let everyone know he is one of the best.

He looks up from his computer, turning around to see his award on the wall. Such a lovely plaque, engraved with his name and title, along with a picture of himself with the headmaster. Sometimes, he just stares at it, remembering all the hard work that went into achieving such an esteemed honor.

The hours he spent at fundraisers and receptions, talking to the board members, convincing them he is one of Belmont's finest.

But today is different.

His Teacher of Year plaque is gone.

47

It isn't often Teddy goes to see the headmaster. That type of meeting is usually reserved for promotions, firings, or a substantial dispute with a student. His stolen Teacher of the Year plaque ranks right up there.

First, though, he has to get through Ms Marsha. The headmaster's pit bull.

Today, he is second in line to speak to her. The young woman in front of him is an aide who accidentally put her security card through the wash and needs a replacement.

He waits, trying hard not to sigh in frustration. Finally, Ms Marsha gets to him.

'Teddy,' she says, looking up at him over her glasses. When she's not wearing them, she keeps them around her neck on a string of pearls.

'Hello, Ms Marsha. May I see the headmaster?'

'He's in a meeting right now. You can't see him.'

'I don't think you understand how important this is,' Teddy says.

'What I understand is that we are five minutes away from the first bell, and you have a class to teach.' She turns away from him, back to her computer monitor. 'Why don't you come back at the break. I can try to squeeze you in then.'

Teddy clenches his hands into fists. 'Ms Marsha, there's been a *theft*. At *Belmont*, for God's sake.'

She raises one penciled eyebrow. 'A theft? What was stolen?'

'My Teacher of the Year plaque is gone.' He throws his hands up. 'Yesterday, it was on my wall. This morning, it's gone.'

Ms Marsha does not look nearly shocked enough. 'How odd.'

'A travesty is what it is.'

'No, Teddy. Murder is a travesty. Your missing plaque is an inconvenience.' She stands up from her desk, straightening her herringbone skirt. 'Check with Joe. You know he cleans at night. Maybe he saw something.'

She gets up and walks away from him.

Teddy has been dismissed.

Dismissed.

The first bell rings before he can find Joe, and now he has to wait. Back to his classroom he goes. He checks the wall as soon as he walks in.

Still gone.

The students are filing in, depositing their phones, and getting settled in their seats. Teddy no longer feels very generous toward them. Anyone could be a suspect – even one of the students. Belmont kids are the type who would steal for fun. It isn't because they need anything.

They don't deserve a treat. Not today.

'Let's begin,' he says, slamming his laptop shut. 'It's time to start our next assignment. I've thought long and hard about this next book, and given that you all have done so well this semester, I feel it's time for you to tackle something more challenging.' He stops to smile at them. 'Which is why I'm assigning you to read Dante's *Divine Comedy*. All three parts.'

Groans. Real, audible groans.

Good.

At the morning break, Ms Marsha isn't even at her desk. Teddy almost knocks on the headmaster's door. Almost. Such a thing would be unheard of, a complete breach of Belmont protocol, but for God's sake, if this doesn't warrant it, what does?

Murder. Always back to those damn murders. It's like he's never going to get away from them.

He goes in search of Joe, whose office – if it can be called that – is so far away, it's a trek just to get there. Maybe Joe knows if any of these cameras are actually working yet. A long shot, given that they're still being installed. But it would be so nice to have the thief caught on camera.

Teddy knocks on Joe's door. He's an older man now, maybe as old as Ms Marsha, and he doesn't move as fast as he used to. Teddy hopes he can get to the door before the four-minute bell rings.

While waiting, he checks his phone for news about this afternoon's press conference.

The door flings open with a surprising amount of force. Joe is standing in front of him, wearing his blue uniform with the Belmont crest on the breast pocket. He's lost most of his hair; just a few grey tendrils remain. Joe has the look of a man who has lived a manual life.

'Oh,' he says. 'It's you.'

Teddy is a little taken aback by this greeting. 'Good morning, Joe.'

Joe nods.

'I wanted to ask about your cleaning last night. Did you by

chance clean my classroom? Empty the trash, that sort of thing?'

Another nod.

'My plaque is missing. My Teacher of the Year plaque was on the wall, and now it's not.'

No reaction at all. Joe's face doesn't register surprise or shock or even dismay. It's as if the old man hasn't heard him.

'Did you – '

'I heard you,' Joe says. 'I don't know anything about it.'

'Did you happen to notice if it was there when you entered the room to clean it?'

'Nope.'

'I see,' Teddy says. 'Is the camera system working yet? Perhaps whoever took it was – '

'Nope.'

All right. Teddy gets it. Perhaps he did mention Joe to the police when they questioned him about Sonia. And, yes, he did say that Joe probably didn't like her because of the way she treated him. Then there's the whole email thing he set up, though it's unlikely the police have figured that out yet.

All of which is neither here nor there. Teddy has never treated Joe badly before, and quite frankly, he is stunned by this total lack of interest – or help – from the school's custodian.

'Might you have any suggestions for how I can look into this further?' Teddy says. 'It was a *theft*, for God's sake. On school grounds.'

For the first time, Joe's face changes. He smiles, revealing a full set of coffee-stained teeth. 'Have you checked the dumpster?' he says. 'I know how much you like to root around in the trash.'

48

Crutcher's in a shit mood today. Not that it's anything new, but today he's treating the whole class the way he usually treats Zach.

The Divine Comedy? A punishment – Zach knows that. Or maybe a judgment, given how much he hates everyone.

'I have allotted four weeks in total for *The Divine Comedy*,' Crutcher says. 'Which means you should finish the first book, *Inferno*, by next week. Pay particular attention to who ends up in each ring of hell and why. Hypocrites, for example. Or thieves.'

Maybe that's it, Zach realizes. Maybe Crutcher thinks of himself as a god, and it's his job to punish people.

At lunch, Zach eats in the dining hall with everyone else. He doesn't bring his own food. Nor does anyone else. Halfway through the break, Zach's phone buzzes. So does everyone else's. They all receive the same news alert.

BREAKING NEWS

DA cancels afternoon press conference.

More to come . . .

'I thought Courtney was getting out today,' Lucas says.

'So did I.' Zach reads through the whole article, which is just a recap of the story so far. 'This is weird.'

Courtney's friend, Daria, appears at their table. 'Did you see this?' she says, holding up her phone.

'We saw it,' Zach says.

'I talked to her dad last night,' Daria says. 'He said they were going to drop the charges today.'

'Maybe they still are.'

She frowns, staring at her phone. Daria is one of those girls with white-blond hair and alabaster skin. Red lipstick is her signature thing. 'Maybe,' she says. 'But this doesn't seem right.'

Daria walks away, moving on to another table.

It doesn't seem right to Zach, either. He considers texting Kay, but a jail guard probably wouldn't have a clue what the DA is doing.

All afternoon, he continues to check the news. Nothing else is announced. No press conference, no mention of Courtney. It makes him wonder if that news alert was wrong. Wouldn't be the first time.

When he walks out of his last class, there's still nothing. No word at all. He gets a text message from Lucas, asking if Zach wants to go to his house. That means get high. Zach stands in the hall, trying to decide if he should go home and start reading or go to Lucas's.

'Zach.'

He looks up from his phone to see Ms Marsha. She has always reminded him of his grandmother. The way she speaks makes him do whatever she says. 'Hi, Ms Marsha.'

'Would you come with me please?' She starts walking away, no doubt assuming he will follow.

He does.

She leads him down the hall and around the corner, away

from the classrooms. Ms Marsha doesn't stop until they reach the last door. She opens it without knocking.

The room is tiny, with no windows and barely enough room to fit a metal desk and a few chairs. Like a closet that's been turned into an office. Two men Zach has never seen before sit on the same side of the desk. Neither one looks like the type to work at Belmont.

'These are Detectives Tate and Oliver,' Ms Marsha says. 'They'd like to ask you some questions about Mrs Benjamin.'

Zach looks at them and then at Ms Marsha.

'If you'd prefer to have one of your parents here, I can call them,' she says. 'It's up to you.'

Holy Jesus, no. He'd rather talk to a hundred detectives alone than have his parents in the room. 'This is fine,' he says. 'I'm good.'

She nods and shuts the door. Zach introduces himself, shaking hands with both men before sitting down.

'Thank for you agreeing to talk to us,' says Tate. He's the older of the two, with that same grizzled look detectives always have in the movies.

Thinking about movie detectives reminds Zach that he shouldn't talk to them without a lawyer. His mom has said that a thousand times. It's practically her own Ward-ism. 'Ms Marsha said this is about Mrs Benjamin?' Zach says.

'That's right,' says Oliver. He's not as old or grizzled as Tate, but he's getting there. 'We were told you edit the school paper, and she was the faculty advisor.'

Zach nods. He almost says he took over after Courtney was arrested, but that seems like too much information.

'How well did you know Mrs Benjamin?' Tate says.

'About as well as any teacher, I guess.' Zach shrugs.

Oliver has a notebook, and he writes that down.

'What did you think of Mrs Benjamin?' Tate says. He looks bored.

'She was a good teacher,' Zach says. 'I learned a lot from her.'

'What kinds of things did you learn?'

Zach groans inside, knowing he'd opened himself up to that one. His mom would be disappointed. 'How to lay out the paper, how to make the articles fit. That kind of thing.'

Tate nods. Oliver writes.

Zach has an urge to ask them what this is about, and what's going on with Courtney, but he knows better.

'Did you see her the day she died?' Tate says.

'Yes. I saw her at school.'

'Do you remember when?'

Zach does remember. He met with Mrs B in the *Bugle*'s office at lunchtime to talk about the paper. 'It was either in the halls or in the *Bugle*'s office. Maybe both.'

'But on that day,' Tate says, 'do you remember when?'

'Not really. I saw her every day.'

Oliver writes that down.

'Is there anyone who didn't like her?' Tate asks.

Zach is surprised by the question but knows he shouldn't be. She was murdered, after all. 'Not that I know of.'

'You never heard anyone speak badly about her?'

'Not to me,' Zach says.

Oliver writes that down.

'All right,' Tate says. 'I think that's about it. Thank you for talking to us.'

'No problem.' He stands up and shakes both their hands, then slings his backpack over his shoulder. Just as he turns to open the door, Tate becomes a full-blown TV detective.

'Sorry, I do have one more question,' he says.

Zach turns back. 'Yes?'

'Did you bribe a county employee in order to see Courtney Ross?'

49

Fallon didn't see Teddy once today. Not even in the halls. He must be avoiding her.

It's almost flattering.

Up until she started working at Belmont, she'd been following him. Teddy doesn't do a whole lot. He never goes out to dinner, out for drinks, or even to a movie. Over the past several months, the only interesting thing he did was clear his yard. The rest of the time, he stayed inside that run-down house, probably dreaming up new ways to ruin his students' lives.

Now, it's more difficult to follow him, because he knows she's in town. She has to get a little more creative.

Lucky for her, this is the twenty-first century. The geniuses in Silicon Valley have invented technology designed to invade privacy. Teddy doesn't know there's a camera hidden right by his mailbox. All she has to do is drive close by and download the data, and then she knows when he was home. Or when he wasn't. Every few weeks, she swaps it out with another camera that has a fresh battery.

The downside is the expense. She's run up quite a credit card balance since returning to town. Ruining someone's life isn't cheap.

She packs up her things, vowing to reread all the books her students are reading, and walks out of her classroom. Although school is out for the day, both students and teachers are still around. Some are in the halls, some in sports practice, and a small crowd is gathered near the front door. Mostly administrators, including Ms Marsha. They're all staring out at the parking lot.

'What's everyone looking at?' she says.

The school secretary answers. 'Zach Ward was arrested.'

Fallon has no idea who that is. Outside, a young guy – a student – is put into a police car.

Ms Marsha is on her phone, hand covering her mouth, whispering so no one can hear her.

'How terrible,' Fallon says, trying to sound as concerned as everyone else. 'Do you know what for?'

No one has an answer.

'I hope it doesn't have anything to do with the murders,' someone says.

The school secretary shakes her head rather hard. 'Zach? Oh, no. No way.'

'We don't know anything,' Ms Marsha says, ending her call. 'So let's not start spreading rumors when we have no idea what's happening.' She gives them all a stern look before walking away.

Fallon gets out of there before any of the gossip starts. Reputations are built quickly at a school like Belmont, and the last thing she needs is to be known as a gossip.

Shut up and smile.

That's what Belmont kids do to survive, and now that she's back, she has to do the same thing. Her only job is to gather the data from her camera, study it, and plan her next move.

The first move was months ago, before she'd even returned. Step one was to break up his marriage.

That was almost too easy.

*

Zach is at the police station, sitting by himself in an interrogation room. He's been booked and fingerprinted, and now they don't know what to do with him. They can't take him to the same jail where Courtney is, and the holding cells are full. Too many reporters: A number of them were caught trespassing. There are a lot of people here.

Which is just fine with Zach. He has never been so scared.

Seventeen years of being told not to screw up.

Seventeen years of having it drilled into his head.

One error in judgment can change everything, Dad always says. The example he uses is drinking and driving. Bribing a jail guard probably applies as well.

Zach has finally screwed up, and it's a big mistake. Big enough to change everything. And the only thing he can do is wait for his mom to show up.

When she does, he can hear her through the door.

'How dare you speak to my son without my permission . . .'

Her voice gets louder as she comes closer, and the door flies open. Mom stands there, and Zach can feel her rage, her worry, her confusion. A bundle of emotions entering the room all at once.

Including disappointment.

She rushes to him. 'Are you okay?'

He nods.

She whips around to face Tate and Oliver. 'Someone better start telling me what's going on.'

'Your son has been arrested for bribing a county employee,' Tate says.

'That's absurd.'

Tate says nothing.

'Mom,' Zach says.

215

'Be quiet,' she says. Doesn't even look at him. She takes a deep breath and straightens her shoulders, transforming from a mother to a lawyer. 'Let's speak outside,' she says to the detectives.

Zach finds himself alone again. No phone. No windows. Nothing to do but think about how stupid he is.

The next few hours go by in a blur. He's taken out of the room, and Mom once again tells him to stay quiet. He stands in front of a judge, who reads the charges and sets his bail. Zach barely listens. He's already thinking of what comes next. What a school like Belmont will do with a student charged with felony bribery.

It can't be good.

Things get even worse after the bail is paid and he walks out of the police station. Dad is right there, waiting for him.

'What in the hell did you do?' he says.

'Not here,' Mom says. 'Wait until we get home.'

Zach opts to ride with Mom, which seems like the lesser of two evils. She's on the phone the whole time, either talking to someone at her office or calling around about criminal defense lawyers.

The pit in Zach's stomach grows bigger.

Mom ends a call as they drive up to the house. 'You have no idea what you've done,' she says.

'I just – '

'Not. One. Word.'

He can't talk, can't explain, can't tell his side of the story. Can't even text Lucas because she took his phone. Sometimes, it sucks having a mom who's a lawyer.

Dad is yelling before he's even out of the car, but Mom puts the kibosh on that.

'Inside,' she says.

Once in the house, Zach is sent to his room. No phone, no laptop, no tablet. No way to communicate with anyone. He can't even talk to his parents. Not until his new lawyer arrives.

Until then, he lies on his bed, staring at the ceiling, knowing everything has changed. One moment, one error in judgment, has altered the course of his life.

Dad was right. Maybe he always has been. Maybe all his Ward-isms aren't as stupid as Zach believed them to be.

Zach hasn't even graduated from high school, and he already wants a do-over.

50

After school, Teddy sits in his classroom for a long time, waiting for everyone to clear out. He never did get to speak to the headmaster. The best he could do was file a formal incident report and send it to Ms Marsha, who has yet to respond.

Teddy works, or pretends to, but all he thinks about is his plaque.

And Joe. And the dumpster.

He always knew there was something he didn't like about Joe. He's been around too long. Knows too much, sees too much. Like the dumpster. He's even worse than Ms Marsha, and she knows just about everything.

Teddy made the right choice setting Joe up. If Joe had never caught Teddy rooting through it, things might've turned out differently.

Teddy wonders if his plaque is in the dumpster, if Joe had actually put it there. Part of him thinks it's ridiculous to go outside and search through it. The other part of him knows that he has to. When he finally gets up and heads outside, a light snow has started to fall. It's dusk, making everything look grey. Appropriate, given Teddy's mood.

He slips. Curses. Gets up off the ground, wiping snow and dirt from his slacks.

When he lifts the top of the dumpster, the snow on top falls backward, landing near his feet. He stomps it off. Curses again.

All of his cursing is directed at Joe.

He moves a crate in front of the dumpster and climbs up. The stench is almost unbearable, just as it was last time, but Teddy searches through it anyway. A few times, he retches. A few times, he climbs down to rest a moment. It takes longer than he remembers from before. Darkness falls, leaving Teddy with just the security lights. His hands start to go numb, even with the gloves. Still, he goes through every inch of that dumpster.

No plaque.

Ezekiel T. Fisher is a huge man. Or at least he seems that way to Zach, who looks up at him from the couch. His new lawyer reminds him of a football player wearing a suit.

Zach still hasn't said a word, but at least he's allowed to hear what his own lawyer has to say.

It's dark outside, long after dinner, though Zach never ate anything. He stayed in his room until he was told to come downstairs, and now his stomach is rumbling. The last thing he ate was a protein bar several hours ago.

'I spoke to the DA.' Ezekiel stands by the fireplace, a cup of coffee in one hand. He's flanked by Mom and Dad, who aren't sitting down, either. Zach is, and he feels like a small child looking up at all the adults. 'A guard told them everything, even showed them calls on her phone that came from Zach,' Ezekiel says.

Kay. She must have been caught. Otherwise, none of this makes sense. They'd had a good thing going. For a while, anyway.

'But as we suspected,' Ezekiel continues, 'this has nothing to do with the bribery.'

'Of course it doesn't,' Mom says.

'But why – '

Zach is cut off by Mom, who raises her hand to shut him up.

'They want to know why Zach had to see Courtney so badly,' she says to Ezekiel. 'Why he was willing to pay a guard to see her.'

Ezekiel nods, his big head moving as slow as a snail. 'Exactly. And it goes beyond that. To be honest, I can't blame them. The timing is . . . suspicious, to say the least.'

Mom nods. Dad looks as confused as Zach feels.

'They want to make a deal,' Mom says.

'They want to *talk* about a deal,' Ezekiel says. 'It depends. Because it doesn't look good.'

Mom looks at the lawyer and shakes her head. 'No. It does not.'

'However,' Ezekiel says, 'you can't just arrest someone for murder just because it *looks* bad.'

'Murder?' Zach says.

'Oh Jesus,' Dad says. He looks from Ezekiel to Zach to his wife. 'Are you telling me they think – '

'Yes,' Mom says. 'That's exactly what they think.'

Dad sits down in a chair, mouth open, staring off into space.

'Zach,' Ezekiel says, finally turning to his client. 'Do you understand what's happening here?'

Afraid to open his mouth, Zach shakes his head no.

'You paid a guard to see Courtney,' Ezekiel says. He holds up his hand, just like his mom did. Must be a lawyer thing. 'Please, don't say anything.'

Zach doesn't.

'You met with Courtney and had a private conversation. No recording, no tape, nothing at all,' Ezekiel says. 'A couple of days later, Sonia Benjamin died from the same poison that killed Ingrid Ross. The specifics of that poison have never been released to the public.' He pauses, letting that sink in. It does. 'Then you paid the guard again to speak to Courtney on the phone. Again, there's no recording of that conversation.'

Piece by piece, the picture comes together in Zach's head, until he sees it the way the police do.

They think the two of them met to come up with a plan to free Courtney. They think Courtney told him what poison to use, and then he killed Mrs B.

After all, he had access to her. Even to her food. She was eating a salad when they met at lunchtime in the *Bugle* office. They probably know that, too.

The police think Courtney and Zach were in it together.

It's insane.

It also makes complete sense.

51

Fallon reviews the footage from today. The camera is angled toward the driveway, so she can see when Teddy comes and goes. She can also see part of the sidewalk. Fallon knows what time the mailman shows up. She knows who walks their dog in the neighborhood and what time they pass by. She keeps a chart of everything. If she ever needs to get into Teddy's house, she knows exactly when to go.

Now she needs to put a camera in his classroom.

One day of working at Belmont has taught her she won't get a lot of chances. Before and after school, his classroom is locked. During school, there are plenty of people around. Lunchtime is her only option. She has to wait until the kids are in the dining hall and Teddy goes to the lounge.

It won't take long. All she needs is about thirty seconds.

Fallon wraps up the camera in a scarf and places it inside her bag. The camera app is already on her phone, making it easy to download the data every day. Even several times a day. She considered but eliminated the idea of hooking the camera up to the school's internal Wi-Fi and having the footage automatically go to the cloud. Too risky. Something a stupid criminal would do.

She opens her computer and checks her inbox. Nothing except bill notices from her former college, an angry email from her former landlord, and a bunch of spam for payday loans.

Next, she logs into the Belmont website. As a faculty member, she has access to areas that students can't see. What she wants to see is student grades – Teddy's students, in particular – but that's not available to her. She can only see grades for her students.

Disappointing. Fallon was hoping to track who he was downgrading, the same as he did to her.

What she can see are class schedules. Since they both teach English, she doesn't expect there to be any crossover. So she looks for students who had Teddy and Sonia as a teacher in the previous years. She makes a list on a spreadsheet.

Most of the names don't mean anything to her. She barely knows the names of her own students, much less Teddy's. The one student she recognizes is in Teddy's class this year and was in Sonia's class last year.

Zach Ward.

And she's heard of him only because he was arrested today.

Teddy is at home, showered, and sitting in front of his computer when he learns about Zach's arrest. He'd gone online to see what students were saying, in case any of them were talking about his plaque, and instead he found out about Zach. Very few details have been released. The police have just said that a 'Belmont student was arrested for bribery.'

Teddy laughs. He laughs so hard, he almost spills his water.

Of course that little bastard tried to bribe someone. The only surprise is that he has to pay the price. Kids like him rarely do.

Hours go by before Zach is allowed to speak. Finally, he is alone with Ezekiel. Late at night, his parents leave them alone in his mom's office. Ezekiel sits, which brings him down to a more reasonable size.

'I guess this has been quite a day for you,' he says.

'You could say that.'

'I'm going to ask you some questions, and it's important you only answer what I ask. Do you understand?'

Zach nods.

'Good. Now, are there calls on your phone to a guard at the jail?'

'Yes.'

'How many?'

Zach thinks about it. 'Five or six.'

'And the GPS in your car. Will it show you went to the jail?'

'Yes.'

'How many times?'

'Once.'

Ezekiel does not take notes. He pauses, clasps his hands together, and stares at Zach. 'Do you have text messages to Courtney on your phone?'

'Not since she was arrested.'

'Is there anything about Courtney's mother in the texts you did exchange with her?'

Zach sifts through them in his mind, trying to remember. That was a while ago. 'Probably,' he says.

'Did she say anything bad about her mother?'

All the time. 'Yes.'

'Did she say she wanted her mother dead?'

'Yes.' Many of the text messages that were made public had originally been sent to Zach. 'But it was just – '

Ezekiel holds up his hand. 'Are there any texts about her mother's death?'

'From right after it happened,' Zach says. 'I told her I was sorry her mom died.'

'Anything else?'

'Not that I can remember.'

'And what about your search history?' Ezekiel says. 'Either on your phone or your computer. Did you read about the case?'

'Yes.'

'Did you talk about it on social media?'

'A little.'

'Did you offer an opinion about whether or not Courtney was guilty?'

'I said she wasn't.'

Ezekiel doesn't look pleased, maybe because Zach hadn't stuck to just answering the question.

'Yes,' Zach says, trying to correct himself. 'I offered an opinion.'

'And what about the employees at the jail?' Ezekiel says. 'Did you look up information about the guards?'

The pit in Zach's stomach, which never really went away, grows bigger again. 'Yes.'

'Personal information?'

'Yes.'

'Did you ever look up any information about your teachers? Specifically, Sonia Benjamin.'

Again, Zach has to think. He almost says no, but then he remembers. He looked her up when she asked him to be the editor of the paper. All information is useful. That's what his mom always said.

'Yes,' he says.

Ezekiel does not look surprised. He hasn't looked

surprised at any of Zach's answers. 'How long ago was that?' he says.

'After Courtney was arrested.'

'What about poison?' Ezekiel says. 'Did you ever search for information about the symptoms or effects of various poisons?'

The shock of that question hits like a physical blow. Of course Zach searched for information about poison, but only to try and figure out what had killed Courtney's mom. Everyone was doing it.

And, yes, it was after he saw Courtney in jail.

'It was only because – '

Ezekiel holds up his hand again. 'I don't need to know why.'

'Yes,' Zach says. 'I searched for information about poisons.'

52

The next morning, Zach goes to school as he always does. He has to, Mom says. No one has convicted him of any-thing, and his name didn't appear in the report released to the media. But everyone knows. They always know.

At first, he tries to act normal. Head up, smile on his face, he walks through the hall like everything is fine.

Then he sees the way people react to him. With shocked, distrusting, accusatory looks. By the midmorning break, he walks with his head down.

'Don't worry about it,' Lucas says. 'You're just the thing of the day. Tomorrow, there'll be a new thing.'

Zach hopes he's right. And he should've taken Lucas up on his offer to get high before school.

The students aren't the only ones treating him differently. When he walks into his English class, Crutcher greets him like a long-lost friend.

'Well, if it isn't Zach Ward,' he says. 'So glad you could join us today.'

'Um, thanks?'

'Sit down, sit down. We have a lot to talk about.' Crutcher turns to the class, still smiling. 'I hope all of you have been reading *Inferno*, because today we're going to talk about the circles of hell.'

A poster of Dante's vision hangs on the wall, right across

the chalkboard. It would be easier to see if Crutcher used a smartboard.

Siobhan raises her hand and says, 'Mr Crutcher, you just assigned this book yesterday.'

'Then consider this a gift,' he says. 'Now, the rings are numbered, with one being best – if you can consider it that – and nine being the worst. Dante basically created his own judgment list. As you look over the various rings of hell and who he has placed where, what stands out?'

Zach searches for the word *bribery*.

'Violence is in the seventh ring,' someone says.

Crutcher says, 'That's right. It is. In our society, murder is one of the most heinous crimes. But according to Dante, others were worse. Look at the eighth circle.' He points to it. 'It's the circle of fraud. Here, he includes those who lie, cheat, and deceive.' Crutcher turns to the class. 'This circle also includes thieves. Dante believed *thieves* were worse than murderers.'

Yesterday, Zach wouldn't have been stuck on the word *fraud*, but today he is. Ezekiel told him bribery is a type of fraud.

'In fact,' Crutcher says, 'the only thing worse than a thief is a traitor.' He points to the ninth circle of hell. 'Interesting, isn't it? So if any of you have lied, committed fraud, or stolen anything in your lives, this is where you would end up.'

He pauses and looks at the class. A few students squirm in their seats, including Zach. It feels like Crutcher is staring right at him.

Great.

Everyone knows Zach was arrested yesterday. They don't

know it has anything to do with Courtney. Not yet anyway, but they know he's accused of bribery.

And Crutcher is going out of his way to embarrass him.

Teddy smiles at his students, because he can't help himself. Sometimes it's good to watch these overprivileged kids get a little rattled.

They all are now, especially after Zach's arrest. He's not quite so cocky today. Good to see him acting humble, the way he should. He really is coming along quite well, if Teddy does say so himself.

But it's not just Zach. Any one of his students could be arrested for the same thing. Maybe they've bribed someone to do their homework, or write a paper, or bribed their way out of a speeding ticket. Every single one has done something that would land them in the eighth circle of hell.

Possibly theft. Someone stole his plaque. And he still hasn't ruled anyone out.

Joe is still on the list, but Teddy's betting on Fallon. She was always a brat, and she's mad enough to do something that stupid. But beyond those two, it could be any one of his students. They're all capable of senseless pranks.

Before heading up to the lounge for lunch, Teddy checks the news. Something is going on at the courthouse, though no one is sure what. Lots of lawyers arriving, including Courtney's.

Good. Maybe they're finally letting her go. Honestly, if the wheels of justice moved any slower, Courtney might be dead before they figure out she's innocent.

He shuts the laptop, locks it in his cabinet, and heads up to the teachers' lounge.

*

Thirty seconds. That's all Fallon needs, just thirty seconds.

She's been around the corner from Teddy's classroom, waiting for him to leave. When he does, she slips into the bathroom until he is up the stairs.

Fallon walks with purpose. No sneaking, no looking behind her. That's something all Belmont students learn, and they learn it early: Wherever you are, act like you're supposed to be there. People will assume it's true.

She goes right into Teddy's classroom and straight to the far corner, assessing the best place for the camera. A pile of books are stacked on top of a cabinet behind his desk. She swipes her finger across them. Dust.

Perfect.

The camera fits right between the last book and the wall. She aims it toward Teddy's desk and takes out her phone to check the angle. One quick adjustment, and she's done. This camera is even better than the one in front of his house. More expensive, too. She wanted one that not only had a microphone, but could also zoom.

Fallon walks out the door and into the hallway. All clear. Not a single person around. The new security system isn't working yet. Ms Marsha told her they weren't even testing it until this weekend.

Not luck. Fallon doesn't believe in luck. This is karma. And that bitch is on her side.

First, she ruined Teddy's marriage. Now, she's going to get him fired.

53

Teddy is in the lounge, eating his sandwich, when Louella comes in screaming. Well, she's always screaming, but today her voice has an unbearably high pitch.

'Press conference!' she says. 'The DA is having a press conference right now.'

Most of the teachers immediately follow her to the Porter Room, where the TV is still set up. Teddy takes his time. Finishes his lunch and makes himself a cup of coffee before he strolls down the hall, too.

He hopes the DA does what's right and lets Courtney go.

One more problem solved.

Then he could concentrate on his other problems: Fallon and his missing plaque.

At first, Joe seemed like the likeliest one to steal the plaque. He has access, he has time, and he even has motive, given what Teddy told the police. But would an old man like Joe really risk his job stealing from a teacher? After all these years?

Silly. That would just be silly.

He's still thinking about this as he walks into the Porter Room. The DA is on TV, his big stupid face filling up the whole screen.

'*Late last night, we filed an emergency motion with the court in the case of Ingrid Ross's murder. This morning, the judge heard our motion and ruled to postpone the trial for one month.*

'*I can't say too much at this point. What I can say is that it no longer appears as if the defendant was working alone. We have a second person of interest in this case, as well as in the murder of Sonia Benjamin.'*

Zach. He has to be the second person.

The DA actually thinks Zach and Courtney are in it together.

Another problem to fix.

If the world wasn't filled with so many incompetent people, Teddy would have so much more time to concentrate on the important things. Like teaching.

Everything is the same. Zach sits on the couch, and Ezekiel is by the fireplace, flanked by his parents.

Exactly the same as last night. Zach feels like his life is running in a loop.

'The press conference was strategic,' Ezekiel says. 'The DA is trying to put pressure on Zach. By now, they probably have your phone records. Maybe even your internet searches. And they want us to know they have them.'

'Are they offering anything yet?' Mom says.

Zach tries to say something, but he's cut off by Ezekiel. He and Mom continue talking like Zach isn't there. 'They want to talk,' Ezekiel says.

'So they're fishing.'

'It appears that way.'

Dad makes an angry noise and looks at his phone.

'He's not going to talk,' Mom says.

'That's one option,' Ezekiel says. 'But then they'll move ahead with the felony bribery charge. They probably won't make a deal.'

'Right, right,' Mom says.

Zach stands up from the couch. Finally, everyone looks at

him. 'Explain to *me* what's happening,' he says to Ezekiel. 'You're *my* lawyer.'

'You're right. I am,' he says.

'In private. I want to talk about this alone,' Zach says.

His parents exchange a look, but they agree. Once again, Zach and his lawyer go into his mom's office. When they're settled, Ezekiel starts to talk.

'The police and the DA want to know why you bribed a guard in order to see Courtney. Not once, but twice,' Ezekiel says. He holds up his hand, stopping Zach from answering that question. 'They think – or rather, they *hope* – that you can confirm she's guilty. Further, if you did have something to do with Sonia Benjamin's death, in all likelihood they are willing to believe Courtney convinced you to do it. That she is the ringleader, so to speak.'

Zach fights the urge to say this is all a lie. Every word of it. Instead, he tries to see it the way the police do. 'So they're willing to offer me a deal in exchange for testifying against her.'

'Exactly.'

'And what if I don't know anything? What if they have it all wrong?'

'They'll still move forward with the bribery charge,' he says.

'What about Courtney?'

'That I don't know. Since Sonia Benjamin was killed the same way . . . I don't know how they can proceed,' Ezekiel says.

Zach turns this over in his mind. Either way, he's screwed. So is Courtney.

'Do you know what kind of evidence they have against Courtney?' he says.

'Not all of it, no, though I've heard some things. They

found the poison at her house, in the yard. A lot of text messages about how much she hated her mom.'

'Do you know what kind of poison was used?'

'You don't know?' Ezekiel looks surprised. He thinks Zach was involved.

'I have no idea.'

Ezekiel thinks about this for a minute, maybe trying to decide if Zach is lying. 'I don't know exactly. Only that it came from a plant.'

'A plant? Like . . . hemlock or something?'

'I suppose. I don't know which one.'

Zach nods, thinking he's going to have to search the internet again. Before, he was just looking up poisons in general. Now that he knows it's a plant, he can narrow down the search.

Not that it will help him.

'Realistically,' he says. 'What will happen to me if they go ahead with the bribery thing?'

'Under normal circumstances, given how young you are and given that it didn't involve political corruption, I could plead it down to a misdemeanor. You probably would have to do some community service.' Ezekiel pauses. 'But with this Courtney thing . . . I suspect they aren't motivated to make that deal.'

'I'll go to jail?' Zach says.

'Possibly. And you may end up with a felony on your record.'

'Great.'

'There's something else to consider,' Ezekiel says. 'The court of public opinion can be more important than a court of law. Meaning it won't be long before everyone figures out the DA is talking about you. Especially after they arrested you at school.' He looks a bit angry about that. 'Again, a strategic move on their part. They wanted people to see it.'

It's not hard for Zach to imagine what the media will be like. He's already seen what they've done to Courtney. He's also seen how many people assume she's guilty.

He and Courtney will be just a couple of rich, entitled kids who think they can get away with murder.

Hell, if it were anyone else, he'd believe it.

'No deal,' he says to Ezekiel. 'I'm not talking to anyone.'

54

While Ezekiel goes out to talk to his parents, Zach slips out the side door and leaves the house. He turns off the GPS in his car, takes the chip out of his new phone, and drives straight to Target to pick up a cheap tablet. For cash. He won't keep it in his room, either, just in case the police search it, so he'll put it in the pool house. No one's using it this time of year anyway.

Half an hour later, he's at Starbucks to do some research that can't be connected back to him.

As he waits for his triple-shot Venti Americano, Zach realizes that no one knows where he is and no one can find him. It might be the first time in his life that's happened. Strange. No one peering over his shoulder. No one watching him. No one checking to see what he's up to.

He likes it. For the first time, he feels free.

That reminds him of another Ward-ism, something he always thought was stupid. It was the kind of saying that belonged on a poster.

Money isn't the point. Freedom is the point.

His dad was right about so many things. If only Zach had believed him from the start, he wouldn't be stuck between a felony and a betrayal. Thinking about that doesn't make him feel very free anymore.

When his coffee is ready, he sits down and goes to work on the internet search:

A second person.

Teddy can't believe this is happening. He especially can't believe everyone is saying the second person is Zach Ward.

Has to be, they say.

He was just arrested the other day, they say.

Who else would it be, they say.

Teddy is sitting out on his back porch, in the freezing cold. Although he's wearing a jacket, hat, and gloves, he can still feel it.

He takes a deep breath of frigid air and can see it as he exhales. Again. Again. He watches his cold breath, and it's almost comfortable. As a kid, he used to do the same thing, when he stood out in the cold, waiting for the bus. One winter, when he was nine, the furnace in the house broke and there was no money to fix it. He could see his breath inside. Sometimes, he'd pretended to hold a cigarette like he was smoking.

He can hear his mom, telling him being cold is just a state of mind. She used to wrap him up in blankets and tell him to pretend he was on a beach, basking in the sun. Sometimes, he was so cold, it hurt.

Now that he's an adult and all bundled up, the cold no longer hurts. It feels good. And hopefully, it will kill the worms rumbling in his stomach.

That's how sick he is about this. How awful he feels. All he wanted to do was help Courtney get out, and now *two* students are implicated in the murders.

How can an entire police department screw up so badly?

More importantly, why does Teddy have to fix *everything*?

Unbelievable.

There's a way out of this, because there's always a way. He just has to figure out what it is. It would help if he were surrounded by people who were a little more intelligent. Since they aren't, he's going to have to be very clear about what he does and how he does it.

Kindergarten clear, as teachers like to say.

It's going to take some work. Good thing Teddy's not afraid of that, not like some people. Fallon, for example. If she put more work into herself, she might not be so angry at him.

Her time will come, though. For the moment, the Fallon problem has to come second. Right now, he's got to save his current students.

But it won't be easy with all those new cameras at the school.

Late at night, Fallon sits on her blow-up bed, watching Teddy's last two classes of the day. So far, that's all she has. The disadvantage of using a camera with a microphone is that Fallon has to hear Crutcher's voice. Listening to him talk about Dante – Dante! – brings her right back to high school, when she was one of the students sitting in that classroom.

His voice was annoying then, too.

And arrogant. That's what she notices now, how arrogant he is. Every single word he says is patronizing, even to the students he seems to like. Though there aren't many of those.

The camera doesn't move, so she can only see him when he's in front of the class, along with a few students sitting in the front row.

When he walks too far away, she can't see anything but his desk.

Which is the point.

She fast-forwards through his last class, unable to listen any longer, and waits until the students are leaving. When the room is empty, Teddy opens his laptop.

He types in his password.

This is why she needed the zoom feature.

She watches him check his email, though the camera is still too far away to see any details. He opens the Belmont website, easy to recognize from the logo on the screen, but again she can't read anything.

She slams the laptop closed and throws her one pillow across the room. It knocks over the lamp, pulling the cord out of the wall, and the room goes dark.

Now she's going to have to get back in his classroom and adjust the camera.

As always, Teddy is a pain in her ass.

55

Fallon never dreamed the answer to her problems would fall right out of the sky. Or walk in the door, as it happened.

Not after she found out about the reference letter Teddy wrote.

It took a lot of begging, and what was left of her money, to get it out of an aide at the admissions department at Columbia. She wasn't allowed to have a copy of the letter – or even take a picture – but she did get to read it. That's when she discovered Teddy had accused her of cheating:

> It is my belief that the papers Courtney Ross has turned in were not written by her. Not in their entirety. While I was never able to find definitive proof of this, I do not believe she is capable of that level of work. Therefore, I cannot recommend admitting her to your fine institution.

Those words, now permanently etched in her mind, explained all her rejections.

She considered filing a complaint to Belmont, but without a copy of the letter she couldn't prove anything. It was his word against hers. She knew which way that would go.

That's when she gave up.

She was no longer in school. After spending two years at State, Fallon applied to transfer to a better school. One with a good name. One that would make her parents happy. She

240

had a 4.0 GPA and a 1590 on her SAT, and still didn't get in. Not anywhere.

In her third year at State, she flunked out. By choice? Maybe. Because she was depressed? Likely.

Either way, after that she was living in an apartment almost as bad as the one she has now, and bartending to keep it.

Then luck finally turned her way.

She was at work, slinging drinks and collecting tips, when one of the Belmont teachers walked in the door.

Frank Maxwell had never been her teacher, but she knew he taught math. She had seen him around, just as he must have seen her.

She started to say something to him. 'Hey, Mr – '

'Draft beer, please,' he said.

She poured it, looking at him over the tap. He stared at the mirror behind the bar with blank eyes. He didn't recognize her. Couldn't blame him, either. She was a cheesier version of herself these days. More makeup, fewer clothes. The tips were higher that way.

The bar where she worked was almost in the middle of nowhere, halfway between the airport and the city. The locals she knew. The others were usually visiting. He had to be the latter.

'So what brings you to town?' she said.

'Conference,' he said. 'Education.'

'You're a teacher?'

He nodded. 'I got stuck at a cheap hotel near the airport. That room was driving me crazy.'

She poured him a shot of tequila and placed it in front of him. 'You deserve a shot. You have a hard job.'

He smiled. She smiled. He drank the shot. And another.

When he was sufficiently intoxicated, she said, 'So tell me what really goes on behind the scenes at school. I feel like teachers have a lot of good gossip.' She never asked where he worked, leaving him free to talk.

He did. The first thing he talked about was God, and the lack of God at his school. He went on and on about how teachers don't live right and, therefore, set terrible examples for their students.

'Like what do you mean?' Fallon said. As a bartender, she had learned pretending to be dumb was considered a good thing. It was the opposite of everything she believed, and she did it anyway.

He told her about two teachers who were having an affair – a science teacher and a health teacher. She could guess who they were. Those rumors had been around when she was at Belmont.

He also mentioned a teacher who was into pagan rituals. That had to be Louella Mason, the art teacher.

Throughout all of this, Fallon kept feeding him drinks, acting like he was the most interesting person she had ever met. 'What's the worst thing you've seen a teacher do, though? Like the very, very worst?' She leaned forward across the bar, waiting for him to look at her cleavage. He did.

'Okay,' he said, lowering his voice. 'But this is really bad.'

'Tell me.'

'There's this English teacher. He's nice enough, but pretty uptight.'

Bingo. There was only one male English teacher at Belmont.

'Yeah?' Fallon said. 'What did he do?'

'He and his wife have been trying to have a baby. It's been

going on for a while now. Not that he talks about it, but she does. My wife knows his wife, because they used to work together at the hospital.'

Fallon nodded, not sure where this story was going. 'So did this guy's wife get pregnant?'

'No. She never did. She told my wife that Teddy got tested and was sterile. He couldn't have kids.'

'That's too bad.'

'Yeah.' Frank paused to take a sip of his beer. He went quiet, but not for long. He had come too far not to tell the rest of the story. 'The thing is, my wife now works for a private doctor. In the billing department.'

Fallon shrugged. 'Okay.'

'This doctor, Tobin, he's a fertility specialist, but he does other things, too.'

'Other things?'

Frank shifted in his seat and looked around, checking to see if anyone was listening. They weren't. It was late, the bar was a half hour away from closing, and people were starting to leave.

'I mean, my wife shouldn't have told me this,' he said. 'She could lose her job, but she just couldn't believe it. See, this teacher had gone to her doctor, only he didn't get a fertility test.'

'Then why did he go?' Fallon said.

'To get a vasectomy,' he said. 'That's what the bill said. A vasectomy.'

'So he lied to his wife?'

'Yes, he did.'

Before Frank had even left the bar, Fallon's mind started to spin. It was like she had just won the lottery and had to figure out the best way to spend the proceeds.

Spend them, she did.

Finding a fertility doctor named Tobin wasn't hard. Dr Leo Tobin, fertility specialist, had an office just a few miles from Belmont. She called the office, and a nice woman named Sandra answered.

'Hi, Sandra. My name is Mary. We'd like my husband to get a vasectomy, and I'd like to know how much Dr Tobin charges for this procedure.'

'That depends on your insurance.'

'I work at Belmont Academy. We have insurance through them.'

'Ah, well, in that case, hold on a moment.'

When Sandra returned, she gave Fallon the approximate price, which she said could vary depending on extenuating circumstances or needs.

Fallon thanked her, hung up, and created a fake bill on her computer. The only 'mistake' she made was on the envelope.

Mrs Theodore Crutcher

Whoops.

56

On the coldest morning so far this year, the roads are slick. Teddy hits a patch of black ice and skids right off the road, almost ending up in a ditch. A man in a checked coat and matching hat stops to see if he's okay.

'You're lucky you didn't go in,' he says, pointing at the ditch.

Teddy grunts. 'Not so lucky I hit the ice in the first place.'

The man scurries away, and Teddy continues on to school. No reporters in sight. Too early, even for them. The sun isn't even up yet.

As he gets out of his car, he notices dirt on the cuff of his pants, no doubt from when he got out of his car near the ditch. An annoying start to the day. If he had come to work at the normal time, some of that ice might have melted. But that wasn't an option. He had to arrive early to check the cameras.

They still aren't fully functional. Not until after the week-end check. Today is Friday, his last chance to take note of where they're located without being recorded.

The halls are still quite dark – the daytime lights haven't turned on yet – and the only sound is Teddy's footsteps. But it's not scary. It's comfortable.

Cameras have been placed in every hallway, recording in both directions. They're over every door leading into the building, inside and out – including the teachers' lounge, given that's where Sonia's salad was kept. But they aren't inside the classrooms, the lounge, or the meeting rooms. And there is no camera outside the headmaster's office, either.

Finally, the dining hall. He swings open the door, looking up at the ceiling. No camera right inside the door. He walks around the entire room, corner to corner, and doesn't see anything.

Maybe no one wants to see the kids eating. Can't blame them for that.

Next, the kitchen.

He sees the light too late.

Joe is in the kitchen, standing at the counter, with a plate of eggs and toast. When he sees Teddy, his fork freezes in midair.

Caught.

How fortuitous.

'What a surprise to see you in here,' Teddy says, glancing down at the plate of food and the frying pan next to it. 'Eating breakfast.'

Joe nods, straightening up a bit, trying to recover. 'Teddy,' he says. 'What are you doing here so early?'

'Working. I heard something as I passed by and came in to check it out. With everything that's happened recently, I almost called the police.'

'They would've been disappointed to find me.'

'Yes,' Teddy says, looking at the plate of food again. 'Nothing to see here, is there?' He turns and walks away, leaving Joe to his stolen breakfast.

Teddy also notes the cameras in the kitchen. After this weekend, the food will be watched.

*

Fallon's morning begins in chaos. She wakes up freezing, because the heat stopped working. Unable to get back to sleep, she spends hours on the internet, researching anything and everything to do with Teddy: His students. His ex-wife.

His family.

Teddy doesn't have one. At least not that Fallon can find. Both parents are dead and have been for a while, one from cancer, the other from a car accident. No brothers, no sisters, no children.

She knows all of this because she has googled him many times. Too many. She keeps hoping something new will pop up, but today it doesn't. With nothing left to google, she gets ready for work and goes in early. At least the school is warm.

The only car in the parking lot, other than Joe's, is Teddy's.

Odd. It's unlike him to be so early. He usually keeps to a tight schedule.

The hallways are empty, as expected, and her shoes click as she walks to her classroom. After putting her things down and warming up a bit, she gets an idea. Maybe a good one, maybe not. Hard to make a judgment with so little sleep.

She decides to go ahead with it anyway and heads straight to Teddy's classroom. He looks up when she appears in the doorway.

The look of surprise on his face is already worth it.

'Fallon,' he says. 'Good morning.'

'Morning,' she says. The temperature feels like it drops a good ten degrees when she walks into his room. 'I didn't realize anyone else was here yet.'

They stare at each other.

All she feels is anger. Not surprising – the anger is always with her. Sometimes, it's buried deep, simmering away at a low temperature; other times it feels like red-hot rage. Right now, it's somewhere in the middle.

'So,' Teddy says, standing up. He walks closer to her, then leans back on his desk. 'How are you settling in at Belmont?'

'Oh, it's been fine so far,' she says.

'Good to hear it. Sonia was always quite organized. I expect her lesson plans are in order.'

'Yes, they are. That's been helpful.' Fallon's voice sounds normal, though she feels anything but. She clears her throat. 'I wanted to apologize to you,' she says.

He doesn't look shocked. Not one bit. 'Oh?'

'Some of those emails I sent were . . . out of line. Stupid, really. I'm sorry about that.'

He shrugs. It's such a casual gesture, as if he'd barely read them. 'Ah, those emails.' He smiles a little. 'Your apology is unnecessary. Sometimes, students get angry. You'll learn that soon enough.'

Fallon shouldn't be surprised, but she is. He sounds so normal. 'Still, they were uncalled for, and I'm sorry.'

'Apology accepted.'

'Thank you.'

Again, they stare at each other. She looks for something in his eyes, something that reveals his true feelings, but nothing's there. 'I better get to work now,' she says.

'Have a good day, Fallon.'

'You too, Teddy.'

She walks out feeling like she'd made a mistake. The whole point was to check his reaction after she left, on the video,

248

and now she's pretty sure there won't be any. He'll probably sit right back down at his desk and go back to work. Like she was never there.

That's how he gets away with everything. By appearing so normal.

57

No more school.

That's what Zach's parents had said. While he was out at the coffee shop, neither receiving nor returning their calls, they'd made use of the time. The decision was made to pull Zach out of Belmont and have him homeschooled for the remainder of the semester.

No discussion. No questions. No negotiation.

His mom, in all her efficiency, had already hired a tutor. No chance she would stay home and teach him herself. First thing in the morning, she notified the school and arranged for his lessons to be sent over. When she moves, she moves fast. And she spends whatever is necessary to get it done.

'After classes begin,' she said, 'Ms Marsha will meet you at the front of the school so you can clean out your locker.'

Zach nodded, trying to look more upset than he was.

By nine o'clock in the morning, he has collected his things, walked out of Belmont, and he heads straight to Starbucks. His first meeting with the new tutor isn't until noon. Mom must have paid a lot to make that happen.

Until then, he's free.

Back to the list of poisons. Narrowing them down isn't difficult. First, he eliminates any that cause symptoms neither Courtney's mom nor Mrs B had. Next, he eliminates anything that takes days, rather than hours, to kill someone. Last, he removes anything that someone would have to eat too much of. The amount had to be small enough that they wouldn't have known it was there. And if the police were right about Courtney's mom, it had to be something that could be added to coffee.

Many of the poisonous plants – like hemlock, snakeroot, and castor bean – cause nausea, vomiting, or diarrhea long before someone dies. Nightshade leads to paralysis. No one had those symptoms.

Only a few of the poisons can be absorbed through the skin. Just touching them can be dangerous. Oleander is one; touching it can cause skin irritations. Another is the inside of a rosary pea seed; it can actually be deadly, especially if it gets into the bloodstream.

But whatever killed Ingrid and Mrs B was ingested, and Ingrid had a heart attack before she died. Not many plants cause that.

One is *Cerbera odollam*, otherwise known as the 'suicide tree.' It's found in India and Southeast Asia, Colombia, and Costa Rica. North America, not so much.

The other is *Actaea pachypoda*, also called white baneberry or doll's-eyes. The plant is found in Canada, and in the mid-western and eastern United States. The berries are the most poisonous part, and the toxins in them can have a sedative effect on the heart. Eating them can lead to cardiac arrest. There it is.

Zach packs up his things and sends a text to his mom. Got my things from school. Waiting for tutor.

Her answer comes quickly. Great. I love you.

Too bad his parents didn't think of this homeschooling thing earlier. It's almost too easy.

Except for that whole felony business.

He heads back into the freezing cold to find out where this plant grows around here. His first stop is the closest nursery on Google Maps. Rare Earth is on the posh side of town, the kind of place where Zach's mom would buy plants. *If* she bought plants.

He greets the woman at the desk with a big smile. She's older, maybe his grandmother's age, with long grey hair braided down her back.

'Good morning,' she says. 'You surprised me. I didn't think anyone would be out in this cold.'

'I'm actually looking for a gift. It's for my mom.' Another smile. 'I bet you can help me.'

She smiles back at him. Even the corners of her eyes turn up. 'I bet I can, too.'

Off they go, into the greenhouse, where Zach keeps an eye out for those doll's-eyes berries.

'Are you looking for flowers?' the woman asks.

'A plant, actually. Maybe something that can stay inside until winter is over, then be planted out in the yard?'

'Smart,' she says, throwing him a smile over her shoulder. 'Does your mother like to garden?'

'Loves it. So I'm looking for something a little unusual.'

'I've got just the thing.'

She shows him a variety of plants, talking about each one at length. Zach gets the feeling she'll talk all day if he lets her. He keeps her going, but only until he sees what he's looking for.

'This is interesting,' he says, pointing to the doll's-eyes plant. 'So unique.'

'And poisonous. Not a good choice if you have pets or small children.'

'Really? It's that poisonous?'

'Yes,' she says.

'And it just grows outside? Naturally?'

'It does, especially here in the Northeast. In the spring, you can usually see it over near the Grove.' The Grove is the old area of town, with big Victorian houses built on huge plots of land. His mom loves those old houses, but his dad always says they're a money pit. Dad won that argument, so they live in a much newer house.

The woman goes on to describe everything about the plant, telling him a lot of what he already knows. She adds that the only reason there are berries right now is because it's in a greenhouse.

While the woman talks, he smiles and nods and half listens. He stops thinking about the doll's-eyes as a plant and starts thinking about it as a weapon.

The berries are the most poisonous part. In theory, you could crush them up and put them in someone's food. But that would mean you have to prepare a specific dish for a specific person. Hard to do that for one person, let alone two, unless you're very close to both.

Which means you couldn't use the whole berry. You'd have to use the juice inside. If extracted or squeezed out, it could be put in anything. Even coffee.

That's how he would do it.

58

Fallon can download the footage from the camera in Teddy's classroom throughout the day. She doesn't even have to be right next to his room. During the morning break, she decides to view the video right from her own desk.

She wants to see his reaction to her apology this morning. What she expects to see is Teddy sit down at his desk and go back to work. What she ends up seeing is much worse.

After she left, he waited for a moment before getting up to shut the door to his classroom. He walked back to his desk and sat down.

Then he laughed.

Not a chuckle, either. He burst out into a big, loud laugh that almost blows the pods out of her ears.

Teddy knew Fallon was up to something – he just didn't know what. Now, it doesn't matter. After her little visit, he's less worried about her than he was before. The way she'd stood in front of him, wearing those designer clothes with scuffed shoes. She was like a child playing dress-up.

A bad liar, too. Constantly shifting her weight, averting her eyes. Nervous, yes, but also transparent. Nothing but a little girl playing schoolyard games.

He should have known better than to think there was more to it.

To think he'd believed she'd stolen his plaque. She's not even capable of that.

After spinning off the road this morning, Teddy didn't have high hopes for the day. But things have really turned around, starting with catching Joe in the kitchen. Then the interaction with Fallon. And right after first period, he received an email from the front office about Zach:

Please be aware that Zach Ward has withdrawn from Belmont, effective immediately. He will be homeschooled for the rest of the semester. Forward your current lesson plan to the school administrator's office ASAP.

Teddy never doubted Zach was the other person the DA was referring to in his press conference. Still, the news that he has left school is better than seeing Joe eating breakfast in Belmont's kitchen, even better than Fallon's little visit. It's the best news he's heard all day.

The second-best comes at lunchtime, when he opens one of the windows in his classroom and pokes his head out. Nothing. No cameras are anywhere near the outside of his windows. He leaves the one in the far corner unlocked.

At exactly twelve o'clock, Zach is at home and his new tutor arrives. His name is Titus.

'Before you ask, yes, that's my real name,' he says. He's a tall guy with glasses, and he's wearing a Dartmouth sweatshirt. 'And, no, not because my family is religious.'

Zach thinks for a minute. 'Shakespeare?'

'Yes.' Titus rolls his eyes. 'My parents met at a Shakespeare festival. During *Titus Andronicus*.'

'Yikes.'

'Tell me about it.'

Zach feels like they're going to get along just fine. Anyone with that much scorn for their parents is okay in his book.

They go into the kitchen, where Zach grabs a bag of chips and a couple of waters.

'If you don't mind me asking, what happened to you?' Titus says. 'Did you get in trouble?'

For a few hours, Zach had managed to forget everything happening in his life. The felony bribery charge. The murders. Courtney. It all comes flooding back. 'Something like that,' he says.

Titus nods and sits down at the table, opening up his backpack. He pulls out a laptop, five books, and a notepad. 'Ever been homeschooled before?'

'Nope.'

'Here's the deal. I give you assignments, you email them to me. We meet in person once a week to review. For tests, I'll be in the room with you.' Titus pauses to look at Zach, who says nothing. 'I'll be straight with you. Your parents are paying me, which means if you miss any assignments or start screwing around, I'm telling them. No question.'

Zach is impressed. Titus is straight-up and fair, which he appreciates. It's always easier to deal with a situation if you know the rules up front. 'Got it,' he says.

They start to work, not breaking for almost two hours. His mom texts once to make sure Titus showed up. She texts Titus twice to make sure Zach is doing what he's supposed to. He is. The work is just as difficult, if not more so, than it was at Belmont. Zach doesn't mind. It keeps him from think-ing about everything else.

During their break, they eat a couple of the premade meals Zach's mom has delivered every week. Zach has a chance to learn more about Titus, who just started graduate school and tutors for extra money. 'My parents think it's a good idea,' he says, rolling his eyes again.

And, yes, Titus did go to Belmont.

'I'm sorry,' Zach says.

'Yeah, it sucked. What the hell's happening over there, anyway? People are getting murdered?'

Zach nods, remembering what Ezekiel and his mom had said. *Not one word. Not to anyone for any reason.* 'Did you know Mrs B?'

'Oh yeah, she was nice.'

'She was.'

'I heard Fallon came back to take her place,' Titus says.

'Fallon?'

'Fallon Knight. She graduated the same year as me.'

'I think I've seen her around,' Zach says. 'I'm in Crutcher's class this year. Or I was.'

'Crutcher.' Titus shakes his head. 'Fallon hated him so much. I'm surprised she'd go back to Belmont, even for a job.'

'She was on his shit list?'

'Apparently.'

'Me too.'

'Sucks for you,' Titus says.

Yes, it does. Or it did. Doesn't matter now, since he's no longer at Belmont. At least that's one good thing.

'What did she do to get on his bad side?' Zach asks.

'I don't know exactly. I just remember her raging about him online. And that was after we graduated. Something to do with a reference letter.'

'She asked him for one? I'd never do that.'

'That's the thing about teachers,' Titus says. 'Sometimes, you don't know you're on their shit list until it's too late.'

59

Teddy feels good when he walks into the school on Monday morning. It's quiet out front, because the reporters have gotten sick of standing around in the cold, waiting for news that doesn't come. The DA hasn't said anything else, nor have the police. No leaks, no rumors. Someone has tightened up their ship.

The only thing new is the sign in front of the school:

SECURITY NOTICE

VIDEO SURVEILLANCE IN USE ON THESE PREMISES

The cameras work after all. Finally.

He wonders if the students will change their behavior. If they'll feel like they have to watch what they say and do. Not a bad thing.

Teddy isn't the only one thinking about the effect on students. In the teachers' lounge, Louella is clutching her crystals, moaning about Big Brother.

'Kids shouldn't have to live like this,' she says, almost spilling her herbal tea. 'They should feel safe and loved, and not like someone is watching their every move.'

'It is a shame,' someone else says. 'But it's also reality.'

Indeed.

Teddy makes his coffee and picks up his things, heading down to his classroom. The door is locked, just as he'd left it. The first place he looks, as always, is at the wall.

His Teacher of the Year award is back.

At first glance, he thinks it's been returned. That someone had snuck into his class and returned it on Friday, before the cameras in the hall were functional. Upon closer examination, he finds a sticker on the edge of the frame.

A new plaque.

Rather than investigate the one that was stolen, the headmaster – or, more likely, Ms Marsha – had another one made. A shortcut. Teddy hates it when people take shortcuts.

Still, his classroom does feel better now that he has an award plaque on the wall. Like everything is as it should be.

Today is going to be a good day. He thought it would be when he woke up this morning and saw that the sun was already shining. The temperature was above freezing, and the ice had already started to melt. It's still winter, but the end is near.

And now that class is starting, he gets to continue talking about Dante's version of hell. It doesn't get better than that. He doesn't even feel like picking at his cuticles.

Everything continues to be smooth. No ripples, no trouble, no surprise announcements on the news. A perfectly normal day of teaching.

Until about one o'clock.

He starts to feel a little light-headed. A little woozy. He's in the middle of fifth period, talking about the circles of hell, and he has to sit down.

'Are you okay, Mr Crutcher?'

A student says this, and Teddy nods. 'I'm fine.'

In the distance, he hears a scream. Or he thinks he does, but it's hard to tell. All he wants to do is put his head down on the desk and make the spinning stop.

60

Fallon opens her eyes, blinks a few times. No idea where she is.

White room, white sheets. Her own sheets are blue. And she's up too high, raised off the floor. Her blow-up mattress is much lower. The curtains are drawn across the window, and she can't tell if it's day or night.

But there's a tube in her arm.

An IV. She's in the hospital.

The first thing she does is move her legs, then her arms. A wave of relief hits her. Everything works.

Fallon thinks back to earlier in the day. The last thing she remembers is being at school, teaching a class, when she heard a scream. She went out into the hallway to check on it.

That's it.

She pushes the button next to her bed. A minute later, a woman appears. She's young and smiley – like they're in a hair salon instead of a hospital.

'Hello there,' the woman says. Her name tag says TAMMY. 'How are you feeling?'

'Why . . . ?' Fallon's voice croaks. The nurse rushes to get her some water, and she tries again. 'Why am I in the hospital?'

'You collapsed when you were at the school,' Tammy says.

'I collapsed?'

Tammy nods, her lips pursed. Not so bright and cheery now.

'What's wrong with me?' Fallon says. 'Why is my throat so sore?'

'We had to pump your stomach. Unfortunately, it does cause some throat irritation because we had to put a tube down your throat. That should clear up soon, though.'

'Why would you . . . ?' Fallon shakes her head, trying to remember what she ate. 'Did I have food poisoning?'

Tammy sits down on the edge of the bed. She wears glasses – oversize, bright green – and they make her eyes look huge. 'There was another event at Belmont. A number of people fell ill.'

It takes Fallon a long time to figure out what that means. 'Poisoned. Was I poisoned?'

'They have to finish the testing, but right now it looks that way.'

Fallon pulls the covers up around her. 'Oh my God.'

'You're fine now,' Tammy says. 'Are you hungry?'

'Not *now* I'm not.'

'I'm sorry. That was a stupid question. You'll be here overnight for observation, and then you can get back home.' She pats Fallon on the leg and stands up, straightening the covers. 'Just press the buzzer if you need anything.'

Tammy walks out, leaving Fallon feeling like she's in shock. Of all the things she had thought would happen when she returned to Belmont, being poisoned wasn't one of them. Exposed for not having a college degree, yes. Fired, perhaps. Maybe even arrested, depending on how far she had to go to get Teddy fired.

But poisoned? Nope. That was not something she'd thought would happen to her. Or anyone else, after Sonia died.

A number of people got sick, Tammy had said. Fallon grabs the remote and turns on the TV. The breaking news banner on the screen makes her sit up so fast, she almost jerks the IV out of her arm.

MORE TROUBLE AT BELMONT ACADEMY: 1 DEAD, 6 HOSPITALIZED

The reporter on the screen is young and blond and wears too much makeup. She keeps talking and talking, and the words swirl together. It's all a reworded version of the banner. Not once does she say the name of the person who died.

Fallon presses the buzzer.

As soon as Tammy appears, again looking cheerful, Fallon says, 'Who died?'

'I'm sorry?'

Fallon points to the TV. 'It says someone died.'

'Oh.' Tammy's face falls into a deep frown. Not good. 'I'm sorry. I don't know. Everyone who was brought here is going to be fine.'

The anger is immediate. Familiar. It's been with Fallon ever since she can remember. Because of her parents, who expected too much. Because of her friends, who were always smarter, prettier, better. Because of her teachers, who asked for more and more and more.

And Teddy, who derailed her whole life.

It's not just the big things, either. She gets angry about a lot of little things. When someone is running late, when she finds a spot on her blouse, when someone cuts her off in traffic: Anger has become her default.

Like now.

Fallon grips the remote so hard that she turns up the volume. The reporter sounds like she's screaming.

'I don't think you understand.' Teddy has to restrain himself from getting angry with his nurse. 'My *wife* works at this hospital. All-i-son Crutch-er. That's her name. Can you page her and let her know I'm here?'

The nurse looks older than God. She shuffles out of the room without saying a word.

Teddy sighs. Why everything has to be so difficult is just beyond him.

His TV is on, and it has been for the past hour. The reporter is so thin, she looks like a bobblehead, and it's highly unattractive. At least her voice is tolerable.

Allison must know he's here by now. She must. And, yes, perhaps she's still angry at him, but for God's sake, he's in the hospital. Being married for over a decade should warrant a visit at least.

He glances over at the phone, wondering if he should call down to the emergency room. How unfortunate he was unconscious when he was brought in. He'll never know if Allison saw him, or even if she helped him. Not unless she comes to his room.

No, he's not going to call. For months, he has not called her, has not reached out at all. In his mind, she just needed time. Betrayals are like that. Shock, anger, and finally, acceptance. Once all the extreme emotions started to fade, he'd expected to hear from her. And he did. It just came in the form of divorce papers.

So dramatic. She was never like that before, and truth be told, it's not a good look.

Yes, perhaps he did agree to have children when they first decided to get married. She was so dead set on having kids, it was the only way she would marry him. He'd had no choice.

'Of course I want kids,' he told her. 'Who doesn't?'

As someone who spent every day around self-absorbed teenagers, kids were the last thing he wanted – even with Allison. So he lied. He'd never expected to have to make good on that promise. He thought he would be able to talk her out of it.

Didn't happen.

'I don't understand why we need to have kids right now,' Teddy told her. 'Don't you enjoy our life?'

'Of course I do.'

They had just finished eating dinner. Teddy was still sitting at the kitchen table, but Allison wasn't. She had stood up to take her dish to the sink.

'I'm just not sure we need to have children,' he said. 'Not right now, given our financial situation. We haven't even finished the house.'

'It's not about need. It's about want. I want kids.' With her back to him, she started rinsing her dish. 'You said you did, too.'

'Of course I do. I'm just thinking about money.'

'If we wait until we're rich, we'll never have kids,' she said.

He didn't answer that, because it was true. The words hung in the air like a bad smell.

'A little while longer,' he finally said. 'Let's at least wait until after the holidays.'

She turned back to him, her eyes hopeful. 'The New Year? Promise me we'll try in the New Year.'

'I promise.'

She held him to that. As the holidays approached, she started talking about going off birth control.

The vasectomy had become necessary. It was also a last resort, after he'd realized he couldn't slip birth control pills into Allison's coffee without her or her doctor figuring it out. He'd had to get the vasectomy. No other option.

When he told her he couldn't have kids, she believed it wasn't his fault. For a few months, everything went back to the way it should be.

Until some inept office clerk sent that bill to his house.

61

Within minutes of Fallon's waking up the next morning, a nurse comes into her room. It isn't Tammy. This nurse is much older and not nearly as cheerful. Her grey hair is shaved almost to the scalp, and her uniform is creased hard enough to break.

'You should be nice and rested by now,' the nurse says. 'It's nearly ten o'clock.'

Fallon scrambles to reach the water on the nightstand. 'Did I miss checkout?'

The nurse glowers at her.

Fallon clears her throat.

'The doctor will be in to see you before you can be released,' the nurse says. She refills the water and walks out.

As soon as she's gone, Fallon turns on the TV.

Game show. Talk show. Sitcom. She flips through the channels, wondering why no one is talking about the news at this hour. The national channels are too busy talking about politics.

The doctor interrupts her channel surfing. He's a young man with a nice smile and big eyes.

'How are you feeling?' he says.

'Much better. My throat isn't as sore.'

'Good to hear.' He checks her chart and listens to her heartbeat.

'So do they know yet?' Fallon asks. 'If it was really poison?'

The smile disappears as he shakes his head no. 'I have no information about that.'

'Do you know who died? I was told someone died.'

'I do not know.' The doctor signs the bottom of her chart. 'I'm going to go ahead and release you, but if you have any issues or if you start feeling light-headed again, come straight to the emergency room.'

He walks out. Fallon starts to get up but realizes the IV is still in her arm. With a sigh, she presses the button for the nurse.

Once she's disconnected, disentangled, and dressed, she walks out of the room, preparing herself for the next step: Before she can leave the hospital, she has to meet with the billing department.

Instead, she is met by two people standing by the door to her room. Both wear jackets emblazoned with the FBI logo.

Teddy is still in his hospital bed, still waiting for Allison, when the FBI agents show up. Not a surprise. A mass poisoning like this one is going to bring in the FBI. Maybe even the DEA. One or two poisonings is one thing, but seven people at once – with one dead? Time for the feds to take over.

A man and a woman, both wearing FBI jackets. They seem professional enough, which Teddy can appreciate. Nothing worse than an unprofessional law enforcement officer.

The bald man is Agent Roland, which is so generic, it almost seems like an alias. The first thing he wants to know is everything Teddy ate yesterday.

'Well, I had coffee at home. One cup, black,' Teddy says.

'At Belmont, I made another cup of coffee before first period – '

'Where did you get the coffee?' Roland asks.

Teddy stares at him. 'As I was saying, I made another cup of coffee in the teachers' lounge before first period. Prime Gold is my flavor. After that, I didn't eat again until lunch, which I bring from home. Bologna on white bread and an apple. I eat the same lunch every day.' He pauses, waiting for a reaction. There is none. 'Yesterday, I did go to the dining hall to get a small carton of milk. I drank it while I ate in my classroom.'

'Is that normal for you? To get a carton of milk?'

'Sometimes, yes. Or I bring a water from home.'

'But yesterday, you definitely drank milk from the dining hall?'

'Yes,' Teddy says, wondering if Roland is a little slow. 'I'm positive.'

'What about your sandwich? Did you make it?'

'I did.'

'Anyone else have access to it?'

Teddy thinks for a minute. Or pretends to. 'No. I always keep my lunch in an insulated bag in my classroom.'

'What about at home?'

Teddy is a bit surprised by this question. 'Home?'

'Do you live with anyone?'

'I can't see how that's relevant.'

'It is,' Roland says. 'We need to know who had access to everything you ate or drank.'

'I live alone,' Teddy says, hoping that will end this line of questioning.

It doesn't.

'Who else has access to your home?' Roland asks.

'I just said I live alone.'

'So no one else has a key?'

Teddy keeps his expression the same and his emotions in check. Otherwise, the hate he feels for this FBI agent might come through. 'My wife has a key.'

Roland looks surprised. 'You said you live alone.'

'I do. We are . . . separated.'

Roland and the other agent, Pruitt, exchange a look.

'Look,' Teddy says. 'This has been one of the most tragic times in the history of the school. As Teacher of the Year, I'm very invested in our students and in their success, and what's happened is horrifying. What we need to concentrate on is who would do this to the school. *To the students.* My wife has absolutely nothing to do with this.'

'We just need to be thorough,' Roland says.

Teddy realizes this is going to take longer than he'd anticipated. 'May I ask a question?' he says.

The agents nod in unison.

'I understand someone died yesterday, but no one has said who it is. Has this information been released?'

Roland pauses before answering. 'It was on the news earlier,' he says. 'The headmaster died.'

Teddy pretends to be shocked.

62

The day after the #HomicideHighMassacre, Zach is right back in the living room with Ezekiel and his parents. Same room, same positions, but it's not the same.

'This is a good thing,' Ezekiel says. 'Zach wasn't anywhere near the school for days before this happened.'

'I knew taking him out was the right thing to do,' Mom says.

Dad puts his hand on Mom's shoulder. 'You were absolutely right.'

A good thing. Six people sick enough to be hospitalized and one dead headmaster. This is what lawyers think is a good thing.

Zach is so angry, he wants to scream.

The only thing that keeps him from doing that is looking like he's lost control. Even if it feels that way inside, he won't show it.

Don't express every single emotion you have. You'll look unstable.

No one wants to be considered unstable. Look what happened to his math teacher, Mr Maxwell. He still isn't back at Belmont.

'That's the good news,' Ezekiel says, looking rather proud of himself. 'However . . . I do have something else.' When no one says anything, he continues. 'As you may have seen on the news, the FBI has arrived in town. They are going over everything from the past events, including Courtney's arrest.'

Ezekiel looks at Zach for the first time this evening. 'And they want to speak with Zach.'

'No,' Mom says.

'Not a chance,' Dad says.

Ezekiel smiles as he pushes up his glasses. 'Obviously, that's what I've told them. However, things are a little more complicated now that the FBI is involved. It's difficult to say no to the feds.'

'What happens if he doesn't talk to them?' Mom says.

'Well, there's no doubt the state will move forward with the bribery charge. And that's just for starters. Now that the FBI is here . . .' Ezekiel spreads out his hands, as if to say *Who knows?*

'Obstruction of justice?' Mom says.

'Could be. They can come up with all kinds of trumped-up charges when they want to. They could even argue those bribery charges meet the federal statute. And if they do that . . .'

Ezekiel drones on, going back and forth with Mom, tossing around legal terms like they're holding a mock trial. They talk about Zach like he's in a video game, being moved around by whoever has the controller.

In fact, he feels like that most of the time.

Usually, he goes along with it because it's easier, because he's young, and because these are the people who are supposed to know what's best for him. Maybe they do. Maybe they are making the best decisions. They just aren't the right ones.

If Zach's father was in this position, he wouldn't tolerate it. And Zach is nothing if not his father's son.

'I'll talk to them,' he says, standing up from the couch. 'Set it up.'

He ignores the protests from his parents, and from his lawyer, and he walks away from all of them.

Feels pretty good.

In the dead of night, Fallon drives to the school. No other cars on the road. Not a person in sight. The only sign of life is the streetlights, and it's a little creepy. Fallon keeps checking her rearview mirror, waiting for someone else to appear.

The school is cordoned off now, taken over by the FBI, but she doesn't need to get inside. She needs to get close to her camera. If she can get within range, she can download the data and delete it from the camera itself.

Assuming the FBI hasn't already found it.

It's unlikely, she thinks. The camera is tucked away behind a book, far from any food or drinks or poisons. Unless they plan on emptying the entire school of every book, paper, and smartboard, it should be safe. She hopes. Because it would be a bad time to get caught illegally recording someone in the classroom of a private school.

She's pretty sure deleting the footage doesn't erase it forever. And if anyone can recover it from the camera, it's the FBI. But she has to try.

The east side of the school is where Teddy's room is, and right now she's the only one on the road. Not surprising at two o'clock in the morning.

She pulls over to the curb and takes out her phone. At first, the app doesn't connect. After three attempts, it finally does. Downloading the data doesn't take long. Again, not surprising. The camera is motion-activated, and the school has been closed since the poisonings on Monday. The last time she retrieved the data was at lunch on Friday.

As she drives away, everything feels a little less creepy. Maybe because nobody stopped her to ask what she was doing.

But the closer she gets to home, the angrier she gets.

On Friday, Teddy had stayed in his classroom during lunch. Fallon never got a chance to adjust the camera, which means she still can't see his computer screen clearly. Now, she's got nothing. Absolutely nothing.

Hard to ruin someone's life without information.

She stomps up the stairs of her building and into her apartment. It feels just as small and suffocating as when she left it. Sleep isn't an option. Not yet. She loads the data into her laptop and starts watching the footage.

Teddy eating lunch. Teddy working on his computer. Teddy teaching his afternoon classes. Teddy gathering up his things and leaving right after his last class ends.

The camera stopped recording at that point.

Until classes began again on Monday morning, the only person who should appear on the video is Joe. He cleans the classrooms every night.

Fallon sees that, as expected.

But then there's more.

63

Two FBI agents walk into the interrogation room where Zach and his lawyer are waiting. One man, one woman, both middle-aged and wearing suits. The man is bald, with small eyes and thin lips. The woman wears no makeup and she has short, simple hair. A sensible haircut, Mom would say. She hates those.

Zach is wearing pressed khakis and a brand-new white button-down, and his hair is freshly cut. He smiles, because he always smiles when he meets someone, even if they work for the FBI and they're investigating him.

His parents made it clear they are 100 percent against this interview. Zach 100 percent does not care. And in this state, he can talk to them without having his parents present.

'Thank you for meeting with us,' the woman says. 'I'm Agent Pruitt. This is Agent Roland.' Agent Roland sits across from Ezekiel, while Agent Pruitt sits across from Zach.

So she's the one who's going to ask all the questions. Good to know.

'This must be a little overwhelming for you,' she says.

'You could say that.' Zach doesn't have to pretend to be nervous, because he already is.

'As I'm sure your lawyer has told you, we're looking into the recent events at Belmont Academy,' she says. 'Your name has come up.'

'I understand.'

'Good. Why don't you start with Courtney Ross?'

'I've known her since we were in the fourth grade.' Zach stops, saying nothing further. Not without another question.

Agent Pruitt waits a beat before asking, 'So is it fair to say you two are close?'

'Yes.'

'So close that you bribed a guard to see her in jail?' she says.

Ezekiel jumps in, doing his lawyer thing. 'That hasn't been proven. Those charges are – '

'I know,' Agent Pruitt says, raising a hand to cut him off. She doesn't look at Ezekiel, only at Zach. Under the bad lighting, her eyes stand out. They're green and brown, a swirl of colors that look different depending on the light. High cheekbones, too. She is anything but plain; she just wants to appear that way.

'Nothing you say in this room can be used against you in that case,' she says to Zach. 'We aren't recording this interview.'

Zach analyzes each word she uses, trying to find the loophole. In *that* case, she said. But they can probably use what he says in *their* case. If they have one.

Except he hasn't poisoned anyone.

'Yes, I saw her in jail,' he says. 'And I paid a guard to do it.'

Ezekiel stands up and says, 'I need to talk to my client alone.'

Zach spent a lot of time thinking about what he would say to the FBI, and he knew his lawyer wouldn't like it. That's why he didn't tell him in advance.

Agent Pruitt is still looking at Zach. 'Do you want to speak to your lawyer alone?'

'No, I'm fine.'

'Zach, I must advise you to end this interview now,' Ezekiel says.

'I appreciate that, but I don't see what's wrong with telling the truth.'

Neither of the agents says a word. They wait until Ezekiel sits back down at the table, hands folded, mouth shut.

'So you did see Courtney in jail?' Agent Pruitt says.

'Yes. I saw her once and spoke to her on the phone once.'

'What did you two discuss?'

'She was really upset. First, because her mother had been murdered. And second, because she was in jail. I tried my best to comfort her, to tell her this was all a mistake and it would work out.' Not exactly a lie, but certainly an exaggeration. Courtney wasn't that upset. She was depressed.

'Did you talk about how her mother died?' she asks.

'I never asked if she did it, if that's what you're thinking,' Zach says. 'She told me anyway. She said she didn't do it, and she wanted me to know that.'

'Do you believe her?'

'Absolutely.'

'What else did you talk about?'

'I told her about things going on at school, tried to give her a little break from her own problems. Just stupid things, gossip. She said she didn't have anyone to talk to other than her lawyer and her dad and she was really lonely,' Zach says. 'Still is, probably.'

'Anything else?' Agent Pruitt says.

'No. I didn't see her for very long. Ten, fifteen minutes at the most.'

'And the phone call? What did you talk about then?'

Zach takes a deep breath. 'That was after Mrs Benjamin died, and I knew Courtney would be upset. They worked together on the *Bugle*. Our student paper.'

Agent Pruitt nods.

'I wanted to see how she was doing,' Zach says.

'And how was she?'

'She was upset. It was all so . . . unreal. Still is.'

'Did you talk about how Sonia Benjamin died?'

'Yes,' Zach says. He looks down at the table, shaking his head a little. An act. 'I hoped Courtney would be released. That after Mrs Benjamin died, the police would realize Courtney wasn't the killer. I told her that.'

Agent Pruitt doesn't say anything. Zach continues looking down, waiting her out, determined not to meet her eye. Not yet.

'Zach,' she finally says. 'You went to great lengths to see Courtney, and put your own self at risk just to talk to her.'

She stops. Zach remains quiet, waiting for the question. He knew this one was coming, and he's prepared for it.

'Why would you do that?' she says.

Now he looks up. 'Because I love her,' he says. 'And I was going crazy without her.'

Agent Roland has been silent throughout the interview. He nods. Just a tiny bit, but it's enough.

He gets it. More importantly, he believes it.

Zach slumps a little, trying to look sad. Trying to look like a lovesick teenager who couldn't stand to be away from Courtney Ross. His unrequited love.

'I know it sounds stupid, but it's true,' Zach says. 'She doesn't even know that . . . Well, anyway. That's why. I really do love her.'

Agent Pruitt looks to her partner, who shrugs a little and turns to Zach.

'Thank you for coming in. I think that's all we have for right now.'

Zach forces himself not to smile until he gets out of the building. His lawyer is so pissed, he won't speak. That's just fine with Zach. He's already done all the talking necessary.

A few months ago, he never would've lied to the FBI. Never would've talked to them at all, in fact. He would've done exactly as his parents, and his lawyer, told him to do. Or at least he would've pretended to do as they said, because that's the kind of kid he is.

Or was. Maybe his parents don't always know what's best.

64

Lissa. The bobblehead reporter's name is Lissa.

Teddy is not surprised.

They are sitting in the studio of a local TV station where Lissa works, and someone connects a microphone to Teddy's shirt.

'Just speak normally,' Lissa says. 'You don't have to shout or anything.'

'I understand,' Teddy says.

'And remember, this is live. If you stumble over a word, just keep talking. Don't stop. But if you do, I'll jump in.'

'That's fine.'

Under any other circumstances, he would never be on TV, would never put himself in the spotlight like this. But these aren't normal times. No one is speaking for Belmont.

With a dead headmaster and a board that would rather stay in the background, only a written statement has been released:

Due to the tragic events at Belmont Academy on Monday, the school is closed pending an investigation by the police and the FBI. Once they are finished, the school will be cleaned and disinfected. We will then begin the process of moving forward from this difficult time.

A separate, private notice went out to all students, offering assistance if they would like to temporarily transfer to another school. While the board gave no estimation of when Belmont would reopen, they said they hoped it would be soon.

That was it.

Teddy has a lot more to say. About the hospital, and how the wonderful, talented staff took care of him. About the students, who are so brave and strong to endure such madness. About the school itself, and its history of resilience.

Someone has to do it.

Teddy looks at the monitor, checking his position. He shifts a little to the left so his profile shows a bit more. The lighting is harsh, and a straight-on angle isn't the most flattering. The three-day scruff is gone. He's clean-shaven and wearing a tie.

He looks down at his hands. At least his cuticles are healed, now that he has stopped picking at them.

Allison will probably see this. Maybe she'll think he looks good.

'I'm going to start with what happened to you on Monday,' Lissa says. 'Are you ready?'

'I'm ready.'

If only the students knew how much he does for them.

Fallon is at a coffee shop when she sees the live interview with Teddy. She couldn't stand to be in her apartment for one more second.

She also can't stand watching Teddy. Every word he's saying is a lie. Every. Single. One.

And she has the video to prove it.

When she'd first watched the video from the camera in Teddy's classroom, she wasn't sure what was going on.

Everything happened after school was out. At six o'clock on Friday, the camera was triggered by Joe, who mopped the floors and emptied the trash. By six thirty, he was gone and the video went dark.

It came on again at one o'clock Saturday morning.

Teddy walked into the room, only he didn't enter through the door, on the left. He came from the right. At first, it was hard to tell who it was. He was wearing a winter coat, a hat, and gloves. His face wasn't visible until he passed directly in front of the desk. He didn't stop, though. Didn't sit down or pause to get anything. He walked straight through the room and out the door. That was it.

Until fourteen minutes later.

Teddy walked back into his classroom through the door on the left. Again, he passed by his desk, didn't stop, and then disappeared on the right side of the room. The recording ended there.

She had to watch it twice until she realized he had climbed in through the window and then back out. On that side of the room, it was the only option.

The goddamn *window*.

That was how he did it. If he had come through the front door, he would have had to scan his security card.

Next, she checked the video from his mailbox. It shows him leaving his house about fifteen minutes before he climbed through the window. He returns not long after leaving Belmont.

Fallon hasn't slept. She has only consumed a muffin and a cup of plain coffee – because it's the cheapest kind – so maybe her mind isn't working right. But it certainly looks like Teddy could've been behind the poisonings.

Part of her thinks it's ridiculous. He's an arrogant asshole, but not a psycho killer.

The other part of her wonders why she didn't think of this earlier.

She looks up at the TV screen mounted above her head. Teddy is still speaking. It's about eight o'clock in the morning, the before-work crowd has arrived, and everyone is watching.

'Our headmaster was an honorable, hardworking man who only wanted what was best for the students. His death is a huge loss for staff, the students, and for Belmont.'

Everything he says sounds like it was written by a PR team. Still doesn't make him a killer.

'I can't say I was scared when I passed out, because I really didn't know what was happening. It was only after, when I was in the hospital, that I realized I may have been poisoned. As far as I know, the police still haven't confirmed that, but it certainly looks like that's what happened to me. To all of us.'

Now that the caffeine has hit her system, Fallon's brain starts to work a little better. She thinks it through using deductive reasoning, working backward from the result to see how it was accomplished.

Just like she'd learned at Belmont.

How do you poison people – even kill a few – and get away with it?

Use something that kills quickly. Do it in a place where you're expected to be anyway, so being there doesn't look odd. Don't kill too many people at once; that would bring too much attention.

One at a time.

Then all at once.

283

Fallon bolts upright in her chair, the same way she used to when she had the right answer in school. When all the pieces fit just right, the answer is easy.

Poison a bunch of people at the same time, including yourself. Hide your real target.

The headmaster.

65

Party at the Grove, 1pm.

Lucas's text arrives one hour before the party starts.

Zach hasn't been to the Grove since he left Belmont. Lucas has been sending out texts for daily parties ever since Belmont shut down, but today is the first day Zach has shown up. First, because he's sick of spending so much time alone.

But also to celebrate, because Courtney is getting out of jail.

The news came from her father, who called first thing this morning to let him know. Zach was still asleep – another good thing about not having school at eight in the morning – and it took a minute for him to get what Mr Ross was saying.

'Did they make an announcement?' he said.

'No, they called and told me,' Mr Ross said. 'But it doesn't matter. She's coming home.'

Zach sat up in bed, wondering if this was a trick. 'They're dropping the charges?'

'Yes. The charges are dismissed without prejudice. Which technically means they could charge her again if they want to, but her lawyer says that's just so the DA can save face.'

'Because they screwed up,' Zach said.

'Yes.'

So they were admitting it without admitting it. Typical.

Zach was one of the first to arrive at today's party. Now,

the place is packed with all the Belmont kids who haven't transferred to a new school. BYOB&D is the name of the game, and the Grove is now filled with bottles, cans, Solo cups, and the smell of weed. At one time, the Grove was an orchard. Now abandoned, it belongs to the teenagers.

Zach is both high and buzzed, a good combination on any day, and it helps. So does the girl who keeps looking at him.

Lana. No, Lena. That's it. Lena just transferred to Belmont this semester, when her family moved out from California. Bad luck for her.

She catches him watching her and smiles.

Lena's cute in that wholesome way. Since Zach doesn't have a particular type, wholesome works for him as well as any other. He smiles and walks over to her.

'Hey,' he says.

'You're Zach Ward,' she says. 'Right?'

'Right. And you're Lena.'

'Do you know my last name?' She shifts her weight from one leg to the other, a finger tracing the edge of her beer bottle.

'If I say no, will you hate me?' Zach says.

She thinks about this. 'Probably.'

'Then it's a good thing I know your last name is Holliday.'

Surprise.

With a last name like that, how could he not remember it? Maybe she's impressed, or maybe she's pretending to be. Doesn't matter. The result is they end up off in a corner, sitting together on a crumbling stone bench.

She's from Southern California, where it never snows, and until this year she never owned a winter coat.

'Tell me about the beaches,' he says.

286

She does, and for a little while Zach forgets they're sitting outside in near-freezing temperatures. He also forgets about the past couple of weeks. The light at the end of the tunnel feels close enough to touch.

Until she asks.

'What's it like to be arrested?'

'I'm sorry?'

'You were arrested, weren't you?' Lena says. 'At least, that's what I heard.'

All of a sudden, Lena isn't so cute anymore. Not after she told Zach he's become *that* guy. 'Yep, that was me,' he says. 'I'm the loser.'

'I didn't say that.' Lena touches his arm. 'I didn't mean any – '

'Cool, cool. I should get going anyway. It's freezing out here.' He stands up and looks around, realizing that this afternoon party has grown pretty big. Too big. Probably won't be long before it gets broken up. 'Nice talking to you.'

Zach walks away, not regretting it at all. He shouldn't be here anyway, because Courtney is getting out of jail today. He should go see her instead.

Teddy sits in his living room, a glass of milk empty, a package of cookies gone. While he normally wouldn't eat so much sugar, today is an exception.

The news replays snippets of Teddy's interview through-out the afternoon. He watches them all, critiquing himself – the way he looks and moves – and critiquing the interviewer. Lissa may look like a bobblehead, but she's not half-bad at her job.

'I want to express my thanks to the staff at the hospital. I was

impressed by their professionalism and the level of care I received. We are very lucky to have this world-class facility in our community.'

That was one of his favorite quotes. It was a stretch, yes. Even bordering on an outright lie. But the care he received wasn't bad, even if Allison never visited him.

He hopes she has seen his interview. Honestly, it would be almost impossible for her to miss.

By late afternoon, the Belmont website has linked the interview. It's right alongside their memorial page to the headmaster, and a page sending well-wishes to the surviving victims: four students, Fallon Knight, and Teddy.

Fallon. She was a fluke, not a target.

Who knew she drank milk? Teddy didn't know. He hadn't paid that much attention to her drinking habits. Nor did he know which students would end up with the milk he'd tampered with. He only knew they wouldn't die.

Probably.

Unless one of them happened to have a heart condition, there wasn't enough poison to kill them. And he was right.

Except for the headmaster, who'd had that unfortunate heart attack last year.

Very few people knew about it, but Teddy did. Thanks to Allison, who'd told him because he's her husband and this is what couples do. They talk about interesting things that happen during their day. The Belmont headmaster showing up in the emergency room was one of those things.

And, yes, Teddy also knew he drank milk. Every single day, he showed up first for lunch in the dining hall. And every day, he drank a small carton of milk while he ate lunch among the students.

So maybe Teddy had had a tiny little suspicion that, of all

the people who drank milk, the headmaster would be the one to die. Not that he *wanted* the headmaster to die; he just knew it was a possibility.

All beside the point. The point, of course, was to save his students. They deserved a better leader, someone who would go the extra mile to save them. Even students like Zach.

A breaking news report lets him know he succeeded.

DAUGHTER RELEASED IN
DEATH OF MOTHER.
CHARGES DROPPED BY DA.

It's about time.

Teddy gets up and goes to the kitchen. As he pours himself another glass of milk – a rarity, given his lactose issues – he wonders how long it will take before the next breaking news announcement. Because they have to blame it on somebody.

Good thing Teddy made it easy for them.

66

Fallon tells herself to go to the police. Repeatedly.

Yet she hasn't done it.

Instead, she stays in her apartment, staring at the ceiling. She thinks about everything that could happen if she goes to the police.

Because Teddy isn't just an arrogant prick. He's also smart. If she brings the video to the police, he's going to turn it around on her.

The video is fake. It's been doctored. Just look at who gave it to you. Fallon Knight hates me because of a reference letter. Here, see these emails she sent to me? See where she called me a 'piece of shit'?

Her motivations will be questioned, along with her character.

If the situation were reversed, she'd defend herself the same way. By attacking him.

Or maybe she's wrong. Maybe Teddy snuck into the school for a completely different reason. Maybe he had to get something and forgot his key card and didn't want to go all the way home to get it.

That would make her feel incredibly stupid.

The police would think she was an idiot, too.

Another option: Put it on social media. Let the court of public opinion decide. But would they recognize Teddy? Would they know who he is?

After that TV interview, they would. And the media is

always quick to convict someone – usually before they're arrested.

But when she thinks it through, it always ends with someone figuring out she's the one who leaked it. Fallon would end up right back where she doesn't want to be: in the spotlight, with her motives questioned. She's no computer expert. If there's a way to hide the source of the video, she has no idea how to do it.

All of which brings her full circle, right back to her original thought.

It takes a while for her to get out of bed. Once she does, it feels like she's on autopilot. Shower, makeup, hair. Nice clothes – her only nice clothes, left over from her previous life. Before she was rejected everywhere, before she flunked out of school.

One final glance in the mirror before leaving. She can't decide if she looks like herself or like an imposter.

It's dark out now, after dinnertime, and the drive feels long. Canary Lane, the house at the end. That's what everyone calls it, the big house at the end of Canary Lane.

Her parents' house.

They don't know she's back. She never told them, never came to visit. They think she's still in school at State. Never told them about that, either. Her name hasn't been in the news – none of the victims have been named yet, except for the headmaster. Everyone at the school knows who was poisoned, but it hasn't been in the media.

Well, except for Teddy. But only because he went on TV to talk about it.

Halfway up the driveway, she stops the car. She imagines herself as a child, locked in her room until her homework was done. Fallon used to sit at her desk, tears streaming down her face, vision blurred, trying so hard to get everything finished before bedtime. At first, she failed. Then she got better. Eventually, she became smarter. Figured out the shortcuts. She had to make her parents happy somehow.

She also imagines explaining why she came back, and why she's teaching at Belmont. Why she placed a camera in Teddy's classroom, not to mention outside his house.

She sees her mother. Elegant, refined, and disappointed. Always disappointed.

And her father. Tall, commanding, almost godlike. When he shakes his head at her, it feels like a curse.

She knows what he's going to say:

Are you still blaming other people for your failures?

Fallon backs up her car and drives away.

Courtney is wrapped up in a plush robe, eating sushi and red Twizzlers, her two favorite foods. Zach brought them over after leaving the Grove. The high he had earlier is long gone, in part because of the food.

'I spent an hour in the bath,' she says. 'It's impossible to feel clean in jail.'

'Yeah, I was there. I smelled you.' He ducks to avoid the Twizzler she throws at him.

'I got a text from Siobhan,' she says. 'She transferred to Pellier.'

'I heard. So did Connor.'

'Are you transferring?'

'Not this semester,' he says. 'I kind of like the home-schooling.'

'I'm screwed. Didn't finish last semester and missed half

of this one.' Courtney shrugs, like it doesn't bother her, but he knows it does. It would bother him.

'On the upside,' he says, watching her pick up a California roll and pop it into her mouth, 'your college admissions essay is going to kick ass.'

'I guess there's that,' she mumbles.

The TV is on. Whatever was on ends, and it's followed by the news. It starts with Courtney's release, and then suddenly Crutcher appears.

'Now here's more of our exclusive interview with one of Monday's victims at Belmont Academy.'

Courtney sighs. 'I'm so sick of myself.'

'I'm sick of Crutcher,' Zach says.

'At least he's not your teacher anymore.'

He reaches over and grabs a Twizzler. 'You know, the teacher who replaced Mrs B used to go to Belmont.'

'Yeah?'

'My tutor knows her. Says she hates Crutcher.'

'Why?'

'She was on his shit list,' he says. 'It's weird she was poisoned, too. Both her and Crutcher.'

'That is weird,' she says, finishing off the last of the sushi rolls and washing it down with Coke. 'Hey, do you think that since they let me go, they have another suspect already?'

'Maybe. Or maybe the FBI just realized the police here are stupid.'

'I hope they know who did it,' she says, staring off toward the TV. 'I hope there's an arrest soon.'

'As long as it's not you or me, I hope you're right,' he says.

'Who do you think did it? I mean, if you had to guess?'

Zach has thought about this a lot. Too much, probably.

293

When he thinks about the people who died – an overbearing mother, a beloved teacher, the headmaster – it doesn't make any sense. No one person benefits from those three deaths. Not that he can see.

So it must be random. It's someone who just wants to kill people, regardless of who. And that's the scariest part.

'I have no idea,' he says. 'But I know what they used.'

'No way. They never released it.'

He smiles. 'I figured it out.'

'Okay, Encyclopedia Brown,' she says. 'What is it?'

'A plant. Well, really it's a berry.'

She nods. She already knows from her lawyer.

But he doesn't stop there. He explains about doll's-eyes: what it is and what it does to the body. The longer he talks, the more upset Courtney becomes. He stops, realizing he's describing how her mom died. It feels like it happened so long ago that he almost forgot.

Just like he almost forgot about searching through Crutcher's desk and finding that book about plants.

67

It's after eight o'clock at night when Teddy walks into the Fairlane Hotel downtown. A swanky place, the kind his students and their parents would stay in. Or own.

The Fairlane is where Belmont holds a lot of its fundraisers, along with the faculty holiday party, the headmaster's inauguration, and prom night. Now that Belmont is closed, the hotel is where the board of directors holds its meetings.

Teddy finds the board on the mezzanine, in a room with ugly carpet and ridiculous curtains, but otherwise it's fine. The chairman sits at the head of the table. He is short, round, and unattractive. But very, very wealthy.

'Thank you for meeting with us,' he says.

Teddy takes the only empty seat. 'Of course. Anything I can do.'

'We appreciate that.' The chairman introduces a new face at the table, Grady Lewis. He's young, with slick hair and a polka-dotted handkerchief in his breast pocket. 'Grady is from a PR management firm in New York. Our lawyers suggested we hire them to help with this . . . situation.'

Grady stands up and walks to the front of the room, where a PowerPoint is waiting. Everything about him screams douchebag.

Teddy is okay with that. For now.

'The tragedy of this situation cannot be swept away or ignored,' Grady says. 'Everyone is scared, from the faculty to

295

the parents, and now you have students who have been, presumably, poisoned. Your enrollment will drop. That's a fact.' He pauses, looking around the room. 'We estimate that by the time the school reopens, you'll have lost at least fifty percent of your students.'

No one says a word, but they look very unhappy.

'At this point, you don't have a lot of options. The investigation is out of your hands – actually, the entire school is out of your hands. But what you can do is keep people informed about what *you're* doing to rectify the situation. Your new security system, for example. And a new system for food controls. All these things need to be communicated to the parents. Because, as you know,' Grady says, almost smiling, 'they're the ones who decide everything.'

A clever way of saying they're the ones who pay the bills.

'Because you have lost your headmaster – a most unfortunate event, in so many ways – our first recommendation is that you designate someone to speak for the school. Give it a face, not just a written statement delivered to the media. You may even want to designate an interim headmaster.'

Grady turns to Teddy, along with everyone else.

If he were an author, he couldn't have written this story any better.

MAD SCIENTIST

Zach stares at the text from Lucas, having no idea what he's referring to. A movie, a cartoon, a video game? A superhero, maybe, or a villain. At this time of night, Lucas could be referring to anything.

It's almost midnight, and Zach is in his room, working on another assignment from Titus.

Zach replies: Is that your new life goal?

Dude. No. Get online. That's what they're calling him.

MAD SCIENTIST.

Zach doesn't have to get online to know that *him* refers to whoever is poisoning people at Belmont.

The first person he thinks of is Courtney. She's going to get online and see that's what everyone is calling the person who killed her mother. When she was in jail, she didn't see all the social media. She didn't know anything about #HomicideHigh or read what everyone was saying. Maybe it was better that way.

That's messed up, he says to Lucas.

So is poisoning people.

Can't argue with that.

Again, he thinks of Crutcher. Of that book in his desk, of his interview on TV. It reminds him of those true crime shows and podcasts. Sometimes, killers can't help but put themselves in the spotlight. It makes them relive the crime over and over again.

But Crutcher?

All of this floats around in Zach's mind as he tries to come up with an answer that never comes. The only thing it does is distract him, and now he can't think about his assignment at all.

Sneaking out has never been a problem – he's been doing it since he was fourteen. The house is more than big enough that it's easy not to wake anyone up.

At first, when he gets in his car, he doesn't know where he's going. No plan, no destination. At least that's what he tells himself. When he ends up on the other side of town, near the Grove, he knows he's been headed here the whole time.

Crutcher's house is set back from the street like all the old houses in this area. Most have been redone, but his is a wreck. Not in that cool old haunted-house kind of way, either. From the outside, his house looks like a teardown.

Except the yard. There isn't one.

Even in winter, the houses around here have gardens and plants. No flowers or fruit, but the plants are there, dormant until spring.

Crutcher doesn't have anything. It looks like the front yard has been bulldozed.

Zach pulls over and turns off the engine. The street is quiet, and all the lights at Crutcher's house are off. Not surprising. He seems like an early-to-bed-and-early-to-rise kind of guy.

Out of the corner of his eye, a movement makes Zach turn. Across the street, a car is parked parallel to his. It's old and a bit run-down, and it's not empty. The woman in the driver's seat looks as surprised to see him as he is to see her.

He waves, like it isn't weird at all to see Mrs B's replacement sitting outside Crutcher's house.

68

Fallon watches Zach Ward drive away, her attention now on the taillights of his car instead of on downloading video from the mailbox camera.

Her first thought is that she's been caught. Up until this minute, she's never seen anyone she knows at Teddy's house, but now she's been recognized. In the middle of the night, no less. It makes her wonder if Zach has seen her out here before. Maybe he even knows her car.

She looks him up online, searching for his address.

He doesn't live near Teddy. Not even close.

So maybe he has friends or a girlfriend around here. Impossible to tell, especially since she barely knows him in the first place. Never even spoken to him.

She finishes downloading the video, resets the camera, and drives back to her place. At this point, she's not even sure how useful the mailbox footage is. All it shows is Teddy coming and going. No one visits. No one approaches his door except delivery drivers.

Ruining his life would be a lot easier if he had a constant stream of sex workers and drugs dealers stopping by.

Of course, he'd probably make them use the back door.

The guys at Belmont used to describe girls like that. You were either a house cat or an alley cat. Some girls would be introduced to parents; others wouldn't be.

Fallon was always a house cat.

Her first boyfriend was Jeremy Locke, a rich kid with a background similar to hers. Same pushy parents, too. They talked about that a lot, talked about the pressure to get into a good school. The pressure to succeed. At Belmont, it was a way of life.

She loved Jeremy, as much as any high school girl could love a boy, and everything was perfect until her parents found out.

'He's a distraction,' her father had said.

'He's not,' she'd argued. 'I swear he's not.'

They didn't believe her, didn't care. One phone call from her mother to Jeremy's ended everything.

'Plenty of time for boyfriends later,' her mom said.

Wrong. Her mother was so wrong about that. Nobody wanted a loser like her now.

Fallon arrives at her apartment building, her mind shifting from Jeremy back to Teddy. Three people are dead, Belmont is still shut down, and yet it feels like she is no closer to getting him fired. Far from it, in fact. He's practically a media darling now.

With a sigh, she pulls into the parking lot of her building. A car passes by behind her.

The taillights look just like Zach's.

The next morning, Titus shows up at 9 A.M. sharp. He's so punctual that Zach is convinced he watches the seconds count down on his phone so that he can knock at exactly nine o'clock.

'You know I cut you some slack last week,' Titus says, walking past Zach and into the kitchen. 'But only because of that thing at Belmont. I'm not going to do it again.'

Zach smiles, his face turned so Titus doesn't see it. Sure he won't do it again. Not the first time he's heard that.

'Thanks,' Zach says. 'I really appreciate you taking it easy on me.' No sarcasm. He prefers to stay on Titus's good side.

'Cool. Now let's talk about the Peloponnesian War.'

Zach has already finished his assignments. He can talk about the war all day if he has to.

Ninety minutes later, they take a break. Zach uses the opportunity to talk about the recent Belmont events, eventually getting to what he really wants to talk about.

Fallon Knight.

He knows a lot more about her now, starting with that run-down apartment building she lives in. And where her parents live. Everybody knows the big house at the end of Canary Lane.

So what went wrong there?

And why did a rich Belmont girl go to State?

It wasn't hard to find the basics on the internet, but what he couldn't find is what happened next. She moved away, went to college, and dropped off the radar until she showed up here, as Mrs B's replacement.

Something wasn't right.

Does he have too much time on his hands? Yes. Zach knows he does. Ever since he switched to homeschooling, he's had a lot more time. And, yes, he did feel a little bit stalkery when he followed Fallon home last night. But it was just so weird seeing her sitting outside Crutcher's house. Like *she* was stalking *him*.

'Did you hear Fallon Knight was one of the victims at Belmont?' Zach says to Titus.

'Seriously? I had no idea.'

'Oh, I thought you kept in touch with her or something.'

'Nah. For a while, our class had an online group, but eventually people dropped off,' Titus says. 'I haven't really talked to her in a couple of years. She went off to State.'

'State? I didn't know anyone from Belmont went to a state school.'

'Yeah, that was weird. She didn't get in anywhere she applied. That happened when we were still at Belmont. Later on, she blamed Crutcher for it.'

Zach nods and keeps his mouth shut, hoping Titus will keep talking. Sometimes shutting up is all it takes. He learned that from his mom, not his dad. It was a tactic she used with witnesses.

'I never really understood it,' Titus says, picking up another veggie chip. 'Something to do with getting into college, but I didn't get the whole story.'

Again, Zach waits. But Titus digs into the veggie chips and shrugs, saying nothing further.

'Weird. Don't colleges need three reference letters?' Zach says.

'Yep.'

'Must be more to it.' Zach grabs a veggie chip, trying to act casual. 'What was she like? In school, I mean?'

'High-strung. Ambitious.'

'So, normal?' Zach says.

'Basically.' Titus starts to pick up another chip but stops. 'I remember some saying she Roarked, but I don't know.'

Roarked is prep-school slang for 'cracked under pressure.' Zach knows the term. Everyone at Belmont does.

So maybe that was it. She cracked, and now it's led to her sitting outside Crutcher's house in the middle of the night.

69

At times, Teddy wonders why he even bothers. His entire life is built around his students – whom he would, and has, *killed* for – yet they still find ways to upset him. It's like they go out of their way to do it.

The evening news is on. All day, he expected the headmaster announcement to dominate the local coverage. It should have, given that his predecessor had died in the most recent poisoning at Belmont.

Was it so wrong to do what Teddy did? Wrong to kill someone, sure. In general. But when it was for the greater good – like saving his students, Courtney and Zach, from a life of hard times – then maybe it wasn't 'wrong' in the bigger sense of the word.

And was it so wrong to want something for himself? It's not like he could tell anyone what he was doing; he couldn't claim credit. Teddy had never had any ambition about becoming the headmaster. Headmasters were always former Belmont students. He'd never thought it was possible until suddenly it was.

They should talk about that on the news. The new headmaster at Belmont is the first one who isn't one of the alumni. Because he's that good.

Instead, he's staring at Veronica.

She's a nice girl. Veronica was in his class when she was a sophomore. A good student – not a great one, but good enough. She's a senior and one of the most popular students at Belmont. The prettiest, too, some would say. Teddy wouldn't.

Veronica was also one of the students poisoned last Monday. Now she's on TV, telling her story.

'*It was about an hour after lunch, and I started feeling sort of light-headed, like I hadn't eaten in a while. But my stomach was still full from lunch.*'

'*What did you eat for lunch?*'

'*A soft-wrap taco and a small carton of milk. Two percent milk. I got both of them in the dining hall. When I got up to leave after fifth period, I felt dizzy. It was like . . . It was like looking through a tunnel, where everything just gets smaller and smaller. That's the last thing I remember.*'

Teddy rolls his eyes. Looking through a tunnel. She should have paid more attention in class. If she had, she would've used a better metaphor.

The interview goes on forever, like they have nothing else to talk about on the news. Not the statement from the board of directors about the new headmaster, not his press conference, not his announcement about the memorial.

The idea for it had come to him all at once, like a siren going off in his head. Due to the death of Ingrid Ross and Courtney's arrest, the school had never held its annual memorial for the first headmaster who died. The statue was never dedicated, and Teddy never got a chance to give his speech.

Now, a memorial is the perfect way to honor *all* of the Belmont victims, and to move on with a new headmaster.

It will be held just outside the school – they still can't go inside, but the front steps and the parking lot have been approved. Teddy already has it all planned out. The top of the stairs will serve as the stage, with the school itself as the backdrop.

Perfect.

Except no one is talking about it. Everybody is listening to Veronica.

He turns off the TV and goes into his office. It's been a few days since he checked social media to see what the students are saying. While he hopes they're talking about the new headmaster – good or bad, as long as they're talking about him – he bets they're talking about Veronica.

And he's right.

While most are sympathetic to the fact that she was poisoned, that doesn't stop some of them from calling her a media whore. Can't argue with that.

They also dissect everything about the interview: what she said, what she wore, how her makeup was applied. Teddy finds himself mesmerized by their analysis. With a little editing, it could be a term paper. A rather impressive one at that.

Using his alter ego, Natasha, he adds in a few remarks of his own. They aren't kind, but they're true.

When he's bored with the topic, he searches for particular students to see what they're saying. Starting with Courtney. She's been out of jail for a day now – plenty of time to get online.

She hasn't. Courtney hasn't made any comments or posts since the day she was arrested.

Probably smart. She's always been an excellent student.

Next he checks in with Zach. He *has* been online, though he doesn't mention Veronica. He also doesn't mention the school's new headmaster, which isn't surprising, given that he is no longer enrolled at Belmont.

Teddy goes back to the conversation about Veronica. She is so lucky to be a senior. Otherwise, he'd have to bring her down a peg or ten.

He stopped.

Fallon didn't remember this until much later, because she was too rattled about seeing Zach Ward follow her. The next day, she was rattled again when she heard Teddy had been named new interim headmaster.

Of course he was.

Everything was beginning to make sense. So much sense that Fallon could actually make a spreadsheet detailing the whole story. Well, most of it. There are still holes to fill, beginning with the death of Ingrid Ross. Fallon has no idea what the story behind that is, but there has to be one.

While reviewing her spreadsheet, filling in all the details she can think of, she remembers Zach stopping.

He drove up to Teddy's house, pulled over to the curb, and turned off his lights. In other words, he parked. Like he was about to go pay Teddy a visit in the middle of the night.

When he saw her, he waved and drove away. Or it looked like he drove away, but really he followed her.

So why did he do that when he saw her? If he really was there to visit Teddy, why would seeing her make a difference?

She researches Zach and his family online. He's a typical Belmont student with two successful parents and a house on the right side of town. His social media is pretty boring. He's not a troll. At least not with his real name. Zach Ward had appeared to be a normal kid, right up until he got arrested and left school.

All of which leads Fallon to a couple of possibilities.

The idea that he would show up in the middle of the night, in his own car, no disguise, to do something bad to Teddy seems ridiculous.

But the idea that Teddy has someone helping him is not.

PART THREE

70

At exactly noon, Courtney turns on the TV. Zach wants to tell her to stop but can't bring himself to do it. The midday news blares out, making it impossible for him to study.

'Just coming in now, a three-car crash on the interstate. Let's go out to the scene with Trevor Harmon for more . . .'

Courtney changes the channel.

'Today, the city council will be holding what should be a contentious meeting about this year's budget . . .'

Click.

'We have no information yet about injuries from the accident, but we are expecting a statement from the state police at any time.'

Click.

'Still no arrests in the mass poisoning at Belmont Academy. But new interim headmaster Theodore Crutcher has announced that the upcoming memorial will be titled "Remembrance and Recovery: A New Beginning." As we reported last week, the event was originally scheduled to honor the death of Belmont's former headmasters as well as all recent victims. It has now been expanded to include a tour of the school, which is currently being renovated with upgraded security.

'Now let's go to weather. Tom, how's the lunch hour looking?'

'That's it?' Courtney says. 'That's the entire news about Belmont?'

Zach grabs the remote and turns the TV off. 'It's because of the FBI. No chance they're going to talk to reporters.'

'Or maybe they just aren't doing anything.'

'They aren't going to let this go,' Zach says. 'It's like a school shooting, but not as violent.'

Courtney grunts.

Homeschooling hasn't turned out to be a good thing for Courtney, though it might be better if she were away from her phone and the TV.

'What else have you found out about that Fallon woman?' she says.

Another mistake of Zach's. He shouldn't have told her about the plant book in Crutcher's office, or about seeing Fallon Knight outside his house. If he'd known another week would go by without an arrest, he never would've mentioned it.

'Nothing. Just that she hates him,' he says.

Courtney stares at him until it feels uncomfortable.

'Seriously,' he says. 'I haven't found anything else.'

She sighs and goes back to her computer. Zach returns to his own work, his head hanging a little lower.

Usually, he doesn't feel bad about lying. Now, he does. Courtney isn't someone he hides things from – or she didn't used to be. She also used to have a mother who was alive, instead of murdered, and everything she knew about jail came from *Orange Is the New Black*.

Since she came home, she's become obsessed with TV shows about jail. She rates them according to how realistic they are.

When she's not doing that, she's searching online about the Belmont murders. Every article, every message board, every chat. It's both completely understandable and completely disturbing.

His parents would say she's trying to process her mother's murder.

This time, he thinks they'd be right.

So he doesn't talk about Fallon anymore. Or Crutcher. He doesn't tell her that he has followed Fallon on several occasions, and that she stops by Crutcher's house once a day. Every day. Never gets out of her car, though. She just drives up, stops, gets on her phone for a minute, and then drives away.

It makes zero sense to him, but it must mean something to her. She keeps doing it.

Fallon keeps following him, too. Zach has seen that rundown little car a few times. Once, a block from his house. Another time, a few cars back at a stoplight.

He doesn't know why Fallon has been following him, but does have fun with her. The first time he saw her, he drove to a maternity store. The second time, to a dog park. With no dog.

But Zach hasn't told Courtney any of this.

He has to lie to her. It's for the best.

The conference room is ten stories up, with a view of the town. In the distance, Teddy can see Belmont.

'We need to decide on the speakers,' Winnie says.

Teddy smiles as he turns to her. It's cute that she uses the word *we*. As the new head of the Parents' Collaborative, she has embraced the power she thinks comes with it. Winnie still isn't a board member, but that takes time. And a lot of schmoozing.

He sits back down at the head of the table. Ms Marsha is

on his left; Winnie is on the right. Everyone else in the room is irrelevant.

'Run down the list,' he says to Winnie.

She recites the names of potential speakers for the Remembrance & Recovery ceremony. It's a pointless task, because he has already decided who will speak, but it gives him something to do since he's not teaching.

Beyond the walls of the conference room, people are busy doing office things. Typing or inputting or downloading. Paper shuffling. Whatever cubicle people do. The business is owned by a Belmont parent who offered a conference room to the school while Belmont is closed. Teddy was quick to take that offer, adding that he preferred to have lots of windows in his work space.

Ask, and he receives.

Winnie finishes the list and looks at him, waiting for an answer. She's not quite as strong or opinionated as Ingrid was. That should make his life a little easier.

'All of the victims should be introduced and brought onstage,' Teddy says. 'It would take too long to have each one speak. Unfortunately, we have quite a few victims.'

'Yes. It's very unfortunate,' Winnie says.

'Perhaps one of the student victims should speak,' Ms Marsha says. 'For representation.'

'You took the words right out of my mouth,' Teddy says. 'I was just about to suggest that.'

Winnie nods a little too hard. It's annoying. 'Great idea. Which student?'

The names run through his mind until he lands on the obvious. 'It has to be Veronica, don't you think?'

'Yes. Absolutely,' Winnie says.

314

'Or has she had enough attention?' Teddy says. 'Perhaps she has already become too synonymous with this tragedy?' He glances over at Ms Marsha, trying to gauge which way she is leaning. She gives nothing away, and it's more annoying than Winnie's enthusiasm. 'I was thinking of Damien. He would make a good speaker,' he says.

Damien Harcourt is a junior, and his parents are among the top ten wealthiest couples in the area.

Now that Teddy is the headmaster, he has to think about donations.

At first, he had resisted. He talked about the school's mission, the high quality of education, the importance of what they were teaching the kids. He wasn't concerned with the parents. Not unless they got in his way.

Then Ms Marsha showed him the accounts. And the lawsuits. A number of parents are suing the school because of the poisonings. As if it's the school's fault.

So, yes, Damien Harcourt will be the one to speak at the memorial. The wealthiest students may be the most annoying, but at least they're good for something.

Teddy glances up at the clock. 'What else do we have?' he says. 'I've got an appointment at three.'

He doesn't mention that the appointment is with the FBI. They want to talk to him again.

71

Every day, Fallon's apartment feels a little smaller. Every day, her bed loses a little more air. Every day, her noisy neighbors become more unbearable. She never imagined she would be here so long. Finishing off Teddy has taken much longer than she thought it would.

Deep breath.

Again.

Again.

She flips open her laptop and checks the news. Checks social media. Checks the news a second time. She watches the video from Teddy's mailbox camera. She's already watched it twice.

Nothing.

If Fallon thought she could get away with it, she would put a camera outside Zach's home. But she used to live in a house like that, and they all have security systems. She can't get close without getting caught.

She knows he is helping Teddy. It has to be him.

She's watched the video from Teddy's classes – before Zach withdrew from Belmont – and she can see it. The way he talks to Zach. Half disdain, half admiration. As if he's pretending not to like Zach.

It's so obvious. It's also circumstantial.

So is everything she's found online. It didn't take long for the hive mind to figure out what kind of poison was used. One of the #HomicideHigh Massacre group chats already googled it to death – pun intended – and came up with a bizarre plant called doll's-eyes, which grows right in this area.

She went straight back to all the videos she recorded outside Teddy's house. How very convenient that he cleared his yard just days after Ingrid Ross was murdered. But does she have footage of a doll's-eyes plant? Nope. The camera wasn't angled to catch those kinds of details.

None of what she has would convince the police or the FBI that Teddy is behind everything. And certainly not if it came from her.

She never should've sent those emails to Teddy, calling him an asshole and a piece of shit. Repeatedly. It makes her look like she's out to get him.

Which she is.

She's not getting anything useful from the mailbox video. She's not getting anything useful from Teddy himself, who appears to be the most boring person on the planet. And she's not getting anything from Zach. She can't even get a picture of Zach and Teddy together, much less talking.

All of which brings her right back to where she is now. In her shoebox apartment.

Maybe today she'll get lucky. Maybe she'll find something. She grabs her bag and walks out. If nothing else, she'll find Zach. He's easy to locate. If he's not at home, he's at the Grove. Or at Courtney's house.

That's where she finds him today, leaving his friend Courtney's house. Or is she a girlfriend? Maybe they just hook up. Hard to know, but they certainly spend a lot of time together.

Another interesting connection. They're everywhere, these little tidbits of information, yet no smoking gun, no bloody knife. No poison in hand.

317

So Fallon keeps going, keeps following Zach in his fancy car. He drives out of Courtney's neighborhood and into downtown. Good. It's easier for Fallon to hide among other cars on the road. She stays three or four cars behind him. More if she can manage it.

He takes a left, away from all the little shops and restaurants, and heads toward an industrial park filled with office buildings. They're ugly and square, tucked away and far from the expensive houses like the one Courtney lives in.

Fallon hangs back, circling through a parking lot while keeping an eye on Zach. He pulls into a spot right outside a flat one-story building with very few windows. He's sitting in his car. Maybe waiting for someone, maybe on his phone.

The sign out front is too far away to read, so she drives around the back of the building. A middle-aged woman wearing all black is getting out of her car, and Fallon pulls up alongside her.

'Excuse me. I think I'm lost,' she says. 'Can you tell me what building this is?'

The woman looks irritated, as if Fallon had just interrupted something important. 'It's the sperm bank.'

The sperm bank. Of course.

Zach has spotted her again, and he's playing with her. Not the first time, either.

Yes, he's a smart kid. She gets that. But she can out think a high school kid.

She just can't follow him without being seen.

With a sigh, she drives out of the industrial park and heads toward a Starbucks. Maybe she needs to go back to following Teddy. But he knows her car from seeing it at school. He

318

might alter his route if he spots her, though he would never be as obvious as Zach. Not because he's smarter, but because he's not seventeen.

Teddy isn't easy to ruin.

Unlike the headmaster who killed himself.

72

Teddy considered bringing a lawyer with him to the FBI meeting. At first. After thinking about it, he decided the worst thing he could do was assume he's a suspect. Several faculty members said they had been interviewed, so it seemed they were talking to everyone. And, as a victim, it only makes sense that they want to speak to him again.

The FBI is working out of the sheriff's headquarters. Teddy walks into a chaotic scene, a blend of FBI jackets and brown uniforms. The man at the front desk looks irritated. Teddy already feels the same.

'I'm Teddy Crutcher,' he says.

The man blinks at him.

'I'm here for an interview with the FBI.'

With a sigh, the man points. 'Over there.'

Halfway to 'over there,' Teddy is greeted by Agent Roland, the bald agent from the hospital. The same female agent is with him.

'Thank you for coming in,' Roland says, gesturing to a chair.

'Of course.' Teddy takes a seat. He hasn't smiled yet, nor does he intend to. 'This whole tragedy has been very difficult for everyone. I want to do anything I can to help find whoever did this.'

'I'm sure you do.'

That's from the other agent, Pruitt. She looks no-nonsense and speaks the same way.

'I guess I should congratulate you,' Roland says. 'Now that you're the headmaster.'

Teddy nods a little. 'I wish it wasn't necessary, yet here we are.'

'Yes,' Pruitt says. 'Here we are.'

No, Teddy doesn't like her.

'I'd like to go all the way back to the day Ingrid Ross died,' Roland says. 'What do you remember from that day?'

Teddy talks about Sonia's anniversary party, describing how these events are always a cause for celebration. 'Because we're a family at Belmont. That's how it works,' he says. 'That's also why this is so . . . unbelievable.'

He lists everyone he can remember from the party, including the headmaster, Ms Marsha, Frank, Louella, Nari, a number of parents from the Collaborative, as well as several students. Agent Pruitt writes everything down.

'And what about the day Sonia Benjamin died?' Roland says. 'Do you remember seeing her or speaking to her that day?'

'Of course. I saw her every day, even if it was just in the lounge,' Teddy says. 'I'm sure we exchanged a hello or said good morning. But, no, I apologize for not remembering exactly what happened on that day.'

Agent Pruitt opens a file and flips through the pages. 'In an earlier interview with the local police, you mentioned that she didn't treat Joe very well. The custodian.'

'That's right. Sonia could be . . . Well, I don't like to speak ill of the dead, but Sonia could be rather elitist in that way.'

'How did the headmaster treat Joe?' Roland asks.

'You know, that's a very good question. I wish I could answer it. But the truth is, I rarely spoke with the headmaster. As you may have heard, most communication went through Ms Marsha.' Teddy pauses and looks down at his hands. 'I really didn't speak to the headmaster very often.'

'But he was in the lunchroom every day,' Pruitt says.

'Oh, yes, of course he was. But that was his time to speak with the students, not the faculty.'

She writes that down.

'And after Sonia was found by Frank Maxwell,' Roland says, 'what do you remember?'

'It was just . . . shocking. At first, everyone was just worried about her. I'm not sure anyone started thinking about a connection between Sonia and Ingrid until after everything calmed down a little.'

'Let's move on to what happened a few weeks ago,' Roland says. 'I know we went through this at the hospital, but let's go through it again. Sometimes people remember things later.'

'Of course.' Teddy recounts what he ate, where he ate it, and how he felt just before he collapsed. Not word for word the same story, but in general.

'Is there anything else you remember from that day? Anything different or strange?' Roland says.

'Actually, there is.' Teddy leans forward a bit. It's the first time he has moved since sitting down. 'It happened the week before, but it was definitely strange. My Teacher of the Year plaque hangs on the wall in my classroom. And one morning, it was gone.'

'Gone?' Pruitt says.

'Yes, gone. It just vanished overnight. Just like that.' Teddy snaps his fingers. 'I asked Joe about it, because he cleans the rooms every night, but he said he didn't notice one way or another. I also tried to speak to the headmaster, because technically it was a theft and should have been treated as such, but Ms Marsha said he was all tied up with . . . well, with Sonia's death and the new security system.'

'Is it still missing?' Roland asks.

'Yes. A replacement showed up on Friday. The last Friday we were in school, before the security cameras were due to be turned on. And right before . . . that Monday.'

Agent Pruitt writes that down. 'Did you ever find out who did it?'

'No, although I have some theories,' Teddy says. 'At first, I thought it could be a student playing a prank. And it might have been.' He takes a deep breath. 'But it also could've been someone who wanted to win that award. Or someone who didn't think I deserved it. Though I have no idea who that would be,' he says. 'What I do know is that it had to be stolen outside of normal school hours. And other than the head-master, only two people have basically unlimited access to the school. The first is Joe, who is always here late, and it wouldn't be unusual for him to be in the building.'

'And the other?'

Teddy had thought about how to answer this question before he even sat down. Accusing someone outright was out of the question. But letting the FBI know who had the easiest, and most plausible, access to the building seemed reasonable.

'Ms Marsha,' he says. 'She distributes all of the security cards, and she maintains the log of card swipes.' Teddy pauses for a second, as if he's thinking. 'Actually, she could enter the school undetected if she wanted to.'

323

The FBI should know this already. But Teddy never assumes anyone does their job correctly.

He also doesn't assume they've already looked through Ms Marsha's desk.

They will now.

73

When Zach isn't with Courtney or Titus, or trying to catch Fallon following him, he goes to Starbucks with his new tablet. He still does all of his research there. Being arrested has made him a little paranoid about his online activity.

This evening, he heads out early, before his parents are home, and drives downtown the way he normally does. He's sitting at a stoplight when he sees Crutcher's car.

The old Saab is hard to miss. First, because Zach had seen it in the school parking lot so many times. Second, because of the Belmont sticker on the front windshield. The strangest part is where it's parked.

In front of a liquor store.

He never suspected Crutcher was a drinker. Zach has seen a lot of drinkers in his life – so many of his friends' parents are – but Crutcher has never shown any of the signs. No broken capillaries on his face, no bloat, no puffy or red eyes.

Maybe it's something he's picked up recently. Maybe it's something worth knowing.

Zach pulls over onto a side road, watching the car through his rearview mirror. Minutes later, Crutcher walks out of Fourth Avenue Liquors with a brown bag.

Interesting.

Zach waits until he drives away before going into the store. The bell rings when he walks inside, and he's immediately surrounded by rows of alcohol. Beer in the back, in the coolers, and hard liquor lining the walls.

At the register, a middle-aged man is watching TV and, no doubt, the security camera. Zach smiles at him and heads toward a cooler, grabbing a bottle of water. He scans the food and picks up a bag of chips.

At the register, he smiles again. 'How's it going?' he says.

The man smiles back. A real smile. 'Oh, you know, living the dream.'

'Nice,' Zach says. 'Hey, maybe you can help me out with something.'

'What's that?'

'I go to Belmont. When I was coming in, I swear I saw one of my teachers walking out. Well, someone who used to be my teacher, because . . . well, you know. It's closed now.'

The man nods, his expression grave. Everyone knows about Belmont.

'Was that Teddy Crutcher who was just in here?' Zach says. 'Our new headmaster?'

'Sure was,' the man says. He offers nothing further.

'Weird. I never pegged him as a drinker.' Zach leans in a little, like he's sharing a secret. 'You probably know we've got some teachers who like to drink.'

The man laughs. 'I'm not about to rat out my customers, but Teddy wasn't here to buy liquor. He drinks milk.'

'Milk?' Zach says. 'He comes in here to buy milk?'

'Sure does. I'm the only one who carries his brand.'

Zach blinks. 'He has a special *brand* of milk?'

'In the back,' the man says. 'I stock it for him, because he only drinks milk out of glass bottles. Says those cartons and

326

plastic ruin the taste.' He rolls his eyes, like he knows how ridiculous that sounds. Because it does.

It's also weird, and not just in the 'weird habit' kind of way. It's weird because Belmont doesn't have milk in glass bottles. Only in the little cartons. Including the ones that were poisoned.

The cheapest place in town to drink, get free Wi-Fi, and not be bothered is called The Hole. And it's there that Fallon sips her gin and tonic, which is awful, and ponders her lack of progress. She's disappointed in herself. Not a new feeling.

She has to rally, has to figure out how to get under, over, or through the cracks in the doors that won't open.

Teddy used to say that in class, back when she called him Mr Crutcher. When they were reading something particularly difficult, like Russian literature, he would say, 'Analyze each word, each sentence, and figure out what it means. Don't just stare at the words. Do something.'

First, another gin and tonic. One had made her sleepy; the second gives her a little more energy. Plus, it tastes better now that she's less sober.

Do something.

So far, Fallon hasn't done anything except try to catch Teddy or Zach slipping. She finishes off her second drink, opens her laptop, and starts typing.

Three emails, all sent to different people. She only signs her real name to one of them.

This isn't her first rodeo. Sometimes, you have to give a little nudge. Just a tiny one. Otherwise, someone might commit suicide.

But that wasn't Fallon's fault. The headmaster hanged himself in his office all on his own.

He was a tiny, meek little man. Not the kind anyone would suspect of having a gambling problem, but he did. Fallon was a sophomore when she came across that information.

She had been called to his office to discuss being a student liaison to the board of directors. They wanted one from each grade, and she was under consideration for hers. During their conversation, he was called away by Ms Marsha, leaving her alone in the office for a moment. Just enough time for her to sneak a glance at his computer screen.

One of the many open tabs on his browser was an online poker site. Fallon snapped a picture with her phone, knowing that gambling had to be against the Belmont rules. It was only later, when she looked it up, that she realized online gambling was illegal.

Illegally gambling on school premises had to be grounds for dismissal.

Which meant she had some valuable information. And what good was information if you couldn't use it?

When she approached him about it, he didn't even argue. He knew what she could do to him. That was all Fallon needed.

Student representative to the board? Done. An extension on an assignment? Done. A higher spot on the nomination list for the summer seminar? Done.

It was so perfect. Or it was until the headmaster killed himself.

And until Teddy accused her of cheating.

It wasn't cheating – not really. All she'd done was gather information and use it to her advantage.

She had done it with the headmaster just as she had done it to Teddy when she ruined his marriage.

It was her thing.

74

Zach's parents have called a family dinner. As soon as he walked out of the liquor store, he'd received an appointment reminder from his dad. Between Courtney, Fallon, Crutcher's milk, and his parents being . . . well, parents . . . Zach is getting tired. Not easy to manage all the people in his life.

'We want to talk about your current situation,' Dad says.

They're in the dining room, all gathered at one end of the table, because it's big enough for twelve. Dinner is salmon again, because Mom is convinced it's a superfood. No milk, though. Never milk.

Zach swallows a bite and clears his throat. 'My situation?'

'Titus tells us you're doing quite well with your schooling,' Mom says.

'That's good,' Zach says.

Dad takes a sip of sparkling water. 'We certainly don't want that to change,' he says. 'However, we are concerned about your lack of extracurricular activities.'

'You had so many at Belmont,' Mom says.

'And now you have none,' Dad says.

If only they knew how he spent his days. He can barely keep up with his 'extracurriculars.'

'Right. I understand,' Zach says.

Dad nods. 'I knew you would.'

Zach says nothing. They already have something in mind. His job is to wait for them to tell him what to do.

'We were thinking of volunteer work,' Mom says.

'It's important to contribute. We've always said community work is important,' Dad says.

'My firm contributes to a number of organizations. I've prepared a list for you to take a look at and see what interests you,' Mom says. 'I'll email it to you.'

Zach nods and smiles and plays along, acting like this is a great idea and he's super happy they thought of it.

When he's finally free to return to his life, he goes up to his room and opens his laptop. The first thing he sees is an email from an address he doesn't recognize. The subject line is MAD SCIENTIST.

After his FBI interview, Teddy spends his evening reading. No TV, no internet, just some quiet time with Henry Miller's *Tropic of Cancer* and a cold glass of milk. It's been a while since he's done this. He used to do it all the time when Allison was around.

She creeps into his thoughts like those worms creep into his stomach.

He can still see her curled up in her favorite chair, reading whatever she was into at the moment. Sometimes a romance, other times a thriller – she read a little bit of everything. They used to do it together, in silence, and it was the most comfortable thing.

They had such a good marriage. Everyone says that, but in his case it was true. They had a great life together until she insisted they have kids.

Now he's stuck reading by himself. It isn't the same.

After getting through just twenty pages, he gives up. The internet beckons, with the news from the day and the message boards filled with theories about the Mad Scientist. He's not sure how he feels about that nickname, but it's the one that stuck. In part, because it's gender-neutral.

As the media keeps reminding everyone, the majority of murders by poison are committed by women.

Teddy already knew that.

He goes into his office, knowing he should check his emails. Ever since he became headmaster, his inbox has exploded. Many messages have been well-wishes and congratulatory, but even more have been suggestions. Parents, faculty members, and even students seem to believe they can tell him what to do.

It's exhausting.

Today he has over a hundred new emails. Some are spam, but others require an answer. He can't ignore the people who pay the bills, especially since so many students have withdrawn. Now, he has to be nice to them.

As he scans down the list, one catches his eye. The subject line is MAD SCIENTIST.

He opens it.

I know it's you.

Teddy stares at the words, his heart thumping. No. Pounding. It's pounding so hard, he closes his eyes and takes a few deep breaths.

Impossible. It must be a joke. Spam. A sick message that has been sent to everyone, not just him.

He's not bcc'd on the email; it was sent only to him. And the address comes from a generic account, the same kind he uses to set up his fake social media accounts. If the email weren't so disturbing, that might be funny.

The email address, though. The first part catches his eye.

LittleBirdie

What are the chances a man would choose that name?

Fallon. Of course she's the first one he thinks of. She already has a bad habit of emailing him, though it's always been from her real address.

But why hide now?

Furthermore, how would she *know*? Impossible. She wasn't even in town when Ingrid Ross died.

As he starts to think of other possible senders, a knock at the door interrupts him.

Teddy freezes, sitting up straight in his chair. Maybe it wasn't the door at all. Maybe it was the pounding of his heart.

The doorbell rings. Not his heart.

He walks out of the office, toward the door, bracing himself for whoever it might be. The police. The FBI. Both.

Deep breath. He can handle it.

Teddy doesn't even glance through the window. He wants his reaction to appear normal. Natural. As if he didn't expect this at all. He opens the door without hesitation. The surprise is immediate, and very much real.

Not the police. Not the FBI.

It's Frank.

75

'Frank,' Teddy says, his heart slowing a bit. 'What a surprise.'

Frank smiles a little, looking embarrassed. 'I know this is probably a bit strange, showing up like this. I should've called.'

'No, no, this is a wonderful surprise.' Teddy opens the door wider, motioning for Frank to come inside. He hasn't seen Frank since he went on medical leave from Belmont, which feels like it was a hundred years ago. So much has happened since then. 'Come in and sit down,' Teddy says.

He leads Frank into the formal living room, which is the cleanest area of the house. Frank sits on the edge of the couch. Teddy sits in a chair next to him, getting a good look at his colleague.

Frank looks thinner, yes. But healthy. The dark circles under his eyes are gone, and there's a glow about him. He also appears calm. Before, Frank was always so hyper. Now he sits so still, he looks like a statue.

Then Teddy sees what he's wearing. Under his jacket, Frank has on a black shirt with a white collar.

A clerical collar.

Frank sees him notice and smiles.

'You've . . . joined the clergy?' Teddy says.

'I have,' Frank says. He pulls an envelope out of his pocket and hands it to Teddy. 'I'm an ordained minister.'

Teddy pulls out a certificate stating just that, signed by

Touchpoint Ministry. It looks like it's been printed off the internet. 'Congratulations. I'm . . . well, I'm very impressed. It must have been a difficult choice.'

'Actually, it was the easiest decision I've ever made,' Frank says. He still has that smile on his face. 'And congratulations to you, on being headmaster.'

'Thank you. Unfortunately, it happened under such tragic circumstances.' Teddy's mind goes back to that email. Frank may have changed his life, but he still has bad timing. Some things never change.

'Yes,' Frank says. 'The events at Belmont have been . . . Well, they've been evil. And I don't use that word lightly. No one in the clergy does.'

Teddy nods, bristling at the word. 'So I expect this new life of yours means you'll be resigning from your teaching position?'

'It does, yes. And of course I wanted to tell you in person.'

'I appreciate that.'

'I also wanted to speak with you about something else,' Frank says.

'Oh, don't worry about your retirement account,' Teddy says with a wave of his hand. 'Belmont only has 401(k)s now, so you can roll it over into an IRA or whatever you like.'

'It's not that. I wanted to ask about the memorial.' Frank leans in a little toward Teddy. It's the first time he's moved anything but his mouth. 'If you're going to have clergy at the event, I hope you will consider me. Although I won't be employed by Belmont, I still care deeply about its future.'

Teddy is tired of this conversation, and of Frank. He needs to get back to his email. 'Of course we want you there.

Frank, no matter where you go, you'll always be part of the Belmont family.' He stands up, indicating that their little chat is over. 'I'm sorry. I've been rude, haven't I? I should've offered you something to drink. My wife isn't home, and I'm afraid she's a much better host than I am.'

'How is Allison? I haven't seen her in a while.'

'She's great, just great. Busy as always, but she's great.'

'I'm happy to hear that.' Frank stands up. 'I should be going. I've taken up enough of your time.' He pauses. 'Unless you'd like me to stay and pray with you.'

'That won't be necessary.'

Teddy walks him to the door and then out to his car, asking about his wife and child.

'Missy and Frankie are at her mother's house right now,' Frank says. 'It's for the best, considering my life transition.'

So she left him. Not surprising. 'Probably a good temporary move.'

'Thank you again,' Frank says, unlocking his car with a click. 'I really want to stay involved with Belmont.'

'Of course.'

Teddy waits for Frank to get into the car, forcing himself to be polite, and he waves as Frank drives away.

Calm. Cool. Collected.

Until he gets back into the house, his mind on that email, and he picks up a glass bowl. A wedding present, one of Allison's favorites. Teddy slams it against the floor with so much force, a piece of glass flies up and lodges itself in his arm.

He spends the rest of the evening cleaning it up.

I know you're helping him.

Zach stares at the email. His first thought is that it's a joke from Lucas. But Lucas wouldn't send an email; he'd send a text. And he sure as hell wouldn't use an email address like LittleBirdie.

Next thought: Fallon Knight.

She's the one who has been following him, the one who's been going to Crutcher's house every day. And she thinks he's . . . what? Helping the Mad Scientist? Because Zach was outside Crutcher's house once?

Insane.

But she also may be right. Just not about him. About Crutcher. Fallon isn't the only one who thinks he may have killed those people. Zach still thinks the same thing, especially after Crutcher was named headmaster. And after learning about the milk.

He sits back in his chair, staring at the words, trying to figure out why she would even send an email like this. What's the point? If she really thinks he's helping someone kill people, why not go to the police? What's she going to do – try to blackmail him?

Part of him wants to go talk to her and see what this is all about.

The other part of him keeps coming back to the same thought: *She's crazy.*

76

Frank. *Frank Maxwell.*

Fallon shakes her head, not understanding. In all the months she has been watching Teddy, he's never had a visitor. Not once. And on the night she sent that email, Frank shows up at his house.

She watches the video again.

It's early in the morning, and she's parked down the street from Zach's house. She's been sitting here for a half an hour, watching the footage from outside Teddy's house last night on her phone.

Frank Maxwell.

The last time she heard about him, he was on medical leave from Belmont. Now, he shows up out of the blue. Fallon was trying to provoke a reaction with that email, and she got one. But this isn't what she had in mind.

Maybe she's sitting in front of the wrong house.

She looks up where Frank lives, and it's not in this rich neighborhood. She drives to the Maxwell house and parks down the block, though it's clear she can't stay for long. This is Willow Heights, a middle-class subdivision where the houses are close together and close to the street. Guaranteed there's at least one neighbor who keeps an eye out for strangers in the neighborhood.

Fallon watches just long enough to see Frank come out of the house.

Lucky. Today, Fallon is lucky. Five more minutes, and she would've left.

She follows him to the interstate, where he drives for about twenty minutes. He takes an exit she's not familiar with and goes through a neighborhood she's never heard of. Frank doesn't stop until he pulls into the parking lot of Touchpoint Ministry.

Church. Not even nine o'clock in the morning, and Frank is going to church.

Maybe he's done something so horrible, he needs to pray for forgiveness.

Zach is pretty sure he's being an idiot.

He shouldn't be sitting here, in his car, outside Fallon's apartment building. First, because it makes him feel like a stalker. Second, because she's probably insane.

Or maybe she just Roarked. She wouldn't be the first from Belmont, though Zach's never seen it for himself.

The term comes from a kid named Roarke. His last name changes, depending on who's telling the story, but his first name is always Roarke. Valedictorian, all the right extracurricular activities: math club, volunteered with children, and in his free time he invented something you might see on *Shark Tank*. Didn't get a lot of sleep, though. And he didn't take failure well.

He cracked under the pressure to be perfect. Set fire to his locker, burning up his books, his laptop, even his phone.

Walked away, dropped out, and was never heard from again.

Is it true? No one knows. But Roarke is a cautionary tale, a fable, the bogeyman for Zach and his friends. Other kids get told to stay away from drugs, hang out with the right crowd, get good grades, and go to college. Belmont students are warned about Roarke.

Maybe that's what happened to Fallon. She cracked under the pressure and walked away, then decided it was Crutcher's fault. Now she's back for revenge.

Or maybe Zach's losing his mind, too. Hard to tell at this point.

What he does know is that he didn't help anyone kill. He's going to explain that to Fallon in a calm, reasonable, factual manner and hope she doesn't pull out an axe or something.

If only she would come home. He lowers the back of his seat, prepared to wait for as long as it takes. Too bad she didn't follow him today. Zach closes his eyes for a few minutes. He opens them when he hears a car door shut.

Someone has arrived and parked off to the right, at the far end of the parking lot. He leans forward to get a better look.

Not Fallon.

Crutcher.

77

Eighteen minutes. That's how long Zach waits for Crutcher to come back out of Fallon's building. He goes straight to his car and drives away.

Zach knows she isn't home. He's already checked, and as far as he can tell, she hasn't returned. The door to the apartment building is visible from where he's parked.

Oh, wait. The back door. There must be a back door.

Zach is terrible at this stalking thing.

He gets out of his car and goes to the door. No buzzer to enter. Just an open door, like it's a hotel. That's pretty much what the building looks like, an old hotel converted into apartments. The lobby even looks that way except there's no desk clerk.

The internet says her apartment number is 104, which means she's on the first floor. It doesn't take long to find it. And, yes, her apartment faces the back.

Zach crosses detective off his list of potential professions. And criminal. He'd be bad at that, too.

He knocks. No answer.

Second knock. Still no answer.

Zach puts his ear to the door, listening for any sound from inside.

Nothing.

Did Crutcher stand here for eighteen minutes? Was he writing her a note that he slipped under the door? Who does that? She works at Belmont – he must have her phone number. Why not just send her an email or a text?

Then again, this is the teacher who refuses to have a smartboard in his class.

Zach starts to leave the way he came but stops. Goes back to look out the back door. There is a row of parking spaces behind the building, but Fallon's car isn't there.

Good. For a second, he thought Crutcher might have done something to her.

With nothing else to do except some assignments for Titus, Zach decides to stick around to make sure. She may be crazy, but she doesn't deserve to be murdered.

Three hours. Frank has been inside that church for three hours. No one can pray for that long. They'd fall asleep. She almost has a few times, and she's not waiting for God to answer her.

Her plan had been to watch from a distance, not to talk to him. So far, that plan has accomplished nothing. After checking her hair and lipstick, making sure she looks appropriate for a house of God, she walks into Touchpoint Ministry.

The outside of the building is deceptive. It's big, yes, but on the inside it's massive. More like an arena than a church.

'May I help you?'

The woman's voice is low, almost hushed. She's middle-aged and dressed in a turquoise suit. She has a kind smile and too much makeup.

'Is it all right if I just sit?' Fallon says.

'Of course.' The woman motions for her to go ahead. No one is on the stage, and Fallon sees just two others sitting down. Both have their heads bowed in prayer.

Neither one is Frank.

Fallon sits down and waits. About twenty minutes later, something finally happens.

A man walks onto the stage. Older, grey hair, wearing a white suit, black shirt, and a white clerical collar. He advances to the podium and picks up a tablet, showing it to a younger man following behind him.

Frank. Who is also wearing a clerical collar.

Oh.

Oh.

He's not here to pray. He's here to . . . work?

Fallon watches them, transfixed by this new Frank, until they leave the stage and disappear. She doesn't wait around to see him a second time.

On the drive back, she tries to wrap her head around this new development. And about why Frank was at Teddy's last night. It's not like *Teddy* was praying for forgiveness.

She's still thinking about this as she parks at her apartment building.

Zach's car snaps her back to reality. Sleek, black, and expensive enough to stand out here.

Not so bright, that kid.

It doesn't look like he's inside. Not until she walks up to it and sees him leaning back in the front seat. Asleep.

Really not so bright.

She considers leaving him there, waiting until he wakes up and comes knocking on her door. But maybe that wouldn't be smart. She'd be trapped in her own apartment, and he's probably stronger than her.

And this is what she wanted, why she sent the email. She wanted a reaction, and here it is.

For a second, she hesitates, gathering her thoughts, trying to brace for the confrontation. When she's ready, she makes a fist and knocks on the window.

Once. Hard.

Zach's eyes fly open. He looks at her, blinks, and sits up.

Fallon steps back as he opens the door. The smell of fine leather wafts out with him. She breathes it in, remembering what it was like to have a car like that. Remembering that this is the kind of car she's supposed to have.

If not for Crutcher.

'Hi,' he says, straightening his button-down. 'Miss Knight, I'm not sure we've actually met. I'm Zach Ward.'

So polite. Even when he was just sleeping outside her apartment.

'Yes,' she says. 'I saw you getting arrested at Belmont.'

This stops him cold. Smile gone, he looks down at his feet. 'Yeah. That was me.'

'And why are you sleeping in your car outside my apartment?' Fallon stands a bit straighter, acting more like the teacher she is supposed to be.

He looks up at her. 'Why have you been following me?'

Not a surprise. Fallon was expecting this question as soon as she saw him. 'Because you're up to something.'

He smiles. This little prick.

'Okay, Little Birdie,' he says.

78

Zach sees the shock in Fallon's eyes. She's not good enough to hide that reaction.

'So you did send the email,' he says, relaxing a little. When he first saw Fallon through the car window, he was sort of scared. No telling what she might do.

Now she's the one who looks nervous.

'I thought it was you,' he says. 'You're the only one who's been following me.'

She rallies a bit, jutting out her chin. 'Must have struck a nerve, or you wouldn't be here.'

Fallon's right. It's just not the nerve she thinks it is.

The conversation isn't going the way he wants it to. She's defensive, yes, but so is he. Wrong approach. Acting like enemies isn't going to get them anywhere. They should be working together, not against each other.

Like Dad always says: *Make more allies than enemies.*

'I can't blame you for thinking that,' Zach says. 'I probably would, too, if I were you.' She looks skeptical, but she's listening. 'You and I think the same thing about Crutcher. We're on the same page.'

'How do I know you're not lying? Maybe you're helping him, and this is part of it.'

'Fair,' he says.

'If I were you,' she says, 'I'd say exactly what you just said.'

She's right. And he has no way to prove otherwise. 'So we're at a stalemate.'

'Looks that way.'

If he had any proof against Crutcher, he'd offer it. All he has is a strong hunch, the plant book in Crutcher's desk, and his milk preferences.

And nothing to lose.

'Okay, here's the thing,' he says. 'I think Crutcher did it. I think he killed all those people at Belmont, starting with Courtney's mom, and I think he did it because he's a psychopath who wanted to become headmaster.' Fallon's eyes widen a little, but not enough. 'I have no way to prove it, but it's what I believe. If you think the same thing, we should work together on this. Because I don't think the FBI has a clue.'

He takes it as a good sign when Fallon doesn't laugh. She doesn't do anything except stare at him.

'If you want to work together, that's great,' he says. 'If you think I'm lying, fine. But that's the truth.' He turns away, only looking at her again once he's back in his car. 'And you can stop following me. You're wasting your time.'

Zach shuts the door and starts the engine, giving her time to tell him to hold on. To say *something*.

She doesn't.

'One more thing,' he says. 'Crutcher was here.'

'What?'

'Before I got here, Crutcher walked into your building and didn't come out for eighteen minutes.'

She crosses her arms over her chest. 'You're lying.'

'I know you think that, but if I were you, I wouldn't eat or drink anything in your apartment.'

*

346

Fallon watches Zach until he turns the corner, out of sight, before going into her building. No sense in following him now. He's not about to go anywhere interesting.

She approaches her door carefully, just in case Zach wasn't lying. First, she checks the handle.

Still locked.

She slips her key in and opens it, looking down at the floor. In case Teddy left a note . . . or something else.

Nope. Not a thing.

Her apartment looks exactly as she left it. Bed unmade, lamp on the floor. Her tiny closet is overstuffed with clothes, the door bulging open as it always does.

She drops her bag on the floor and heads straight to the mini-kitchenette. That's what the landlord called it. A fancy name for a sink, microwave, and refrigerator. All the food she has is in the fridge so it doesn't attract bugs. Nothing inside except a box of crackers, some condiment packets, and a carton of orange juice.

It all looks the same, but Teddy wouldn't be stupid enough to move things around. He would put them back exactly as he found them.

She shuts the refrigerator door without touching a thing.

On her laptop, she searches around for labs that can test food for poisons. There aren't many companies who will do this for regular people like her, and the ones that will are very expensive. It would be worth the money if it would prove Teddy tried to poison her. But that assumes Zach is telling the truth.

He did sound sincere.

Not that she'd expected him to be a bad liar. But if he was lying, he's better than she'd thought.

347

And if he was telling the truth, he's right. They should work together.

It would be amazing to have him – or anyone – as a partner in this. Someone to bounce ideas off of, someone to help figure it all out and put it together in a way the police would believe.

The police. Zach's reputation with them is probably worse than hers even if they read the emails she sent to Teddy.

She goes back and forth on it, finally deciding she needs to test him. Like in her Belmont science classes, where they'd taught her to come up with a hypothesis and then test to see if it was true. The scientific method could be applied to Zach.

Hypothesis statement: If Zach is telling the truth, he would be a good partner.

But she can't use Bunsen burners and test tubes to figure out the answer. Back to the internet she goes, refreshing her memory on the rest of the method.

Statements must be tested, and the tests must be replicable.

Maybe that's the wrong method to use. She needs to be more like a lawyer, asking questions she already knows the answers to.

Maybe she needs to ask him about what she knows.

That would mean revealing some of the information she has, but at this point she has nothing to lose. Still no answer from Teddy other than a visit to her apartment. And no answer to the third email she sent, either.

She sits down in front of her computer and types out an email to Zach, explaining what she knows about Crutcher. Including the video of him sneaking into the school – although she doesn't mention how she got it. He doesn't need to know that.

Fallon gets about halfway through before fatigue sets in. It's late, and she can't think clearly enough to finish.

Tomorrow, she will. She'll finish it and send it to Zach. Maybe then she'll know if he's telling the truth.

79

Teddy misses Ingrid Ross.

He's back in the tenth-floor conference room. Winnie hands him the final invitation list for the memorial. It's coming up fast, and the addition of Frank Maxwell means they need to include clergy members from all religions.

Ingrid would've known whom to invite. She knew everyone.

So does Ms Marsha, but she's not here this morning.

'I've called her twice,' Winnie says. 'She hasn't called back yet.'

Teddy glances up at the clock. It's twenty minutes past nine, which means Ms Marsha is twenty minutes late. That doesn't happen. The woman is more punctual than a Swiss watch.

And it probably means she's not coming at all.

'We're running out of time to decide,' he says to Winnie. 'Make up a list of possible religious leaders, and let's go through it.'

She nods and starts typing on her laptop.

Teddy picks up the invite list and reviews it again. Allison Crutcher's name is not there. As his wife, it's assumed she is already invited and that she will show up. He hopes she at least has the courtesy to do so, given that she hasn't bothered to congratulate him yet. Not even an email that says:

Sorry about the tragedy at Belmont, but you'll do a great job as headmaster.

Nothing. Not a word.

She has been infuriatingly quiet. Being loved is one thing, being hated is another, but there's nothing worse than being ignored. Which is why he still hasn't signed those divorce papers or returned her lawyer's calls.

Winnie gets up and leaves the conference room. She's a brisk, efficient woman, though not particularly intelligent. Maybe that's what he needs in an assistant. Someone who does what he says without putting too much thought into it.

But he can't start looking for a new assistant quite yet.

Zach and Courtney are studying at Starbucks when she suddenly throws her pencil down.

'I don't like my tutor.'

'I know,' he says.

'Why couldn't my dad just hire your tutor? It doesn't make any sense.'

Zach doesn't look up from his own work. They've been through this before. 'Because Titus is a young guy, and your dad thinks he'll hit on his little girl.' That's why her tutor is an older, retired woman, who used to be a teacher.

'I'm not a little *girl*,' she says. 'I've been to jail, you know.'

'Your dad didn't buy that argument, I'm guessing,' he says.

'Nope.'

It's about ten thirty, in between the morning and lunchtime rush, so the coffee shop is empty. Other than the employees, they have the whole place to themselves. Still, they keep their voices low. Courtney doesn't advertise she's the one who was in jail. She even cut her hair and dyed it a darker brown. It looks weird to Zach, but he keeps his mouth shut.

He keeps his mouth shut about Fallon, too. No chance

he's going to tell Courtney about their conversation yester-day. But he keeps thinking about it. Wondering if Fallon will decide to believe him.

Courtney turns around in her seat to look at the TV screen. Again.

'Nothing's happening,' Zach says. 'They're watching a talk show.'

'I know. Nothing's ever happening.'

'The memorial is,' he says. 'You going to go?'

'Have to, because of Mom.' Courtney doesn't look happy about it.

'I'll go with you. Even though I'm not a *Belmont* student.'

'Loser.' She smiles.

He's about to call her a jailbird when a breaking-news ban-ner appears on TV. Courtney hears the news theme and whips her head around to see.

Ms Marsha appears on the screen. In a mug shot.

But she's not alone. A second mug shot appears next to hers.

Joe.

The assistant to the headmaster and Belmont's custodian have both been arrested.

It's about time.

Teddy watches the breaking news in the conference room, along with Winnie and some of the administrators. Someone hooked up their computer to the smartboard so they can see the report in all its HD glory.

Ms Marsha looks a lot different when her hair isn't done and she isn't wearing lipstick. And Joe . . . Well, he looks exactly the same. Unhappy.

'My God,' Teddy says. 'This is . . . It's just unbelievable.'

'But *why?*' Winnie says.

The bobblehead reporter is already on it.

'Marsha Fowler and Joseph Apple have both been employed by Belmont for over twenty years, and now both have been accused of murdering three people and poisoning half a dozen others, including students. If this is true, the only question is why? What would make them do this?'

Relief. Teddy has to stop himself from visibly relaxing in front of everyone. The FBI finally got it right, and it feels like a miracle.

'Reporters are already calling,' Winnie says.

'We have to send out an email to the faculty and staff,' he says. 'Direct all inquiries to the headmaster's office.' Teddy looks around the room, knowing that Ms Marsha would have been the one to send that email. His eyes land on Daphne, Belmont's registration and admissions secretary. She's a young, somewhat awkward woman, the kind people feel a little sorry for. 'Daphne,' he says. 'Can you arrange this?'

Her eyes widen, but she nods. 'Yes. I can.'

'Good.' A lot more will need to happen over the next couple of days – meetings with lawyers, with the board, with the faculty – but first things first. 'We also need to issue a statement, expressing how heartbroken we are to hear the news of these arrests.' He's still looking at Daphne. She sits down and starts typing as Teddy dictates.

Winnie stares at the TV, tears streaming down her face. For the second time today, Teddy misses Ingrid. She was a lot of things, but she wasn't a crier.

She was a mistake anyway. One he has spent months correcting, starting with Sonia and then having to poison the milk and plant the evidence. A receipt for syringes buried in

Ms Marsha's desk. The remnants of a sprig of doll's-eyes in Joe's office. He did, after all, have a habit of sneaking into the kitchen to make himself breakfast. Alone.

And who else would have become so sick of catering to rich kids and parents but the two employees who had been at Belmont the longest? Especially when they were posting anonymously on a blog complaining about it? All that research into fake profiles had been more useful than Teddy had ever expected, like knowing how to set up an IP redirect to the school's server. He'd used thinly veiled email addresses and confidential information that only they would know – both signs of people who *don't* know what they're doing. Like Ms Marsha and Joe.

Finally, it had worked. Courtney was released, Zach was no longer under suspicion, and now Belmont could get back to the business of educating the students.

80

'It actually makes total sense when you think about it. I mean, at first it didn't seem right, because we had talked about Crutcher so much, you know? But then when I think about Ms Marsha and Joe, and all the shit they've put up with from kids like us. Can you imagine cleaning up after us year after year? Or taking all those calls from angry parents? I'm not saying I'm not pissed. I'm just saying, like, I can see the motive . . .'

'I know, right?' Zach says, reminding himself that it's good to see Courtney happy again. Not stressed about the news, not obsessively checking social media. Just happy.

Even if he does have reservations about these arrests.

They're in his car, heading back toward her house, and the radio is tuned into the news. Courtney pauses to listen, then talks, listens again, repeat. Zach isn't about to interrupt. And he's not about to tell her that the FBI could be wrong.

But maybe he's the one who's wrong. Maybe it was never Crutcher.

But the book.

The milk.

Fallon.

Maybe she's the craziest one of all.

Courtney's dad calls, and she spins off again, repeating everything she just said. Her reasoning grows bigger. Stronger.

'It's so obvious, don't you think . . . ? Exactly, why didn't anyone . . . ? That's what I'm saying! How did we not see it? Thank God for the FBI, right? . . .'

When she hangs up, she turns to Zach. Beaming. She is literally beaming.

'Awesome, right?' she says.

'Obviously.'

'My dad and I are going out to lunch to celebrate. Wanna come?'

Zach shakes his head. 'Can't. I'm meeting Titus.'

'Boo.'

'I know.'

He isn't meeting Titus, but Courtney believes it because Zach doesn't lie to her. No reason to. Usually. But he's been lying for a while now, if only by omission.

After dropping her off at her house, he pulls over to the curb to think about where to go next. The Grove? No doubt everyone will be there, according to the text from Lucas.

TWO Mad Scientists?! Get thee to the Grove to discuss, STAT.

In Lucas lingo, *discuss* meant 'get high and talk shit.' Not a terrible option. Although Lucas doesn't know anything about Crutcher, or Fallon, and the last thing Zach wants to do is let any of it slip. If he's high or drunk, it might.

No to the Grove.

Then there's Fallon, whom he could try and talk to again. Not the best idea, not the worst. She hasn't contacted him, though, so the idea of going to see her again makes him really feel like a stalker.

Home. He could go home and study while watching the

356

news. Boring, but probably the best option. He's not an FBI agent, he doesn't have access to the evidence and interviews and everything else, so why even think about it? Not his problem.

Still, it bothers him. Not being able to do anything is the worst feeling of all. Dad doesn't have a saying for that.

Teddy is back at home, watching the news. Once in a while, everything is just as it should be. Today is one of those days.

Except Allison isn't around to see it.

That's the one thing he can't fix. He can't take back the lie, can't even come up with a reasonable explanation for it. And he's tried. God knows, he's tried. And he's not even sure if he believes in God.

All of it could've been avoided if he had agreed to have a child. Just one. Everyone would still be alive, and Allison would still be here.

Thinking about this makes the worms start to move around in his stomach.

He turns up the TV louder, forcing himself to enjoy his success. And he does enjoy it, right up until the doorbell rings.

81

Frank. Again.

Teddy stifles any frustration, shoving it deep down inside so Frank can't see it.

'Twice in one week!' Teddy says, opening the door to let Frank inside. 'How nice to see you again.'

Frank smiles without showing his teeth, and it's strange. 'Sorry to barge in on you again. I tried calling, but I know you must be so busy.'

Teddy smacks his forehead with his palm. 'I'm so sorry. I had it on my list to return your call, and then the news came on and . . . Well, I'm sure you've seen it.'

'I have.' Frank's smile disappears. Solemn face. 'It's devastating. Simply devastating.'

They walk into the living room, where Frank again sits on the couch.

'Can I get you something to drink?' Teddy says. 'Some tea, perhaps?'

'No, no, that won't be necessary. I'd just like to go over the program for the memorial, if that's all right.' Frank reaches into his pocket and pulls out the agenda distributed to all the speakers. 'Do you mind?' Frank says.

'Of course not.' Teddy sits.

For the next half hour, Frank reviews every item on the program. His idea is to insert a prayer whenever possible. After every speech, ideally. Teddy explains, repeatedly, that representatives from other faiths will be there and that, yes, they will be leading prayers as well.

A negotiation ensues.

'I believe it's important that I lead the final prayer,' Frank says. 'Given that I'm family.'

Family. The Belmont family is an exclusive one. As head-master, Teddy is now part of it.

Frank is not.

'The official programs have already been printed,' Teddy says. And they were damn expensive. No chance he's going to reprint them. 'I'll announce at the beginning that we'll have prayers throughout the day. The master list will be at the podium for everyone to see. And, yes, you will go last.'

'Thank you, I do appreciate that.' Frank smiles for real, with teeth and everything. 'Now, before I go, I'd really like it if you would pray with me.'

'You want me to what now?'

'Pray with me. Please. After the terrible news today, I think the two of us should pray for Belmont,' Frank says. 'And for you.'

'For me?'

'Of course.'

As headmaster, Teddy knows he has to pick and choose his battles, because he can't fight all of them. He can fight some, though. After saying yes to everything else Frank has asked for, it's time to say no.

'I respect your beliefs and support your right to have them,' he says. 'However, your beliefs aren't necessarily the same as mine.'

Frank reaches over and places his hand on Teddy's shoulder. 'I understand that. I also think the best thing for us to do is pray for forgiveness for our past sins. Together. Only then will all of us, including Belmont, be able to move forward with a fresh, cleansed start.'

Teddy moves away, causing Frank's hand to drop. 'I think it would be better if you prayed with your fellow believers.' He stands up. Their time together is over.

Frank sighs.

They walk to the door, which Teddy is more than happy to open for Frank. Before leaving, Frank turns to him.

'I will pray for you,' he says.

'Thank you. I appreciate that.'

As soon as he's gone, Teddy goes back to his office. He probably has a hundred new emails to catch up on, not to mention the latest report on the school's financial situation.

But first, the news. The website for the local newspaper is already pulled up on his computer, and he refreshes the page. He's been watching the Metro section, waiting for news about Fallon.

Zach has a headache. Not because he's sick, but because he's been thinking too hard about Crutcher. That must be it. The man is nothing but a headache – always has been.

And a dick.

But would the FBI believe Zach? After he'd presented himself as some lovestruck teenager willing to break the law to see Courtney, probably not. That alone could make him seem unbalanced. A good idea at the time. Not so much now.

Maybe he should've done what his parents and his lawyer said and kept his mouth shut.

Exhausted. He's exhausted trying to figure out the best thing to do every minute of the day. He almost feels like giving up.

Maybe that's what he should do: give up on trying to get Crutcher, give up on trying to do the right thing. Maybe he should just be a teenager and get high, eat junk food, and crash on the couch.

Which is exactly what he does.

He turns on the TV. All the local stations are talking about Ms Marsha and Joe. Interviews with their neighbors and friends, pictures from their personal lives, all cobbled together into a story that ends with murder.

Click.

Zach turns on an action movie instead. He lasts ten minutes before flipping back to the news.

He surfs through the local news channels, looking for any glimmer of hope. Any sign that the FBI has figured out their mistake. But they're done with Belmont, and someone gives the weather report, the sports report . . .

Then he sees a picture of Fallon's apartment building.

'A twenty-three-year-old woman is found dead of carbon monoxide poisoning in her Hidden Palms apartment. Police say an old water heater may be to blame. Tonight at ten: how to make sure your . . .'

Fallon.

Zach doesn't have to think twice about who died, or about who's responsible. When he saw Crutcher at her building, he should've known better.

Well, he did know better. He saw Fallon and spoke to her, and she was fine.

But he should've done more. Stopped Crutcher. Talked to him. At least taken a picture of him walking into the building. Anything other than just watch.

That almost makes him feel complicit.

Fallon knew the truth. She always knew. Otherwise, Crutcher wouldn't have done this.

Zach paces around the room with his phone, googling more information about her death. Not much else is out there. Carbon monoxide, an old water heater, a terrible accident.

Back on the TV, there's a report about Belmont, the murders, the arrests, and the new headmaster. A picture of Crutcher appears, making Zach feel sick.

Crutcher's going to get away with everything.

82

The day is cool and sunny, too beautiful for a funeral. But Teddy isn't complaining. The last thing he wants to do is stand outside in gloomy, rainy weather.

There was no question he had to attend. Not only was Fallon a former Belmont student; she was an employee when she died. No. Passed away. People say 'passed away' when the cause is anything but murder or suicide. And Fallon's death was just a tragic accident.

Even the police said it was. For a minute, reporters had jumped on the fact that she was teaching at Belmont when the school had closed. But once the detectives saw the water heater, and the owner of the building came forward and said the rest of the heaters would be replaced, the case closed with a hard slam. Sometimes, people just die. The bobble-head reporter, Lissa, even said so. That makes it true.

The service is held right at the grave site. Fallon's parents are here, surprisingly, since they clearly didn't support their daughter financially. They're right in front, dressed in expensive black clothing. Mom crying, dad somber. All very appropriate.

A number of other Belmont teachers are also attending, along with former students who knew Fallon. Teddy recognizes several, and all appear to be doing much better than Fallon was. Or at least their parents haven't cut them off.

Frank is here as well, standing right next to Teddy. He's a

bit miffed by that; people might think he's gone and found God or something. But it's hard to tell a man in a clergy collar to get away at a funeral.

The man who leads the service also wears the white collar. He's old and distinguished-looking, with a deep baritone voice to tell a lot of mistruths about Fallon.

'Fallon Meredith Knight, beloved daughter of David and Olivia Knight, was the kind of woman who tried to help wherever and whomever she could. Just recently, she returned to Belmont Academy and volunteered to step in for one of the recent poisoning victims. Her love for the school, and its students, was deep enough that she put aside her own goals in order to help.'

Teddy clears his throat. An unintentional reaction. After all, this man has no idea that Fallon's death never would've happened if she hadn't sent that final email.

And if she hadn't lived on the first floor of a former motel, it wouldn't have been so easy. Too easy, really. The motel was cheaply built, no maintenance, no updates, and cheap windows. Almost as easy to get into as Belmont.

Plus the old water heater. Just a tiny leak made it run constantly, causing the buildup of that deadly gas in her small apartment.

Everything had fallen into place, almost like it was meant to be.

Teddy had a backup plan, of course. Another poison, a product used to kill rodents. The kind one might find a lot of in a run-down building like that. Luckily, he didn't need to use it.

All that's left is right here, right next to her coffin. A few final words, a few tears, and then it's over.

Not that he's proud of it. He can't be. Fallon was, above all else, a Belmont student. One of *his* students. Teddy had a responsibility to help her and, no matter how hard he tried, he failed. This is what weighs on him now, at her funeral. Thinking about it makes his stomach hurt a little, like the worms are starting to wake up.

He reminds himself that, as much as he wants to, he can't save everyone. Some people just refuse to be saved.

Fallon's father is speaking now. He's the chief financial officer of a bank, and he looks the part.

'My daughter had a good soul. A pure soul. Perhaps too pure for this world.' He pauses, looks up at the sky. 'I remember when she was about five, we were out in the garden and she saw her first ladybug. It was alone, wandering around on the grass, and Fallon wanted to help him find his friends . . .'

Teddy tunes out, glancing around at the crowd and trying to calculate the net worth of everyone in attendance. The total would keep Belmont going for the next hundred years. He makes a mental reminder to send out another donation letter.

This keeps him occupied until the coffin is finally lowered into the ground, and the first shovel of dirt is thrown on top of it. Teddy immediately goes to Fallon's parents, offering his condolences.

'Your daughter was a lovely young woman, and such a tremendous asset to Belmont,' he says. 'I am so sorry for your loss.'

As he shakes Mr Knight's hand, someone catches his attention. He turns to look.

Zach Ward.

He's dressed in a dark grey suit, looking much older than

his seventeen years. Freshly cut hair, shiny shoes. Sort of like his father.

He's looking right at Teddy.

Zach had a feeling Crutcher would show up. How could he not, being the headmaster and all.

Plus, he probably wants to gloat.

Zach stares at him until Crutcher has no choice but to walk over. But just as he's about to say something, Frank Maxwell interrupts.

'How nice to see you, Zach. Though I'm sorry it's under such tragic circumstances.'

Zach nods, shocked to see his math teacher for the first time since he left the school. Also shocked to see that white collar around his neck. 'Hello, Mr Maxwell. It's nice to see you, too. I hope you're doing well.'

'I am. Thank you so much.' He smiles, his face so calm and serene, it makes Zach wonder if he's high. That would explain a lot. 'I hope you'll be coming to the Belmont memorial.'

'Wouldn't miss it,' Zach says.

Mr Maxwell nods and smiles and moves on, giving Crutcher a chance to move in.

'I didn't realize you knew Fallon Knight,' he says.

'I did,' Zach says. He keeps his hands in his pockets so Crutcher won't see them shake. That's how nervous he is.

'Is that so?' Crutcher tilts his head up, appearing to think about this. 'Well, it's a terrible thing. Just terrible. And a good reminder for everyone to have a carbon monoxide detector.'

'My parents bought eight of them,' Zach says. 'And a brand-new water heater.'

'Good for them. Better safe than sorry.'

'It's funny, I was just telling Fallon that the other day,' Zach says, bringing the conversation back to the point. 'Her apartment wasn't really in a good area.'

Crutcher looks surprised. 'Oh my, you two really were close.'

'She helped me out with my homeschooling.'

'Did she now?'

Zach nods. Under his suit, his heart thumps against his chest so hard, he wonders if it's visible. Crutcher's a dangerous man. Deadly. In the safe confines of Zach's home, talking to Crutcher seemed like a good idea. Now he isn't sure. This shouldn't be his problem, and he shouldn't have to solve it.

But if he doesn't, then who will? No one left but him.

'I saw you there,' he says to Crutcher. Voice low, blank expression.

'You saw me where?'

'At Fallon's building.'

Crutcher looks at him like the idea is preposterous. 'I'm sure you're mistaken.'

'I was there the day before she died. We were meeting to go over an assignment I have.' The lie comes out smooth, just like the truth. 'When I drove up, I saw you walking out of her building. You went straight to your car. The one you drove to Belmont every day.'

'I have visited with all the faculty members since the school closed,' Crutcher says, waving away Zach's words with his hand. 'You can check.'

'But you just said you weren't there,' Zach says. 'Now you say you were.'

Crutcher stares at him the way he used to in class: with a

whole lot of contempt. It used to confuse Zach, to make him want Crutcher to like him. Not anymore.

Crutcher's mouth morphs into a smile, a shift so sudden, it takes Zach by surprise. 'We're all very upset today, Zach. You'll have to forgive me for speaking in error.'

'Which part?' Zach says.

'I don't understand.'

'Which part was wrong? Were you there or not?'

Crutcher is still smiling, but his eyes aren't. Something changes in them. It's a look Zach hasn't seen before, and it's terrifying.

'Good to see you, Zach.' He starts to walk away.

Zach braces himself.

He's got nothing but a theory. No evidence, no proof, no nothing. But Fallon might. Maybe on her computer, which no one is looking at because her death was ruled accidental. Maybe someone should look at it.

'One more thing,' he calls out to Crutcher, walking toward him.

Crutcher looks angry, but he nods. 'Go ahead.'

'The milk,' he says. 'You drank the milk at school, didn't you?'

'Yes. What of it?'

'Just weird, since you only drink milk out of glass bottles.'

Crutcher clenches his jaw, his skin rippling all the way up to his eyes. His hands clench into fists. For a second, Zach thinks Crutcher is going to punch him.

Zach isn't scared. Because now he knows for sure.

'Goodbye, Zach,' he says. Crutcher turns and walks away, toward the parking lot. Away from the funeral and away from Zach.

Zach watches until he can't see Crutcher anymore.

Shut up and smile.

Not this time.

He takes out his phone and punches in the number he has memorized.

'Hi. This is Zach Ward,' he says. 'Do you remember me?'

'Yes, of course I do,' Pruitt says. The FBI agent has a good memory.

'I want to give you some information. Can I come in and talk to you?'

83

Glorious. Simply glorious.

It's been two weeks since Ms Marsha and Joe were arrested. The shock has passed, and now the healing can begin.

Teddy stands at the top of the stairs, just outside the entrance to Belmont. In front of him, the crowd is beginning to swell. Parents, students, media ... Everyone is here. *Everyone.*

Behind him, a banner is strung from wall to wall:

REMEMBRANCE & RECOVERY
BELMONT FOREVER

The podium is set up here, in front of the chairs for the clergy members.

And the rock. Finally, the memorial rock can be unveiled. Because of the weight, it's already in place, albeit covered in a red velvet throw with gold tassels. Winnie took care of that. She's good at decorating – Teddy will give her that. The flowers are stunning: blue asters and huge golden sunflowers, chosen for the school's colors. They're mounted in stone planters, providing a floral walkway from the parking lot to the front of the school.

Because the ceremony is expected to take the whole morning, they have to serve food and drinks. No small thing, considering what happened at the school. Teddy and his team spent hours trying to decide what to serve, where it should come from, and if people would feel comfortable eating, or even drinking coffee, at the event.

The Calisto Catering van is right next to the seating area, visible to all. It's the caterer of choice for those who can afford it. Every wedding, every charity event, every corporate golf outing is catered by Calisto. If people won't eat *their* food, they won't eat anything.

Already Teddy can see they *are* eating and drinking. Thank God. It cost a fortune.

Winnie appears at his side, with Daphne right behind her. Together, the two of them have taken over Ms Marsha's duties. For now, it works. By fall, he'll have a new assistant.

With a clipboard in her hand, Winnie rattles off a list of updates. 'All the speakers have checked in. The mayor called and said he'll be arriving about five minutes before the program starts. But we have to set up a few more rows of chairs, because' – she looks out into the crowd – 'I don't think we'll have enough.'

Teddy glances up. He's been staring down at his cuticles, which look awful. Ever since Fallon's funeral, he's been biting them again.

'Hello, Teddy.'

Frank. He's looking at Teddy with that same weird smile.

'Frank, good to see you.'

'You look well,' Frank says, glancing around. 'Where's Allison? I'd love to say hello.'

Teddy restrains himself from looking as irritated as he feels. 'She's trying to get away from work but may not make it. Hospitals do need their nurses.'

'Allison must be very busy these days. Missy said she hasn't talked to her in a while.'

'Yes, she's been busy.' Teddy turns away from Frank and back to Winnie. 'We definitely need more chairs,' he says. He walks away, down the three steps to the seating area.

'Twenty minutes!' Winnie calls.

He doesn't turn around. A group of parents stand near the front row, and Teddy stops to greet them. Press the flesh. Smile and nod and hope they contribute a lot. Before Ms Marsha's unfortunate arrest, she'd explained that this was a big part of his job. Public relations. 'You have to be the face of the school,' she said.

Here he is, doing just that, working the room.

If he were still a teacher, he wouldn't have to do any of this. As Teacher of the Year, he would be reviewing his speech. And if he hadn't been named Teacher of the Year, he would be having a snack or showing up a few minutes before it started.

Such is the life of a headmaster.

It's not what he'd expected. Still, it's better than being a teacher who was never considered part of the Belmont family.

The worst part is dealing with the families of the victims. They're all seated in the front row, to the right of the center aisle. Together, they are a sea of black clothing drenched in the smell of death. If Teddy had known this, he would have told Winnie to seat them farther back.

First, he must greet them. He begins with his predecessor's wife. Before her husband died, she was a stern, no-nonsense woman. Now, she appears almost weak, with a stooped posture and a veil covering her face. She only nods when Teddy expresses his condolences.

Next, Dr Benjamin. Sonia's husband wears a grey suit, and his hair is longer than a typical professional's cut. *Professors* can get away with that. He's also much bigger than he was the last time Teddy saw him, and that was at Sonia's memorial. Perhaps grief makes him hungry.

'Thank you so much for coming,' Teddy says, shaking his hand. 'I realize this if of small comfort, but we will do our best to honor your wife in a way that you find fitting.'

'I appreciate that,' he says.

On the upside, at least Sonia never had children. Teddy hates dealing with small children.

The last of the mourners is Courtney and her father. Teddy steels himself to be gracious and humble, because there's still a chance Courtney will return to Belmont in the fall. Her father can afford it.

'Mr Ross,' he says. 'It's nice to see you again, though obviously not under these circumstances.'

'Of course.'

'And I can't tell you how happy I am that the FBI stepped in and cleared up the awful misunderstanding with you,' Teddy says to Courtney.

She nods, tries to smile a little. 'Thank you.'

Teddy sees someone behind Courtney, who must be sitting with them.

Zach Ward. That little shit.

'Hi, Mr Crutcher,' Zach says.

'Thank you so much for coming,' Teddy says. 'Especially since you're no longer a Belmont student.'

Zach doesn't blink. 'I wouldn't miss it.'

Teddy turns away from him and back to Mr Ross. 'Please, let me know if you need anything.'

'I will. Thank you again.' Mr Ross nods at Teddy, who walks back up the steps to the podium. No one is going to ruin this day. Not even Zach.

It's time to start the show.

84

When Crutcher is gone, Zach turns his head to look around.

The FBI is coming today.

When he met with Agents Pruitt and Roland, they listened to him. They asked questions – a lot of them. Just like before, Pruitt did most of the asking. Zach told them about the milk, about the plant book, and about Fallon. 'She knew something. Maybe there's information on her computer. I'm not sure. I didn't get a chance to find out before she died. But please, check.'

'Of course we're going to check this out,' Pruitt said.

'And the memorial is coming up. It's a big event, and he's the headmaster now, and . . . I don't know if he plans to kill anyone else, but it would be a perfect time. A lot of people will be there,' Zach said. 'For all I know, he wants to kill me.'

Pruitt reached out to him, not touching his hand but almost. 'Are you afraid for your life?'

He shrugged her off, even though he was kind of scared. Just a little. 'I won't eat or drink anything at the memorial, that's for sure.'

'You sure you want to go?'

'I have to. Because of Courtney.'

Pruitt nodded and looked over at Agent Roland, who had been taking notes. 'You've given us a lot of good information,' he said. 'We really appreciate you coming in.'

'Is there anything else I can do?' Zach asked.

'We'll take it from here,' Pruitt said. 'But please, for now, stay away from Teddy Crutcher.'

Up until today, he had. And he'd never mentioned anything about it to Courtney.

Because they're sitting in the front row, he keeps turning his head to see if he can spot the FBI agents.

'Who are you looking for?' Courtney says.

'No one. Just checking it out.' He settles down, facing front again. 'You okay?'

She nods, shrugs, shakes her head. That means no. And it makes Zach feel sort of guilty.

Up at the podium, Crutcher is greeting all the speakers sitting on the stage. Winnie is fussing around everyone, trying to fulfill her position as head of the Collaborative.

But what really catches Zach's eye is the man straightening the chairs behind the podium.

'Is that Mr Maxwell?' Zach says.

'Looks like it.' Courtney leans forward a little. 'Wait, is he wearing a white collar?'

'Um . . . yeah. He is.'

'He's a minister now?' Courtney says.

Zach doesn't answer. He'd seen Frank Maxwell at Fallon's funeral, but he never told Courtney about it. Didn't even tell her he went.

They both watch him finish with the chairs and move on to the velvet throw on the memorial rock. He straightens and smooths it, making sure it drapes evenly on all sides.

Courtney looks at Zach and shrugs.

'Weird,' she says.

'Yeah.'

Their conversation is interrupted by Winnie, who taps the

microphone. A thump reverberates through the air. 'If everyone could take their seats, we're about to start.' She stops and then adds, 'We're right on time!'

As soon as the event begins, Teddy straightens his jacket and gives the crowd a sad smile. Seems appropriate for the moment.

'Thank you all for coming today,' he says. 'As you know, a number of tragedies have occurred at Belmont over the past few months. We designed this event, first and foremost, to honor those we've lost.' He pauses, looking out at the audience with the gravest expression he can manage. So many people. Far more than they anticipated, which only adds to the importance of this day, but the pressure doesn't make him nervous. It makes him better. 'We also want to look forward, to what's next for Belmont. To survive, we must move on, and I appreciate all of you showing up to help us do that.'

Applause. Muted, yes, but that's to be expected at a memorial. It's not a rock concert.

He introduces the first speaker, Sonia's husband. Dr Benjamin rambles a bit, as grieving people tend to do, but it's not too bad. Mr Ross is next. He is the only one who will talk about Ingrid. Courtney declined the invitation.

Teddy steps back from each speaker but remains standing, giving him a view of the audience. Courtney cries while her father speaks, and Zach gives her a handkerchief. Teddy hopes it's clean.

The wife of the former headmaster also declined to speak, which is a good thing. She's in no condition for something like this. Originally, the plan had been to have Ms Marsha speak in her place, but obviously, the plan changed. They couldn't broadcast her in from a jail cell.

Instead, the headmaster is represented by Nari Tam, the history teacher. A bit of diversity never hurts.

She drones on, boring Teddy enough that his mind wanders. It continues to wander after she's done and the first clergy member steps up to the podium. She's a female minister from a nondenominational church, and she offers a prayer for those who would like to participate. All very respectful.

Teddy steps to the podium again to introduce the next part of the program – the victims who were poisoned but lived. Damien Harcourt walks up the stairs, and Teddy shakes his hand. His very wealthy parents are seated in the front row, though on the other side of the aisle from the grievers.

Teddy steps back again, grateful the sad time is almost over; that's what he calls the first half of this event. It's unpleasant but necessary. He's anxious to get on with part two, the recovery: the unveiling of the rock memorial, followed by a tour through the school.

It's been scrubbed and cleaned and has a brand-new kitchen with locks on every refrigerator, freezer, and pantry. Even the drink machines require key cards.

Yes, Belmont takes security seriously. Very seriously. That kitchen has to be the most expensive, most secure facility at any school in the country.

When Damien is done with a dramatic retelling of his not-so-near-death experience, Teddy announces that they will take a twenty-minute break before the second part begins.

It's been nearly perfect so far. Nothing has gone wrong. Nothing has been out of place.

And certainly no FBI.

Oh, yes, he knows Zach talked to them. Those two agents,

Pruitt and Roland, came to his house and peppered him with a bunch of questions – including about the milk he drinks. That's how he knew.

He even asked them about it. 'This information you have, by any chance did it come from a student named Zach Ward?'

'We can't divulge our sources,' Roland said.

'Of course. I understand that. But I do suspect it came from him. Let me tell you about Zach Ward.' Teddy went on to tell them all about his young student. 'He's obsessed with me. Ever since last semester, when he received a grade on a paper he didn't agree with, he's been . . . rather angry, let's say. His parents even came in and asked me to change the grade. Obviously, I said no.' Teddy shuddered when he thought about that. He wasn't acting.

Well, maybe just a little.

'After that, Zach started engaging in some very disturbing behavior. He has followed me, and I bet you can check that on his GPS. Normally, students don't scare me, even if they're upset, because this is Belmont we're talking about. But Zach . . . there's something wrong with him. And, as I'm sure you're aware, he was arrested for bribery.'

Teddy stopped then, shaking his head. 'It's a personal failure to me when any of our students strays so far from the right path. But what Zach has done is particularly painful, especially now that I'm headmaster. I feel like each Belmont student is my responsibility.'

The agents had thanked him – *profusely* thanked him – for his time.

Courtney had already been wrongly arrested for the crime. Did they really want to admit a second mistake had been made when they'd arrested Ms Marsha and Joe?

Certainly not. Teddy gave them what they really wanted: a way out. They grabbed right on to it, wanting any excuse to avoid more bad press.

Yes, he'd taken care of that pesky FBI problem. With ease.

He looks down at Zach now, sitting in the front row. He's wearing the same suit he wore to Fallon's funeral, except Zach no longer looks like his father. He looks like a little boy.

Zach glances up, catching Teddy staring at him. Zach smiles. No, he smirks. The little bastard smirks at him.

Teddy shakes his head no. A slow movement that would go unnoticed to anyone who wasn't paying attention.

Zach's smirk disappears, replaced by shock. Then anger. Finally, he looks away and stares down at the ground.

That's right, Zach.

Teddy wins. Again.

85

From his vantage point, Frank can see everything. He sits at the end of the row of chairs onstage, giving him a full view of the audience and a side view of Teddy at the podium. Between them, the rock memorial is still covered.

When the second half of the program begins, Teddy talks about how the rock came into existence. Years of work had gone into it, so many ideas and designs considered, but Teddy makes it sound like it happened yesterday. Like he was the one who decided everything.

'What would be worthy?' Teddy says. 'What kind of memorial would be fitting for those we have lost at Belmont? I wanted something that would serve as a reminder and as a symbol of the school, something that would honor those we have lost and celebrate those to come.'

Frank's heart flutters. The longer Teddy talks, the stronger the feeling gets.

Nervousness, yes.

Remorse, no.

He's known for a while about Teddy. How he lied to his wife, how he got a vasectomy behind her back and told her he was sterile. The closer Frank has gotten to the church, the more he has seen how morally bankrupt Teddy is.

Frank had tried. *God* knows he tried, too. Frank went to Teddy's house – twice – and asked that they pray. Almost implored him to do so.

Teddy refused.

'The Parents' Collaborative has been instrumental to Belmont, and to this memorial,' Teddy says, smiling out at the crowd. 'Please, let's give them a round of applause to thank them for all their hard work.'

Frank claps along with everyone else. He doesn't look at the audience, though. He looks at Teddy's hands.

Those cuticles. He first noticed back when he was still teaching. Teddy's hands weren't always like that, not until he lied to his wife. That's when Frank noticed the change. How ragged they looked, sometimes even bloody.

They're still like that now. A symbol of the deeper rot inside him.

Guilt doesn't go away. It stays with a person, burrowing itself deep into the soul, where it starts to grow. Almost like love, except it feels horrible instead of good.

Frank had been willing to let it go. To be patient, to wait until Teddy was finally ready to ask God for forgiveness. You can't force that.

But then Missy called.

She's been staying with her parents since Frank decided to become a minister. He understood her decision, because this has been a big change. A good change, the right change, but Missy had said she needed time to adjust. He understood that.

They check in a few times a week, usually when Frank calls to talk to his son. But a few days ago, she called him late at night. Despite what he'd told Teddy earlier, Missy *had* spoken to Allison recently. A lie, yes, but it was for the greater good.

'I just got off the phone with Allison,' Missy said.

'How is she doing?' he asked.

'Not well,' she said. 'She said she received a strange email from someone named Fallon Knight. She claimed to be a former student at Belmont and she accused Teddy of poisoning all those people at the school.'

'I don't understand,' Frank said. 'Fallon Knight is – '

'Dead,' Missy said. 'I know. Allison told me. She thought the email was crazy until she heard Fallon had died. That's when she left town.'

He shook his head, trying to make sense of what Missy was saying.

'Frank,' she said. 'Allison is scared Teddy might hurt her.'

What Missy said was so shocking, Frank didn't move. Even after they hung up, he stayed right where he was, sitting in the living room. No TV, no radio, no sound at all except the thoughts in his head.

He knew Teddy was a liar, knew Teddy was a godless man who refused to pray or ask for forgiveness. But he had no idea Teddy was capable of hurting someone. And killing someone, or several people, seemed . . . unthinkable.

Frank prayed. He prayed for guidance, for help, for some kind of clarity. Any kind. All night, he stayed in his seat, not moving until the sun came up.

Something had to be done. And Frank was the one who had to do it.

This knowledge didn't come to him by accident. He was meant to know it. Meant to do something about it. No one else was doing anything about Teddy Crutcher, so it was up to him.

Teddy is a monster. A monster who made Allison physically afraid of him. A monster who has lied multiple times and does not seek forgiveness.

A monster who is leading Belmont Academy.

It cannot stand.

This is *Belmont*, a school with a history of sending its students to the finest universities in the country. A school that has taught one vice president and countless leaders in business, philanthropy, even the church.

He takes a deep breath, quieting the fluttering of his heart. This is right. This is just. This is how it must be.

'And now, without further delay,' Teddy says, 'it's time to unveil our path forward. Our motto, our creed, our rock. Ladies and gentlemen, I present to you the official Belmont Academy memorial.'

Frank watches Teddy grasp that velvet throw with one hand. Everyone applauds when it's been removed. The rock does look lovely in the sunlight, the bronze glow shining like a beacon. As he looks at it, Frank thinks that it should be officially blessed at some point.

He turns his eyes to Teddy's hand. He's still clasping that velvet throw. When he finally drops it, he rubs his fingers against his palm, like there's something on his hand.

There is.

Frank can see it. A light dusting of reddish brown powder on Teddy's palm and fingers. The powder was invisible on the red throw.

Teddy is still talking, but he continues to scratch his hand. He must think it's dirt, or maybe pollen, and he keeps rubbing it in, getting it all over his fingers.

That crushed rosary pea will be absorbed into Teddy's skin.

The idea of using a plant came from the Mad Scientists – Ms Marsha and Joe, apparently – and it wasn't hard to find a plant that killed on contact. There are only a few, and the fact that one of them was called rosary pea felt like another sign: Frank was doing exactly what he was supposed to do.

So easy to research, so easy to get. The now-empty vial is in Frank's pocket. All he'd had to do was offer to help set up and then sprinkle it across the velvet throw as he straightened it.

Now, it's all over Teddy's hand.

He may survive a day. Perhaps two. Hard to know, given that this is the first time Frank has ever poisoned someone. What he does know is that Teddy will die.

It's a shame, yes. But it had to be done.

If there's one thing being a minister has taught Frank, it's that not everyone can be saved.

Epilogue

The dorms at Granite Hill Prep are even nicer than Zach expected: huge rooms, two beds, two desks, one whole wall of bookshelves. It's about seventy degrees in Vermont, and the windows are open, flooding the room with sunlight.

Not a bad place to be, even if they do have classes on Saturdays. That's one big downside of a boarding school.

His parents have left, and his new roommate hasn't arrived yet. Zach picks the bed near the heater – because it's Vermont – and starts to unpack. It doesn't take long. He didn't bring much besides his clothes, computer, and other gadgets. Before it gets too cold, he'll have to go back home and get his winter gear.

When he's finished, he sits down at his new desk and looks around. Nothing is grey. Nothing is gloomy.

Four months have passed since the memorial ceremony. Four months since he walked away from the Belmont campus for the last time, and yet so much has happened.

Two days after the ceremony, Teddy didn't show up for a meeting. The new head of the Collaborative went to his house and found him.

Dead.

He had been dead for a whole day.

At first, the rumor was suicide. Next, a heart attack. Finally, murder.

Everyone went apeshit all over again. Maybe Ms Marsha

and Joe weren't the Mad Scientists. Maybe the real killer was still out there, and the FBI and the police were *still* incompetent. Around and around it went, though Zach hardly paid attention. He couldn't do it a second time. Besides, he was a little busy doing his two hundred hours of community service. That was part of the plea deal for the bribery charge, but at least it wasn't a felony. The advantage of having an expensive lawyer wasn't lost on him.

The poison, however. That was different. Crushed rosary pea had been sprinkled all over the red velvet throw. Teddy wouldn't have died so quickly if it hadn't been for his cuticles. Open cuts brought the poison right into his bloodstream.

When Frank Maxwell was arrested for the murder, not only was everyone shocked, but they started saying it must be Belmont. Like the school was cursed. After all, Mr Maxwell did have a breakdown while working there. And he had checked into a mental facility, against his will at first, before being released and becoming a minister.

He knew how to kill Teddy, but he didn't have a clue about how to get away with it. Everyone at the memorial had a camera, and the whole ceremony was recorded by a professional. The FBI found footage of Mr Maxwell taking something out of his pocket and fiddling with the cover on the memorial rock. Remnants of the crushed rosary pea were found in his garbage disposal.

The day he was arrested, Zach saw him on TV. Mr Maxwell was handcuffed, being led into the police station, and he was smiling. The same smile he'd had at Fallon's funeral, the one that had made Zach think he was high.

'My God,' Mom had said.

'It's a good thing we took you out of that school,' Dad had said.

Zach had said nothing.

He should've been shocked, but the feeling never came. The past year had used up all the shock he had. Nothing was left.

He wasn't even shocked when the FBI claimed that its agents had been investigating Crutcher. Zach didn't believe it for a second. He bet that didn't start seriously until after Crutcher died.

Nevertheless, they had released some of the evidence they'd gathered. Because Crutcher was dead and there would never be a trial, it didn't matter if they showed footage from the cameras set up by Fallon outside his house and in his classroom. She finally got credit for her work.

But Crutcher's computer records were the most damning. Fake emails to frame Ms Marsha and Joe, not to mention the fake profiles. All young, all female. Crutcher had pretended to be a teenage girl online – and that, most of all, convinced everyone he had to be guilty. No normal man does that.

'Sick bastard,' Courtney had said.

Zach had said nothing.

Now he's here, in Vermont, far away from all of it. Almost all of it.

His phone buzzes. Courtney.

'Hey, baby,' she says.

Zach smiles. 'Hey, you.'

'How's your room?'

'It's amazing. Yours?' he asks.

'Fantastic. Have you met your roommate?'

'No, he's not here yet. Hopefully, he's cool.'

'Yeah. Mine seems like it.' He can hear her smiling. 'Should we go explore?'

'Obviously. Ten minutes?' Zach says.

'Meet me outside my dorm.'

He's still smiling, now at the thought of seeing her. They're together, he and Courtney. Really together. It seems so obviously perfect now that he has no idea how he missed it for so long.

More than once, he's wondered if they had Crutcher to thank. If all those horrible things hadn't happened at Belmont, maybe he and Courtney wouldn't be a couple.

Zach goes to the closet and changes into a clean shirt, checking himself in the mirror on the inside of the door. Next to the mirror, high on the right-hand side, a Teacher of the Year plaque is already hung up.

Crutcher's award.

One day after school, Zach had slipped it right into his backpack and walked out. He was angry that afternoon. Angry that Courtney was still in jail, that so many people thought she was guilty, that Mrs B was dead instead of Crutcher. He hadn't planned to keep the plaque, but after his parents pulled him out of Belmont, he'd never had a chance to return it. Now he's glad.

Because of Crutcher, Zach has changed his mind about his future. Forget finance, and forget becoming a lawyer.

Zach is going to become a teacher. And when he does, he'll return to Belmont.

Someone has to save the kids. It's for their own good.

Acknowledgments

Somewhere along the way, *For Your Own Good* became my most personal book. Although I didn't attend a private school and I don't come from a wealthy family, experiences I had as a teenager inspired a few events in the book (the non-murderous ones). That includes some of the behavior by teachers, as well as the friendship between Zach and Courtney. I won't name the people involved here for obvious reasons, but thank you all for your contributions . . . good and bad.

Many, many people went into making this book a reality. I'm going to try very hard to include them all . . .

A thank-you is not enough for my warrior agent, Barbara Poelle; my incredible editor, Jen Monroe; as well as the tenacious publicity duo of Lauren Burnstein and Dache Rogers; the absolutely unstoppable marketing team of Jin Yu, Jessica Mangicaro, and Fareeda Bullert; and eagle-eyed copy editor Elizabeth Johnson. Without this team and everyone at Berkley, you would not be reading this book.

And across the pond, the stellar UK team, thank you for all your hard work! Joel Richardson, Grace Long, Ellie Hughes, Katie Williams, Ruth Atkins, and everyone at Michael Joseph.

A special thank-you to the talented designers who created the book covers!

Over the past couple of years, I've been able to attend a number of book club meetings across the country. I appreciate this so much, and it's such a thrill to talk with all of you! Fresno Book Club, Books & Brunch, Gresham's Book Club, Celeste Fox, and Sara Henry, thank you so much for reading, and thank you for allowing me to join your meetings.

My critique partners, as always, were invaluable when I was writing this book. A special shout-out to Marti Dumas, who is not only a critique partner but also a former teacher. She kept me on point about the finer details.

A number of authors were kind and generous enough to read an early copy of this book and their words mean so much to me. Thank you, Megan Miranda, JP Delaney, Lisa Unger, Sarah Pekkanen, B. A Paris, Chandler Baker, Gilly Macmillan, and Hannah Mary McKinnon!

To the booksellers, there is simply no way to thank you enough for your time, for including me in events, and for recommending my books. Mary O'Malley, Pamela Klinger-Horn, Barbara Peters, Maxwell Gregory, and Alex George – just to name a few. And thank you to all the incredible bookstores I've visited online or in person: Garden District Book Shope, Gresham Bookshop, Skylark Bookshop, Murder by the Book, An Unlikely Story, Poisoned Pen, Mystery Lovers Bookshop, Book Passage, Parnassus Books, The Novel Neighbor, Lake Forest Book Store, Books & Books, Magic City Books . . . and so many more. Without all of you, I wouldn't have a third book.

Bookstagrammers, bloggers, and reviewers, you have a special place in my heart. Thank you for your never-ending passion for reading, your enthusiasm, and your support. You are simply the best!

I can't forget all the wonderful librarians and libraries. My love of reading came from regular trips to the library when I was a kid – and that love is the same reason I eventually started to write. Thank you, librarians, for doing what you do.

Last but never least, my friends and family, thank you for everything.